The Divided Heart

Heart Series, Book Three
Marie's Story

In memory of my friend,
Barbara Arthur Brown,
who introduced me to the books of
Georgette Heyer many years ago
and started me on this journey.

Acknowledgements

Some people are irreplaceable in my life.

Foremost is my husband, James T. Ellis. He has been my unfailing support in too many ways to count throughout our fifty-four plus years of marriage and especially during those times when my mind was so busy with characters vying for my attention that I didn't hear him.

No one produces a book without considerable help from others. I'm fortunate to have known and worked with people who willingly listened to me as I droned on about my stories.

Dawn Aldridge Poore (author of Regency mystery and romance series (https://www.amazon.com/Books-Dawn-Aldridge-Poore) and my niece, who chooses to be anonymous, did major jobs nitpicking my Regency novels.

Elgin and Melissa Cook gave expert assistance on the cover picture. https://www.melissacook.us

Randolph Shaffner shared his publishing expertise in the publication of this book.

My endless appreciation to all.

Books by Peggy Lovelace Ellis

Regency
Heart Series
The Uncertain Heart, Book One
The Merry Heart, Book Two
The Divided Heart, Book Three

Short Stories
Silver Shadows, Stories of Life in a Small Town

Anthologies
Challenges on the Home Front, World War II
(Second Edition)
A Beautiful Life and Other Stories
Lest the Colors Fade

The Divided Heart

Heart Series, Book Three
Marie's Story

Peggy Lovelace Ellis

Faraway Publishing
Black Mountain, N.C

Peggy Lovelace Ellis
76 Wagon Trail
Black Mountain, NC 28711-2565
https://www.peggyellis.com

First Edition
2023

Cover Design: SelfPubBookCovers.com/dianecostanzastudio

Published by
FARAWAY PUBLISHING
125 Spring View Drive
Black Mountain, N.C. 28711

Printed in the United States of America
ISBN: 979-8-9881761-1-4 (pbk.)

Library of Congress Control Number: 2023943573

The Divided Heart
Heart Series, Book Three
Marie's Story
By Peggy Lovelace Ellis

1. Historical Romance; 2. Regency Romance; 3. Regency Morals and Manners; 4. The Regency *ton*; 5. Napoleonic Wars; 6. Wellington; 7. Regency Nobility; 8. George III; 9. The Prince Regent; 10. Regency Vernacular; 11. Orphans

An Overview of the Heart Series

In 1774 three ten-year-old girls living in Somerset, England, made a decision that had a far-reaching effect on their lives.

Bright sunshine had found its way through the barred windows of the nursery at Shelburne Park, reflecting on the tousled curls of the three young misses sitting on the window seat.

Becca, the fair-haired pampered daughter of the earl who owned this estate, held sway over her two visitors: Louise, the raven-haired only child of a duke, and Marie, the auburn-haired offspring of a vicar.

Suddenly, Becca bounced to her feet and whirled around the room. "I have the most wonderful idea! When we grow up, we will each have a daughter and give her all three of our names. They will be best friends, just as we are."

"Will the names not be confusing? I mean, with mother and daughter having the same name?"

"No, Marie. We will give our daughters our own names as their third name."

Becca continued without waiting for another question. "My daughter will be Marie Louise Rebecca. Your daughter will be Louise Rebecca Marie, and Louise's daughter will be Rebecca Marie Louise."

After some squabbling over the best order of their names, both Marie and Louise capitulated to Becca's insistence.

Years passed, as years will do. These three girls became young ladies and entered adulthood, still the best of friends.

Table of Contents

Prologue

Kent, England, 1800

"My name is Marie, and I'm five years old. Who are you?" She spoke around a mouthful of juicy apple.

The other child grasped the trunk of the tree even tighter and turned her brown eyes, huge in her startled face, toward a limb above her head. A pair of blue eyes peeked at her from beneath a tumble of fair curls.

"Susan, and I'm five too," she replied in a whisper, a giggle escaping her tiny mouth as she confessed, "I'm hiding from my nanny. Why are you up there?"

"I'm hiding from my nanny, too. Mama calls her Nurse Robinson, but I call her Robbie. Does your nanny have a name?"

Susan nodded. "Jane."

"That's what I call my doll. I left her in the nursery because I can't climb a tree while I hold her. I like being in trees, high above the ground, do you?"

"Yes, people can't see us, but we can see them. Trees are my favorite place to hide from my brothers. They don't know I can climb, and I'm not going to tell them."

"I don't have any brothers to hide from, but perhaps we will stay up here forever," Marie exclaimed. "Would that not be fun?"

"What would we eat when all the apples are gone?" came the prosaic answer.

"Oh. That might be a problem," Marie agreed. "Quiet! I hear someone coming."

The girls smothered their giggles with their hands as a frantic voice called, "Miss Marie, where are you?

Marie Louise Rebecca Haverford, if you do not answer me on the instant, I shall tell your Mama, and that means no sweet biscuits for you at tea!"

With a disgusted sigh, the child started down the tree, picking her way from limb to limb. She couldn't bear to miss the sweet biscuits. Cook had promised her macaroons. "You must go down, too, else I cannot."

Susan felt for footing as she scampered to the ground.

"You are not the young lady I called," a surprised voice told her.

Before Susan could speak, Marie slid to the ground. "Here I am, Robbie."

"And just look at you, you naughty girl, dirt all over your gown, and what have you done to your face? Never mind, come along home, and let us get you cleaned up before tea."

Marie took her hand and said, "Robbie, this is Susan."

"Good afternoon, Susan. Have you escaped your nanny too? Tell me where you live, and I shall take you home."

"I live at the Meadows over that way." Susan waved one hand toward a dense stand of trees off to their right.

"You must be the vicar's child."

"Yes, I'm Susan Elizabeth Connors." She took Robbie's other hand and skipped to keep up with her longer strides.

Marie peeked around her nanny to ask Susan a question. "Why do you only have three names? I have four."

"I do not know, but it would be nice to have another one."

"You shall have one of mine, and we will be almost sisters," Marie exclaimed and added, "Which do you want, Marie or Louise or Rebecca? You choose."

Susan carefully muttered the names several times. "Susan Elizabeth Marie Connors, that's me!"

"Now that we both have four names, we will be best friends," Marie assured her as she slipped her hand from its nesting place in Robbie's hand and joined Susan on the other side.

Their joyous laughter rang out, attracting the attention of another flustered female, who hurried toward them.

"Susan Elizabeth Connors, I've looked everywhere for you!" Turning to the older woman, she said, "Ma'am, my name is Jane Borders. I'm nursemaid to this young lady. I do hope she has not been a bother to you."

"Not at all. I was just now returning her to you. Both these little imps escaped us, did they not? Well, there's no harm done as I can see. I'm Nurse Robinson, and my charge is Marie Haverford, daughter to Sir Julian and Lady Becca. She and Susan have become fast friends already."

"I will take Susan off your hands now, Ma'am." With a curtsy, she clasped the little girl's hand and hurried away.

Susan's words floated back to Marie, "My name is Susan Elizabeth Marie Connors now. Do you have four names, Jane?"

"Good-bye, Susan," Marie called. "I shall ask Mama if we can play together tomorrow."

Marie bubbled with glee when she told her mother of her new friend. "But, Mama, she only had three names until I gave her one of mine. Should she not already have four?"

Lady Becca chuckled. "No, my dear, three is the usual number of names for people. You have four because I named you for my two best friends and myself."

"Do I know them?"

"No, I fear I lost touch with them some years ago. Their names were Louise Carlton and Marie Stanford, and we agreed when we were ten years old that we would each name our daughters after all three of us. I wonder if they did." Lady Becca's wistful voice faded.

Marie patted her hand. "If they said they would, I'm sure they did. Don't fret, Mama. Perhaps you will find them someday."

"I would love that," her mother answered. "Now tell me more about Susan. I do hope you and she will be as close as I was with my special friends."

"Oh, yes, Mama, and what fun Susan and I shall have together. Always!

Chapter 1

The Sprite

Kent, Spring 1813.

"Oh, Susan, say it isn't true!" Marie wailed as she gazed at her friend reclining on the day bed. "Without you, the Season will not be any fun at all, and I had such wonderful plans for us."

Marie Haverford and Susan Connors had giggled their way through childhood and romped their way through their first Season without shocking their elders beyond reason. There were some near misses on that point, as each girl admitted when pressed. They must abandon their plans for another Season of setting the *ton* on its ear. Influenza had left Susan too weak to travel, and the doctor said she must miss this Season. The news devastated Marie.

Susan smiled. "Tell the truth, Marie, you will not even miss me. You will be much too busy with your new friends, the girls you met last summer who share your names."

Marie shrugged when she remembered Rebecca Blackwell and Louise Mansfield, whom she had met late the previous summer. The coincidence of their having the same three names, only in different orders, had led to the discovery that their mothers had been closest friends in their own youth. Now Rebecca was betrothed, although unofficially, to Marie's uncle, the Earl of Shelburne, and Louise was happily married to Major George Stafford, over the strenuous objections of her family-proud grandparents.

Marie tossed her fair curls. "Oh, Rebecca and Louise are all right, but they can never enter into my sentiments the way you do. Their lives have been so different, growing up in an orphanage and then being obliged to earn their keep. They are so sedate they will not be any fun."

"Sedate? Did you not tell me that Louise raised a considerable number of eyebrows last autumn? Just think—attending a masquerade ball!"

"Yes, she did, but that was only a temporary aberration because of her strict grandparents. Rebecca assured me they both lived a very dignified life at the orphanage and in Town last year. Do you realize they have never even climbed trees?" The horror of such a terrible childhood colored her voice.

"They've had a deprived life, indeed!" Susan grinned at her friend. "Do you remember the time your groom had to rescue you from the top of that huge oak tree at the bottom of the garden?"

"I wish I could forget it." Marie grimaced, as she recollected the stern reprimand she had received. Moreover, she had to forego sweet biscuits with her tea for a sennight. "Do you remember how you hid in the tree outside your bedroom window and spied on your brothers?"

Susan laughed. "To this day, they don't know how I could tease them about the things they talked about with their friends."

"Teasing? Tormenting is a better word."

"You enjoyed those extra sweet biscuits as much as I did, so if I'm guilty so are you!"

They reminisced over their occasional questionable behavior until Marie grew quiet. "I'll miss you so much this Season, Susan."

"Tell me your plans for new gowns." Susan knew how to cheer up her old playmate.

"Oh, I do look forward to visiting the modistes. I never want to see another white muslin gown!" As her friend agreed, Marie continued, "I asked my father if I could have diamonds, and he said perhaps one on a chain with matching ear studs. He won't even consider a tiara, no matter how much I begged. However, I am to have a double strand of pearls this year. One for each of my seasons, I suppose."

Their laughter rang out as they contemplated the possibility of six seasons. "I can see it now—six strands of pearls holding up the triple chins I will surely have by that time!"

The friends talked a little longer before Marie gave Susan a quick hug and took her leave, promising regular letters from London.

London

A few days later, the Haverford traveling carriage, with attendant outriders and baggage wagons, stopped before an imposing brick house in Berkeley Square. The petite blonde with sparkling blue eyes jumped from the vehicle, ignoring the outstretched hand of the footman waiting to assist her. She ran up the broad steps and beamed at the butler, who opened the door for them. "Symms, I vow it is marvelous to be back in Town for the Season, do you not agree?"

"I agree that it is, Miss Marie." The butler gave her an indulgent smile and turned to greet her parents. "Sir Julian, my lady, I trust you had an enjoyable journey."

"Thank you, yes, most pleasant." Sir Julian handed over his hat and Malacca cane, and then he turned to assist his lady in removing her cloak. "We would welcome a tea tray, Symms."

A few minutes later in the small sitting room at the back of the house, Marie was silent while she devoured a plate of macaroons and drank two cups of tea. After wiping her mouth on a table napkin, she commented, "I do regret that Susan could not come for the Season. I don't know how I shall go on without her."

"Of course, you will miss her, Marie, but others may well rejoice there is only one of you here for this Season," her mama, known to everyone as Lady Becca, commented with a twinkle.

Her unrepentant daughter dimpled at her. "They should enjoy the respite while they may because Susan will come to Town later, if the doctor agrees she might. Still, that doesn't solve my problem of a friend in the meantime."

"Goodness, child, whatever can you mean? You have scores of friends," Lady Becca exclaimed, as she stared in wonder at one of the most popular girls in last year's Season.

"Yes, I know I do, Mama, although acquaintances might be a better word to use. Yet you must see that all of them have their own special friends, as I had Susan last Season."

"Have you forgotten your two new friends?"

"I like Rebecca and Louise well enough, what little I know of them, but do you not think they will be busy with their new families? Perhaps they will not have much time for me."

"In that event, you will befriend one of the girls making her come-out this season," Lady Becca told her. "Any one of them would appreciate having someone to show her how to go on in polite society."

Marie drank another cup of tea while she sat in thought for several minutes. "I met someone last season I liked. Deborah Langford. Do you recall her? She came to Town late in the Season and did not find it easy to make friends."

"Is she the plump girl with dark hair whose mother didn't quite know how to dress her?"

Marie wrinkled her pert little nose. "I never saw so many ruffles and ribbons on one gown as was on every one of hers. I'm sure she was self-conscious, and that's why she was so loud at times. Still, I liked her. When it was just the two of us together, she conversed quietly. She didn't indulge in repeating *on-dits* about others either, like some girls do."

"Perhaps you can help her by being her friend." Sir Julian passed his teacup for a refill.

Marie spoke after a moment's thought. "I know, I shall invite her to visit the modistes with me. That should lead to something. I shall send a note round to her on the instant."

Sir Julian shook his head in mock despair. "Poppet, do you think you could wait at least until tomorrow to advise the *ton* that we're giving them the honour of your presence?"

She stared at him in surprise. "I did not intend to tell everybody, only Miss Langford."

"And she will tell one person who will tell someone else and so on. I would like a peaceful evening because I know it will be the last one for three months."

Lady Becca joined her daughter's laughter, but she agreed with her husband. "Yes, Marie, you must wait until tomorrow to report the news of our arrival. This will be the last quiet we will have for an appreciable time, too, as you know."

At breakfast the following morning, surrounded by the aroma of freshly brewed coffee, Marie inquired, "How soon may I send a message to Deborah Langford?"

Sir Julian twinkled at his beloved daughter. "I suppose we have deprived you of her company for as long as we can expect. By all means, send your *billet doux*."

Lady Becca brought up an important point, an innocent expression on her face. "When do you plan to visit the modistes? Or are you content with last year's fashions?"

Her daughter gave her an impertinent grin even as Sir Julian said he should live to see the day.

"I'm going shopping this very day, and I warn you here and now that I draw the line at white muslin. I want bright colors, sunshine yellow, perhaps, or muslin the color of grass. No, green won't suit my blue eyes."

"Blue the color of the sky would bring out the color of your eyes, Poppet, like the gown your mama is wearing."

Mother and daughter stared at him in amazement. Since when did he even notice what they wore?

With a wink, he planted a kiss on his wife's cheek and strolled out of the room.

Recovering from her surprise, Marie said, "I shall invite Miss Langford for a coze over teacups this afternoon and invite her to shop with us on our next visit to Bond Street."

The ladies spent the rest of the morning at the salon of Madame Bouchét where they perused the latest fashion plates. Lady Becca called a halt after they chose designs for morning gowns, carriage gowns, ball ensembles, and walking gowns.

"But, Mama, we have only begun. We must see the glover and the shoemaker, as well as visit the drapery shop."

"Tomorrow is another day, Marie. To tell the truth, my feet are complaining," she added with a sigh, as she settled against the squabs of their carriage and motioned to the footman to close the door.

"Oh, poor Mama," Marie teased. "I shall ask Miss Langford to shop with me tomorrow, and you can stay at home and rest your weary bones."

"Oh, no, you won't! I shudder to think what the two of you would order, considering what you put me through today."

Silvery laughter greeted this sally. "Now it's my turn to tell the truth. I did not really expect to order the crimson satin gown with the hem above the ankles and the deep décolletage. I was only funning you." She kissed her mother's cheek. "I'm so glad I have a mother I can tease, and you do rise to the bait so nicely."

The ladies entered Haverford House well pleased with each other.

A couple of hours later, Marie welcomed Miss Langford into the drawing room. After a quick glance, she spoke impulsively, "You're so much thinner than when we last met."

Her visitor beamed her pleasure. "Thank you for noticing, Miss Haverford! I have walked miles, simply miles, every single day since last summer. At times I didn't think the fat would ever go away."

"Oh, please, can we not dispense with formality? I shall call you Deborah, and you call me Marie."

"I should like that very much, Marie."

"You were not fat, only a little plump," Marie assured her. She turned as the door opened to admit the butler carrying a tea tray. "Put it here, please, Symms."

When he left the room, Marie busied herself with teacups and asked if Deborah would attend the Smythe ball the following evening.

"No, because my parents insist that I must visit my paternal grandparents that evening."

"Parents can be unreasonable, can they not? I must say I'm in discord with my father," Marie announced.

Deborah grimaced in sympathy. "I am always upset with mine, it seems. But tell me what yours has done."

"I had my heart set on a diamond tiara, and he refuses even to consider it. Is that not abominable? Well to be fair," she hastened to add, "he said I could have one diamond on a chain and matching ear studs."

"I must admit I have not asked for a tiara, but it would not help if I did. My mother says only pearls are suitable for young girls, and I have a double strand."

Marie replenished their teacups and passed a plate of angel cakes. When her guest declined a second helping, she too resisted the temptation, although it caused her a pang.

"I'm to have a double strand this Season too. One for each of my seasons, I suppose," she announced, hiding a smile as she recalled her last conversation with Susan.

"Now tell me about your new gowns," Deborah urged.

"Not even one white muslin gown," Marie declared with satisfaction. "However, I did order a morning gown in sprigged muslin with yellow rosebuds and green leaves on a cream background. Just wait until you see the Pomona green walking gown."

"I shouldn't think you would care to wear that shade of green with your blue eyes."

"I thought that too, but I couldn't resist it. It has a matching Spencer striped with narrow bands of yellow. It's perfect for breezy strolls in the park. Besides, I cannot wear blue all the time. I shall wear the green gown when I'm with Uncle Edward and flatter his green eyes, no matter what the color does for me."

Deborah sighed over the mention of the Earl of Shelburne's green eyes. "I wish Miss Blackwell had not already snagged him."

"Their betrothal is not yet official, so perhaps you can lure him away from her." Marie didn't believe a word she said but wanted to bolster the other's self-confidence.

"If you believe that, you haven't noticed the way they look at each other," Deborah replied. "I saw them in Hyde Park yesterday, and they didn't know anyone else was in existence."

"You're probably right," Marie conceded and changed the subject. "Would you care to come shopping with me? Madame Bouchét has all the new fashion plates, so perhaps we can choose some styles together. Shopping is always more fun with a friend, so please say you will."

Deborah's answer was hesitant. "As yet Mama has shopped with me, but perhaps she would permit it."

"I know the very thing. We will shop with both our mothers, because mine insists upon being in attendance also."

"Oh yes, I'm sure Mama will agree to that."

Marie gave a satisfied nod. "That is settled. As soon as I speak to my mama, she will send a note around to yours setting a time, but tomorrow for sure."

After chatting a few more moments, Deborah took her leave, and Marie went in search of her mother.

After a busy morning of shopping, during which Mrs. Langford agreed to Lady Becca's guidance, Marie and Deborah made their way to Hatchard's bookstore, where their presence attracted the eyes of three gentlemen standing nearby. The young ladies, being ladies indeed, pretended to ignore their admirers, although they watched from the corner of their eyes and listened to their conversation.

"Do either of you know who they are," inquired one young sprig of fashion, his cherub face alight with curiosity.

"The fair-haired one is Marie Haverford. Her father, Sir Julian, is only a baronet, but her mother is Shelburne's sister. Miss Haverford and her friend, Miss Connors, were all the rage last Season. There's something familiar about the other one, but I cannot quite bring it to mind," replied the second gentleman, who waved a scented handkerchief, sending the odor wafting outward in a large circle. "She is not Miss Connors, however."

"Miss Haverford appeals to me," commented the third gentleman, whose starched shirt points placed his eyes in danger of injury. "Sprightly little thing, ain't she?"

"I should say she is," agreed the cherub face. "Little Sprite is the perfect name for her. I shall call her that. I shall be the first."

It was fortunate for the Little Sprite's composure that the gentlemen stopped ogling her through their quizzing glasses and went on their way before giggles overtook her.

"Well, Little Sprite," Deborah teased, "perhaps you will meet your admirers at the Smythe ball this very evening. I should like to be there and see for myself which of your three conquests is the first to wheedle an introduction."

Marie tossed her curls. "Perhaps they will be there. However, I do hope that one gentleman leaves his handkerchief at home. The scent was overpowering, even at this distance. I'm sorry you can't be there. Perhaps that same gentleman might recall why you are familiar to him."

"I would rather he does not recall me and all my fat from last Season." A droll expression crossed her face.

"You're slimmer than you were, but your beautiful smile is the same. It should have all the gentlemen at your feet in no time."

"I don't care about all of them. I shall be content with one."

"It would be wonderful if you meet that special one this Season."

Deborah agreed.

"Good evening, Your Grace, Lady Rebecca." Marie, with her mother beside her, greeted the Duchess of Amesbury and her granddaughter on the stairs of Smythe House.

The duchess turned to Becca. "I haven't seen Lady Olivia recently. I trust she is well."

"Oh, yes, Mama is in good health, Your Grace. She merely chose to stay at home this evening."

With the greetings complete, the younger ladies turned to each other. "Please call me Rebecca and allow me to call you Marie. Given names are so much friendlier, do you agree?"

"I shall be delighted, especially since I shall soon call you '*Aunt* Rebecca'," Marie replied with a sly glance.

"I draw the line at that," Rebecca warned, bringing soft laughter from her companions.

"Crowded stairways are the bane of my existence," Marie murmured and frowned in exasperation at the overweight lady in front of her. "Everybody knows that gentlemen prefer petite ladies. I dare say it makes them feel superior, but being small has its drawbacks."

"You're in your second Season, Marie, besides the entertainments you enjoyed last autumn. You should be accustomed to the crowds."

"Oh, I'm accustomed to them, Your Grace, but that does not mean I enjoy them. Is this line moving at all? You ladies don't realize how fortunate you are to be tall enough to see what's happening." When the crowd jostled forward from behind her, Marie clutched Rebecca's arm for support and spoke in a low tone. "I wish we could go back to wearing hoops."

"You would be as wide as you are tall. Would you want to be called a dumpling?" Rebecca quizzed her with a mischievous grin.

Marie's ready laughter bubbled as she declared her resistance to that idea.

When at length they reached the landing, Marie was able to look around. Spotting herself in a large mirror, she admired her artfully tousled curls with the stray tendrils feathering her ears. Her wide blue eyes had inspired many odes in her previous Season, and her rosebud mouth, which could pout so adorably, had captivated all the young bucks. Her gaze lowered to take in the blue spider gauze gown shot through with silver threads that caught the flickering candlelight as she moved, shimmering like light on the lake at Haverford Park. With a self-satisfied smile, she turned to her friend.

"Spring Season is so much fun after winter in the country. Town is still rather thin of company, but within a few days everyone who is anyone will be here. That's when the pleasures will truly begin." She chattered of theater parties, rides in Hyde Park, musicales, al fresco excursions, and the balls. "I do hope you enjoy dancing, Rebecca, because on some evenings, there will be two or even three balls. Many nights you won't get to your bed before dawn."

"Dance until dawn? Must I attend all the balls on offer? That will be another major change in my life." Rebecca's blue eyes sparkled. "What fun I shall have, to be sure!"

After greeting their hostess, they parted inside the ballroom with Rebecca escorting her grandmother toward the gilt chairs lining the walls. Watched by her smiling mother, Marie fluttered her eyelashes at the crush of gentlemen who surrounded her, and her dance card soon had no blank spaces left for late arrivals. Her three admirers from the afternoon were not in attendance.

Marie lived up to the nickname of Little Sprite as she swept through dance after dance. Her dimples on constant parade, she divided her attention among the coterie of young bucks who showered her with compliments, each one more extravagant than the last. She twinkled with amusement when Mr. Robert

Desmond cut her out of the pack for the supper dance, leaving the others hotly contesting his temerity.

Later, Marie snuggled against her pillows and smiled as her thoughts drifted back over the evening. Without doubt, this would be a marvelous season.

Chapter 2

The Spy

Although it was close to dawn before she slept, Marie woke before the maid brought her chocolate. Bounding out of bed, she flung open the drapes and saw that the sun was trying its best to break through the early mist. A glorious day awaited her.

First, she must tell Susan the latest *on dits*. Settling into a straight-backed chair at her writing table, Marie was soon scribbling her thoughts in their usual jumble.

> *. . . and I adore my new sobriquet, Little Sprite. Is that not simply delicious? I'm becoming acquainted with Rebecca Blackwell and getting better acquainted with Deborah Langford. You will have a difficult time recognizing Deborah since she has changed beyond all belief. I like them very well, yet neither can take the place of my own dear Susan. I pray you will hurry and get strong because I cannot feel whole without you by my side. Hannah has come with my chocolate so I must stop, but send my affection across the miles.*

There! She had crossed and recrossed her lines and could only hope her old playmate could decipher the scrawl.

Now she must dress for whatever adventures the day held.

A short while later, Sir Julian peeped around the side of his newspaper as the breakfast table chatter penetrated his concentration. He eyed the stacks of invitation cards scattered amongst the coffee cups and asked his daughter, "Is there anyone who has not sent you an invitation?"

"Is it not marvelous?" Marie enthused. "I shan't have a moment to myself—breakfasts, luncheons, teas, dinners, balls, and rides in the park. I must visit Madame Bouchét this very day."

"I seem to recall a sizable delivery from her already."

Marie cast him a glance of pure mischief. "True! However, a new riding habit is essential for my ongoing happiness. Blue velvet, I believe, with a matching toque hat and a peacock feather. A high plume would make me more visible in crowds of more statuesque ladies."

Heaving a mock sigh, Sir Julian turned to his wife. "What are our plans for entertaining this Season?"

"If you agree, I have in mind that we should schedule a relatively small dinner party fairly soon."

"Dare I inquire how you define 'relatively' small?"

"Oh, perhaps fifty people," she answered, while Marie hid a smile in her table napkin.

"Compared to Prinny's dinner parties, that is small," he conceded.

"A dinner party sounds nice," Marie agreed, "but are we not to have a ball?"

"To be sure we are. However, I would rather have it toward the end of the Season. That will allow us to take inspiration from others yet plan something different."

"Yes, and perhaps Susan will be here. Let us have something no one else does. We shall put our heads together and think of something truly original. What fun that will be."

"And what expense," Sir Julian murmured.

Amid their laughter, the door swung open, revealing the butler attempting to restrain a man of no more than average height with a narrow patrician face dominated by a pair of piercing dark eyes. "I apologize for interrupting, Sir Julian. I did explain that you are at breakfast."

"All right, Symms." Sir Julian nodded dismissal to the butler and turned to his visitor. "John, have you broken your fast? Then, shall we retire to the study away from the feminine chatter?"

"Mama, who is he? I've never seen eyes that shade of brown, and did you notice his long lashes?"

"Goodness, child, how could you see so much in so short a time?"

"I don't know how you could have missed his eyes. Is he always so somber? I wager I could bring a smile to his face."

Lady Becca laughed. "I would not be sure about that. Viscount Beaufort is a business acquaintance of your father's, something to do with intelligence."

"Intelligence? Is he a spy?" She shivered.

"Marie, you will ignore what I just said."

Startled at her mother's unyielding tone, Marie stammered, "Of course, Mama, if you say so." She paused. "I wonder why I have not met him before. What do you know about him? Is he married?"

"No, but it is not from lack of opportunity. He ignores the matchmaking mamas, although they never cease in their efforts to gain his attention for their daughters.

"That's only because he has not met me. I shall invite him to the Langfords' Venetian breakfast, but first things first." She blew her mother an airy kiss and left the breakfast parlor, her mother's words following her.

"Remember, dear, pride goes before a fall."

Hurrying up the stairs, she called for her maid. "Hannah, a carriage gown, please. No, not the sprigged muslin—the pink one with the leaves embroidered around the hem." Moments later, Marie nodded at her appearance and placed a new pink bonnet on her curls, tying the ribbons in a perky bow beneath her left ear. Flinging a saucy grin over her shoulder toward the maid, she hurried down the stairs where she hovered until the study door opened.

When Sir Julian and his visitor entered the hall, Marie stepped forward and showed her dimples. "My lord, it is really too bad of my father to keep you all to himself."

With scarcely a glance in her direction, Beaufort accepted his hat from the butler, muttered "Business," and hurried out the door.

Marie gasped, as her father erupted into laughter.

"Never mind, Poppet. He's a very busy man with several meetings to attend today. You should stick to those cubs who hang around the door. You can't say you lack for company," he remarked, as the doorknocker sounded. "Symms, my hat, please. Tell her ladyship to expect me for dinner."

While Marie outwardly enchanted her morning callers and inwardly fumed about insensitive men, Lord Beaufort and Sir Julian arrived at Whitehall and met in Colonel Hayes's private room. There, they conferred on the problems caused by yet another stolen army payroll. As always, absolute secrecy had surrounded this shipment. Only the three gentlemen now present and the courier, who met his death on the road to Plymouth the previous night, had known the date and route of the shipment. Even the courier's guards had not known until the last moment.

Colonel Hayes cleared his throat. "Gentlemen, I do not for a moment suspect either of you, and I certainly know that I am not guilty of having a loose tongue. So how do the leaks occur? Do you have any ideas, any suggestions?"

Beaufort answered. "Colonel, I, too, have complete confidence in all three of us, and it stands to reason the courier would not talk since three previous couriers met their deaths in robberies. Are we sure we have committed nothing to paper?"

Sir Julian answered, "Not to my knowledge, so even the clerks cannot know. Furthermore, we always speak behind closed doors. Is it possible that someone follows everyone leaving here on the chance we might lead to something?"

The colonel considered the question. "That is possible, I suppose, cumbersome though it sounds. Can you suggest an alternative to our usual procedure?"

"After the last robbery, we ruled out using a carriage and several outriders because they might draw too much attention," Beaufort reminded them.

"That would also raise the possibility of someone talking out of turn," Colonel Hayes added. "Yet perhaps we should rethink that option."

They discussed the matter at length, reaching only the conclusion they must obtain more money. They could imagine what Lord Wilberforce would say about that. His understanding of financial matters was well above average, but his ability to see all sides of a situation would be the deciding factor in disbursing additional funds. Certainly, they did not want another courier murdered, yet it was equally certain they must deliver funds to Wellington. The war depended on men and horses, none of which could march on empty stomachs and threadbare boots. The men went their separate ways, arranging to meet again on the following afternoon.

The following morning, Marie entered the breakfast parlor with a joyous "good morning," but her mood changed when she saw her mother's somber face.

"Mama, what is wrong? Papa, is there bad news?"

"No, no, Poppet. We're discussing something your mama has on her mind."

"Can you tell me?"

Lady Becca turned to her daughter. "You will recall Rebecca and Louise, the daughters of my two closest friends, lived much of their lives in an orphanage."

"I do recall," Marie assured her.

"Yesterday, while you were busy with Deborah, I called upon Gertrude Maitland, who, you may know, has various philanthropic interests. One of her concerns deals with females in the poorer sections of Town. The sight of so many wan-faced children on the streets hurt my heart." She used her table napkin to wipe away tears.

Marie clasped her mama's hand and turned to her father. "I don't like seeing Mama unhappy. What can we do about it?"

"We were discussing that when you joined us."

Becca refilled her teacup. "I will add that my interest isn't as sudden as it appears. The plight of little girls has been on my mind since Shelburne brought Rebecca and Louise to us. I would like to open a home for little girls, but I don't know how to go about it."

"The solution to that is simple enough," Julian assured her. "We will consult the Duchess of Dorchester."

Marie clapped her hands. "This is so exciting! Will the home be in Town? I realize that's where the girls are, but wouldn't the country air be better for them? They would be away from Town temptations too."

"That's excellent reasoning, Poppet. I'm proud of you for your interest." He turned to Becca. "My dear, as soon as I can get away from business for a day or two, we will visit the Duchess. I promise. Now, don't allow the plight of those street children weigh so heavily on your mind that you can't enjoy time with friends."

He bestowed smiles on his ladies and then left the room.

Becca heaved a deep sigh. "That is good advice, Marie. What are your plans for the day?"

Marie's lighthearted mood returned as they talked of their plans.

Over the next couple of days, Marie surveyed every room she entered and found the company flat when she didn't see the patrician face with the distinguished eyes she sought.

On the second evening, Marie arrived at the Callandar townhouse and, after a quick survey of the assembly, decided she would rather be elsewhere. Nevertheless, she smiled and allowed her eager suitors to fill her dance card. Onlookers could not say she displayed her usual sprightliness early in the evening, but the lure of the music soon drew Marie into a better frame of mind, and she became almost her normal bubbling self.

Midway through the evening, Marie stood beside the gilt chair her mother occupied and wafted her fan as she surveyed the room. She didn't see Beaufort but brightened when she saw Rebecca and her betrothed coming in their direction.

"Shelburne, without doubt you are the most modish gentleman I know," Marie informed him. "If you were not my uncle, I would lure you away from Rebecca."

He tweaked one of her curls and grinned. "I might have something to say about that, you abominable brat."

"So might I," Rebecca reminded her.

"Alas," Marie mourned with a heart-felt sigh, "all the truly charming gentlemen are already taken."

"Marie, behave yourself."

The unabashed girl flashed her dimples at her mother and asked for Rebecca's indulgence. "The lemonade seems to have gone to my head!"

Shelburne shook his head and wandered toward the card room, leaving the ladies to have a comfortable coze.

"Will your friend Louise be here this evening? I have not seen her yet this Season."

"No, I don't expect to see her," Rebecca replied. "They have not yet come to Town and perhaps will not. You see, she is *enceinte* and not feeling quite well."

"I wonder if you miss her as much as I miss my friend Susan." Marie was eager to hear what she would answer, because Rebecca and Louise had been friends as long as she and Susan.

"I do miss her, but must admit not as much as I expected. I suppose it's because I have Shelburne on my mind. Also, she's a married lady now, and that of necessity changes our focus, something neither of us ever expected to happen."

Marie thought about that a moment. Would she and Susan grow apart when one or both married? A twinge of pain settled somewhere deep inside her being. Perhaps growing up was different from what she'd thought it would be. She was not sure she wanted anything to be different, at least not between her and Susan. Glancing around the room, she met the gaze of a modish gentleman, who nodded. She returned the nod. Turning to Rebecca, Marie guarded her lips with her fan. "Do you see the gentleman in the green coat?"

"Do you mean Mr. Simon Abernathy?"

"I didn't realize you are already acquainted with him."

"I know who he is," Rebecca replied. "Shelburne warned me against him some months ago, but I found him quite likeable in our one brief conversation."

"Mr. Abernathy is out to snare an heiress, so it is as well you know in advance to avoid him. Although, with Shelburne in your pocket, I cannot believe you are in danger of succumbing to Abernathy's charms."

Over teacups in Marie's sitting room the morning after the Callandar ball, Deborah teased her about the preceding evening. "You paid no attention to your dance card, judging by the mayhem you left in your wake."

"Not quite that, but I admit to causing confusion."

"*Mayhem*," Deborah insisted with a grin. "Someone has captured your fancy, and he was not at the ball. Who is the lucky gentleman?"

Was her interest in the elusive gentleman so apparent? "Do you know a viscount named John Beaufort?"

"I do not believe so. Who is he?"

"An acquaintance of my father who came here on business, but I have never seen him anywhere else."

"What is he like? I cannot imagine your falling head over ears for one of your father's friends. Is he dreadfully old?"

Marie's voice grew dreamy as she described the handsome dark-haired gentleman with the grim mouth. "A smile would transform his appearance beyond words. And his eyes! I have never seen that color before. Just plain brown does not do them justice. Mahogany, perhaps."

"You are in raptures. Is he your father's age?"

"No, no, he cannot be as old as that. I suppose he's in his late twenties, old enough to be interesting after all the callow boys I see every day."

"Have you always considered your friends callow? Or only since you met this gentleman?"

Marie came down to earth and wailed, "He barely acknowledged my existence, and I was wearing my prettiest morning gown and a new pink bonnet."

"By all that's marvelous, why were you wearing a bonnet in the house?"

"I hoped he would take me for a drive, you ninny!"

The girls laughed and turned the subject to their evening's entertainment.

"Do you attend the Lorimer ball? Perhaps your mysterious lord will be there."

"He isn't mine—yet!" Marie dimpled but grew solemn, a side of her personality she kept hidden from public view. After all, gentlemen expected young ladies to be frivolous. Everybody knew that. "I really do want to see him again."

Marie got her wish. Midway through the evening, she stood at her mother's side surveying the crowd. Her breath quickened when Beaufort entered the room, glanced right and left and edged around the ballroom. "Good evening, ladies." He nodded to Marie and turned to Lady Becca. "I hoped to find Sir Julian here."

"He escorted us, but went to White's."

When he turned to leave, Becca asked, "Might it not cause questions if you leave so soon? If I may suggest it, perhaps you should stay to dance and talk with a few people."

"You're right, of course." He turned to Marie. "Will you do me the honour?"

From the dance floor, Marie cast a grateful smile at her mother.

There is little opportunity for conversation during a country dance, but could he not at least speak when the movement of the dance brought them together? Marie was conscious of his light touch as their hands met throughout the dance. No one ignored Marie, not even high-minded lords, so to gain his attention, she chattered and simpered by turns. Was he as bored as he appeared? Impossible. Marie Louise Rebecca Haverford was never boring. So it stood to reason, something drastic must occupy his mind. He returned her to her mother, sketched a bow, and strolled away. Marie managed not to stare as he made his way around the room talking with various people before making good his escape.

A short while later, Marie and Deborah stood together near Lady Becca's chair, while their cavaliers went in search of lemonade. Marie waved her fan before her flushed cheeks. "He came."

"Who came?"

"Lord Beaufort, of course."

"Oh, good! Point him out to me, do."

"He didn't stay. He came to find my father and only danced with me to be polite." Marie refused to reveal his boredom but was unable to pretend even to herself that his touch had been anything but indifferent.

"Perhaps at the next ball he will stay longer," Deborah offered what comfort she could.

"Perhaps."

The rest of the evening passed with Marie deciding on the one hand she would never speak to Beaufort again and declaring on the other she would see him on his knees before the Season ended. She would listen to his abject apologies and his proposal of marriage, but then with complete dignity, she would crush his pretensions. Yet if she wanted that, why was she still determined he would escort her to the Langford's Venetian breakfast? For that matter, why did her fingers tingle at the memory of his touch?

When Sir Julian returned to escort them home, he did no more than grunt when she inquired if Lord Beaufort had found him.

Chapter 3

Danger!

The day of the Haverfords' dinner party began with a heavy mist. Marie stared morosely out the window, feeling quite sorry for herself. Lord Beaufort had sent his regrets, claiming a previous engagement, but she doubted that excuse. If the truth were told, he wanted to avoid her. That set the tone of her day. Neither the mist nor her spirits lifted.

Midway of the afternoon, Marie decided, if she stayed in the house another minute, she would go berserk and do something drastic. She rang for her maid.

"Hannah, I need some exercise."

"Miss Marie, you're never going out on a day like this!"

"Yes, I am. The mist isn't heavy enough to hinder us. Do you care to accompany me, or shall I request the services of a footman?"

"If you're determined to do this, I shall accompany you." Hannah's glum voice came from deep within the satinwood wardrobe from which she emerged, clutching a Clarence blue cottage cloak with an attached hood. After fastening it around her mistress's neck, she hurried away for her own drab outerwear.

Moments later, the thud of horse hooves matched their footsteps as they made their way to the park. Standing at a corner waiting to cross the road, their first realization of danger came when they heard the loud neighing of a horse coming close. As the huge black animal reared on hind legs, front hooves clawing the air, a pair of arms closed around Marie and Hannah and dragged them to safety.

The sudden backward movement caused them to lose their footing, and both landed in a heap atop their rescuer. Scrambling to their feet, they offered heartfelt apologies and gratitude.

The slight gentleman rose to his feet and bowed. "Gervais Hadley at your service, ladies. I hope neither of you suffered injuries. Perhaps I should escort you to your destination."

Hannah brushed Marie's cloak, muttering about chance-met gentlemen while he searched the roadway for his high crowned beaver.

Her mistress ignored her. With a smile at Mr. Hadley, she introduced herself as Miss Haverford and thanked him again for his heroic action. "I believe we should return home at once."

"I will see you to your door. In Berkeley Square, I believe."

When Symms opened the door to them, Marie asked where she would find her father. Upon learning he was in his study, she allowed Hannah to remove her cloak, and then she led Mr. Hadley toward the back of the house. There she tapped on the study door and then opened it.

Taking a deep breath, she asked, "Papa, may we interrupt? This gentleman is Mr. Hadley whose quick action saved me from the hooves of a rearing horse. I have expressed my gratefulness, as has Hannah, and I believe you will want to add your appreciation."

"Yes, of course, I do." He shook the younger man's hand. "Marie, you will explain to me later why you were out and about on such a day. In the meantime, you may leave us."

Recognizing the note of steel in his voice, she scurried away to find her mother, who hurried toward her, arms outstretched.

"Darling, Hannah said you were almost killed by a runaway horse!" Running anxious hands over her daughter, she asked, "Where are you hurt?"

Marie clasped her mother's hands and held them still. "I sustained no injury, Mama, I promise, and I apologize for scaring you. Let us ring for tea in my sitting room, and I shall tell you all about it."

She finished her tale of woe with a long sigh. "I deserve whatever censure you and Papa give, and unless I mistake, those footsteps we hear are his."

The next hour was one she preferred to forget, as she later told Susan in a letter. She confessed she didn't know which had unnerved her more, the rearing horse or her father's scold.

> *He has confined me to the picture gallery for exercise if there is even a hint of inclement weather. At least it's a long gallery, so I can stretch my limbs. After giving the matter some thought, I decided this is better. I won't be constrained to ladylike steps! Susan, I can almost hear your voice—hoydenish behavior indeed! The mortifying truth is that I am just as bird-witted as Lord Beaufort believes. Most remiss of me not to have mentioned him sooner, considering how often he's in my thoughts. He's handsome, though sober of face, and has the most compelling eyes it has ever been my*

privilege to see. Beaufort is Papa's business acquaintance and does not yet recognize my existence, but he will! Now I must stop this scribble and dress for dinner. Susan, dear, do please get healthy soon!

Marie was more shaken than she cared to admit and dreaded the dinner. Nevertheless, she recalled her duties as daughter of the house and received their guests with a smile.

Throughout the elaborate meal, Marie concentrated on her dinner partners, and the horror of the afternoon receded from her thoughts. The ladies left the gentlemen to finish their meal without feminine chatter and gathered in the drawing room. Here, Marie entertained their guests with a few melodies on the piano and passed the cups when Symms brought the tea tray.

Beaufort had taken his dinner at White's and afterwards joined a card game. He was content to end the evening with only a minor drain on his resources, so he bid his companions a pleasant evening and strolled home. He was not aware of exactly when a pair of beguiling blue eyes invaded his thoughts, but invade they did, and he turned accusing.

Why had he avoided the Haverford dinner that evening? Surely not because of her. No, that could not be. That dainty little miss was the daughter of a business acquaintance, nothing more. Besides, he had met her kind before, all appearance and no substance.

That was not what he wanted in a female, so he would not allow dainty, blue-eyed Marie Haverford to invade his thoughts again.

A few days later, Marie watched from the shadows at the top of the stairs as Symms escorted Beaufort to her father's study. When the butler left the hall, she strolled into the study, stopping just inside the door, her eyes growing wide in assumed surprise.

"La, sir, you startled me! I believed the room to be unoccupied," she prevaricated without blinking an eye.

He rose to his feet. "Good morning, Miss Haverford. Symms asked me to wait here for Sir Julian."

"My father is a punctual person, so he must have been unavoidably detained." She seated herself in a straight chair, arranged her skirt into neat folds, and waved him to a chair opposite her.

"Except for the Lorimer ball, I have not seen you at any soirées, and we missed you at our dinner party. Do you not care for society?" Marie played with her fan and favored him with a dazzling smile.

He resisted that smile with every ounce of his being and spoke abruptly as a result. "I have little time for such tomfoolery."

"I know you work with my father, and he escorts us most evenings. You could find the time to attend some balls, could you not? They are such fun!" She didn't give him an opportunity to answer.

"Perhaps you prefer daytime social engagements? Deborah Langford is planning a Venetian breakfast for the day after tomorrow, although I do not know why it is called breakfast since it is held in the middle of the afternoon. However, that is of no importance. Do say you will be my escort!"

"Ah, I believe I hear your father now." Beaufort turned toward the open door, while Marie bit her lip in chagrin at the unfortunate interruption.

"Run along, Marie. Lord Beaufort and I have business to discuss."

"Must you conduct business all the time, Papa?" With a saucy smile across her shoulder at Beaufort, she left the room.

Sir Julian's lips twitched as he read the relief written so clearly on his visitor's face. He settled behind his desk and waived Beaufort to a chair. "Have you had an opportunity to speak privately with Lord Wilberforce?"

"For a few minutes only."

"And?"

Beaufort grimaced. "To put it mildly, he is not pleased. He said to approach him again *after* we solve the delivery situation."

"We couldn't expect a different answer, could we?"

"No, but he's forewarned of our eventual request."

"You're on better terms with him than I," Sir Julian conceded. "Do you believe he has sufficient influence to persuade Parliament to part with more funds without delay?"

"Yes, I do. In fact, I'm confident he is even now considering how to obtain the funds with the least amount of controversy."

"It behooves us to solve the problem without further delay, but I admit to being mystified about how to go about it. My thoughts go around in circles."

"Mine, too." Beaufort rose. "We can only keep thinking through what we know until something new breaks through the mass of details."

The days passed too swiftly for Marie. She did not encounter Beaufort, although she watched for him at every event.

She arrived at the Langford's breakfast with her mother—not her chosen escort. That was enough to put any personable young lady in a temper, and Marie was no exception. The fact that several gentlemen gazed upon her with adoring eyes did not mend matters. She hurriedly glanced around the room, even as she greeted Mrs. Langford. Beaufort was not there, nor had she expected he would be. Deborah's commiserations didn't mend matters either.

"I insisted Mother invite Lord Beaufort, even though we have never laid eyes on him. He sent his regrets."

Marie tossed her curls, and an inelegant snort greeted this information. "I doubt his lordship even eats." She couldn't resist the twinkle in Deborah's eyes, and her silvery laughter rang out.

They joined a table crowded with chattering young people. As the gentlemen vied for attention with exaggerated tales of derring-do, Marie grew quieter and soon sat staring into space, her thoughts elsewhere. She roused herself to join in the general fun when she felt Deborah's gaze. She concentrated on her surroundings for a short while before her thoughts again wandered.

By keeping a smile pasted on her face when she was not chewing her food, Marie believed no one realized her abstraction. However, she did not deceive Lady Becca, who tapped her on the shoulder as soon as she finished her meal.

"Come, Marie. We must leave."

After a glance at her mother, Marie rose to her feet.

There was an underlying note of steel in Lady Becca's pleasant words. "Do you think you can pay attention long enough to thank our hosts?"

Marie gathered her wits and assured Deborah she had a very pleasant time and would see her at the Swanborough's musicale that evening. She knew she deserved the homily her mother issued on the carriage ride home.

"Whatever is wrong with you, Marie? How could you be so rude to your friend? We can return to Kent if you find the Season so boring."

"I'm sorry, Mama," Marie replied. "I should not have allowed my disappointment to show."

"What possible disappointment could you have had? You appeared to be the only person who did not enjoy the occasion."

Marie equivocated, "The boys seemed so young."

Lady Becca laughed. "Is that all? They *are* young, you absurd child. Understand this, Marie. Your father and I did not rear you to be a spoiled darling of the *ton,* and we expect better behavior from you. Is that clear?"

"Yes, Ma'am. I do apologize for embarrassing you." Marie gave her mother a quick embrace, and they were at peace as they talked of coming entertainments.

When their carriage approached Haverford House, Lord Beaufort mounted his horse and rode in the opposite direction, much to Marie's chagrin. A moue of frustration crossed her face. How like him to be here when she was some other place.

She managed to laugh it off a few hours later when she met Deborah at the Swanborough home. First, however, she apologized. "Deborah, I truly am sorry I failed to pay attention this afternoon and after looking forward to your breakfast too. Can you ever forgive me?"

Deborah squeezed her hand. "Of course, you ninny! I knew why your thoughts wandered, and it's all right. Truly, it is. I only wish his lordship had been there, because I want to meet this paragon of yours."

"He was not at your house because he was at mine," Marie told her with a rueful smile.

Deborah closed her gaping mouth and commented on the hand of fate.

"Fate cannot deter me from asking him to escort me to the Buxteds' picnic. He can't go on denying me forever, because I shall find a way to wear down his resistance." Marie preened, as she thought of her new rose carriage dress with the long sleeves and the wide-brimmed leghorn bonnet with matching ribbons. The perfect ensemble for an al fresco engagement.

"Oh, see who is approaching," Deborah whispered behind her fan. "He must be coming to you because he looks straight through me."

"Andrew Saunderson looks straight through almost everyone. He appears to believe that, as the son of an earl and as wealthy as Golden Ball, being toplofty is his due. He paid close attention to Louise Mansfield last autumn, much to her grandparents' delight and her own dismay." She turned on a smile. "Good evening, Lord Saunderson. Are you acquainted with my friend, Deborah Langford?"

He dipped his head a fraction and stood by their side a few moments before the music started.

"Do you see what I mean?" Deborah asked when he strolled away. "He looked straight through me. I might as well not exist."

"He truly is a rude person. Although he joined us, and not we him, and stood by our side for an appreciable time, he never uttered one word, not even in greeting. Belinda Creighton is besotted with him, and I cannot understand why."

Deborah sighed. "We had best return to our seats and try to ignore the caterwauling."

"That's a forlorn hope, I fear, but if we don't regain our chairs, Mama will have something to say and not something I want to hear."

The following morning, Marie had another opportunity to waylay the unwary lord. Crossing the front hall, she glanced out a window just as a carriage pulled to a stop. Beaufort alighted. After a quick glance around the empty hall, she slipped into the study and stepped out of the immediate view of anyone entering.

"Please wait here, my lord, while I inform Sir Julian of your arrival."

"Thank you, Symms."

When the door closed behind the butler, Marie presented herself to Beaufort's view. "Good morning, my lord! This is another beautiful day, is it not?"

Beaufort turned toward her, a quick frown marring his brow before he smoothed it away. He stood behind a large leather chair, his hands gripping its high back. "Good morning, Miss Haverford."

"I did not see you yesterday, either at the Langfords' breakfast or at the Swanborough musicale. You missed two enjoyable occasions, my lord. Perhaps you prefer outdoor activities? The Buxteds plan a picnic and boat ride on Saturday. Do say you will be my escort!" Her smile faded as she heard footsteps approaching.

Sir Julian perceived the situation at a glance and nodded dismissal to his daughter. "Marie, I daresay your mother is in need of your presence."

With a pert grin, she left the gentlemen to their business. Outside the door, she admitted that her prey had outwitted her yet again and hoped for another opportunity to see him before Saturday.

Late that evening, Beaufort sat in his study, going over in his mind the details of the recent robberies. A blazing fire took the chill off the room, and he gazed into the flickering flames. Unfortunately for his objectives, a pair of blue eyes insisted upon intruding into his thoughts. The third time this happened, he erased his frown and allowed his mental vision to expand beyond the sparkling eyes and take in the entire face. Shaking his head in resignation, he recognized the Haverford chit.

It was bad enough that he encountered the silly chit so often in her own home, but he drew the line at allowing her to intrude on him in his. He had no time for schoolgirls, not even the daughter of his friend and cohort. Still for that reason, and only that reason, he assured himself, perhaps he should be nicer when he next saw her.

He pushed away the vision of her saucy smiles and returned to his cogitations.

The rattle of drapes across the windows caused Marie to open one eye. "Hannah? Is it time to get up already?"

"Yes, Miss, if you want breakfast before the Buxteds' picnic. Drink your chocolate." The maid flitted around the room, preparing a bath and laying out the rose carriage dress.

By the time Marie entered the breakfast parlor, her enthusiasm knew no bounds. "Good morning, Mama. Is it not a beautiful day for a picnic? Has Papa gone out already?"

"An early appointment with Lord Beaufort required his attention, but he said to wish you a pleasant day."

"How can they work on such a beautiful day? I feared it would be too cool for a picnic so early in the season, but Hannah assures me it is already warm."

"I had my doubts about the weather too, but I'm sure it could not be better. I remember James and Alice Farnsworth are chaperones, but remind me who else will attend the picnic."

"I can only name those who will stop for me, although I'm sure there will be others. There's Robert Desmond, of course. Lady Alice Farnsworth is his sister, and we will use their carriage. Deborah Langford and Richard Anstey make up the rest of our party."

"Lady Farnsworth can be forgetful at times, so be aware of your behavior, even if she doesn't pay attention," Becca cautioned.

"I will remember." Marie reverted to her favorite subject. "Lord Beaufort would have much more fun if he escorted me to the picnic." She gave her mother a naughty grin. "You should have seen his face when I suggested it. Horror does not begin to describe his reaction."

"I'm not surprised," her mother responded. "I did warn you about him."

"I consider this a minor setback." Her curls bounced as she cast a sly glance toward her mother and vowed, "I shall snare him yet!"

"Snare? Don't you ever let me hear you use that word again, unless you are talking about rabbits!"

"I knew that would get a rise out of you, Mama! I don't want a husband I have to snare, I assure you, although I won't mind if the one I choose realizes how lucky he is to have snared me!"

Lady Becca glared at her daughter but joined her mirth. "You are incorrigible, did you know that?"

"My lady, Mr. Robert Desmond and his party have arrived." Symms's voice brought the laughter to a sudden halt, and Marie jumped to her feet.

"I shan't be above a moment!" She hurried up the stairs, calling for Hannah, and soon came tripping down again, her curls peeking from beneath a wide-brimmed straw bonnet tied with rose ribbons.

Lady Becca accompanied her daughter to the carriage and greeted Alice and James Farnsworth.

"Don't worry about your daughter, Becca," Alice trilled. "We shall take good care of her."

"I'm sure of that, Alice." Becca turned to Lord Farnsworth, whom she had known since they were in leading strings. "I appreciate your willingness to contend with these young people, James. I don't envy you."

"No trouble at all, I assure you, Becca," Farnsworth told her. "Keeps me young, don't you know."

Some people believed James was not quite right in his upper works, but Becca knew of old that his seeming forgetfulness was a ruse to avoid doing anything he didn't choose to do. With a smile, Lady Becca turned to the other members of the expedition, Deborah Langford and Richard Anstey, and wished them a pleasant day. She stood on the steps and waved until they were underway.

Mr. Desmond and Mr. Anstey chose to ride and now moved in front of the barouche carrying the others. The escorts said little, but inside the carriage the girls chattered like magpies as they made the hour's journey to Buxted Park.

There, alighting from the carriage, Marie shook out her skirts and greeted her hostess. "Mrs. Buxted, what a delightful idea this is. I vow I can hardly wait for the boat ride."

With a smile, Mrs. Buxted waved her hand in the general direction of the gardens. "The other young people are strolling through the rhododendrons. You will find them there."

As the girls moved in that direction, Marie glanced back across her shoulder. Mrs. Buxted had turned to Lady Farnsworth. "There are few plants in bloom, but that son of mine insisted on being the first to entertain al fresco this Season."

Alice wafted her fan with a languid movement and sank into a chair under a large shade tree. "They will enjoy being out of doors on such an agreeable day and won't even notice the lack of flowers."

And enjoy themselves the young people did. Marie forgot she had considered her friends immature and joined their boisterousness. "Oh, look at the ducks. Let us follow them."

"They're only going to the pond, Miss Haverford," Timothy Buxted assured her.

"Could we feed them some bread crumbs?"

"I believed you would enjoy that, so I stashed some near the pond."

With a joyous whoop, they followed the ducks and were soon competing to see who could throw the crumbs the farthest. With the crumbs gone, the gentlemen began skipping stones across the pond. The young ladies insisted upon trying, much to the amusement of the gentlemen. Their jeers grew quiet, though, as Miss Patterson made hers skip three or four times. With the other girls cheering her on, she admitted that her brothers had taught her the secret of turning her wrist just so.

Marie tried but soon admitted defeat.

Strolling back through the gardens, she smiled to herself when Lord Beaufort's face intruded into her mental vision. She could not imagine him skipping stones across a pond. With a shrug, she quickened her steps when a bell rang, summoning them to the food spread on tables on the side lawn.

"I vow I don't know when I enjoyed myself more." Alice Farnsworth gently fanned herself.

Marie and Deborah exchanged a grin. They doubted that their chaperone had so much as moved from the lawn chair since she sat down upon arrival—and was not likely to move until necessary.

Marie forgot all about ladylike nibbling at food when she heaped her plate with cold chicken, cheese, and fruit. Strawberries from the succession houses were especially welcome with large dollops of Devonshire cream. She sat on a rug next to Miss Patterson, whom she had not previously met.

"I must say you routed the gentlemen with skipping stones. Having brothers is educational."

She laughed. "Thank you, Miss Haverford. Do I gather you don't have brothers?"

"I have no siblings, and I can't decide if that's a blessing or a curse."

"Having a sister would be nice, I believe, but I assure you that brothers can be altogether different when they play tricks."

"My friend, Susan Conners, has brothers, and she has said much the same thing about them."

"I don't believe I've met her. Is she here today?"

"No, she's recovering from influenza but hopes to come to Town later in the Season. I will be sure to introduce her, if she does join us. I daresay you will enjoy comparing tales of your brothers' pranks." Marie set aside her plate and rose. "I will speak to Lady Farnsworth, after which I understand we must walk some before the boat ride."

"Do you join us on the boat, my lady? I'm sure you will enjoy it above all things." Marie could not contain her enthusiasm. "I have only been on a boat for the short ride to Vauxhall Gardens, and I look forward to a longer trip."

Her chaperone raised her eyebrows. "I believe I shall forego the pleasure, child."

After the young people strolled again around the grounds, the Buxteds ushered their guests to the landing stage where boats waited. Footmen tried to hold the boats steady while the landlubbers stepped into them but were not altogether successful. Amid shrieks and laughter, everyone settled onto the cushioned seats, and their cruise on the Thames began.

The cool breeze was pleasant, and the river stench so common in London did not reach this far into the country. For this, Marie gave silent thanks and chatted with her friends, exclaiming over the prowess of the sailors. As the speed increased, however, she grew quiet. Her stomach rolled with the boat—perhaps that last serving of strawberries and cream had not been a good idea. Sun glaring on water gave her a headache, and rivulets of perspiration slid into her eyes making them burn. She refused to disgrace herself, so she fixed a smile on her face and joined the talk around her. Would this nightmare never end?

When Marie stepped off the boat onto the landing stage, her knees buckled. She smiled at the jokes and accepted Mr. Desmond's arm.

"How pale you are!" He peered into her face. "I'm afraid the sun is too bright for you."

"I only need to sit in the shade a few minutes." Marie glanced around. "Deborah can sit with me, while you fetch some lemonade."

"You poor dear, have you suffered beyond bearing?" Deborah's words tumbled over each other. "I enjoyed myself so much I failed to notice how the ride affected you. Is not Mr. Anstey wonderful?"

Marie almost moaned aloud. She was pleased beyond measure that Deborah's new style of dress had increased her self-confidence. She even admitted she had enjoyed helping the other girl choose various gowns. However, she did not want an exhibition of Deborah's newfound confidence at this moment. She wanted Susan, who wouldn't chatter on and on about a mere gentleman when her friend needed sympathy.

"Marie, my dear, I understand you are unwell." Lady Farnsworth's worried face turned this way and that, trying to locate her husband. "We must leave on the instant."

"Oh, no, my lady, that is not necessary." Marie's voice was so weak Lady Farnsworth called for their carriage. With a sigh of relief, Marie rested her head against the squabs and vowed never to set foot on a boat again.

As her eyes closed, a sudden thought made them pop open again. What if Lord Beaufort saw her like this? He not only would smile—he would probably laugh. She was spared that humiliation at least. Perhaps this was an omen warning her away from Beaufort.

`Chapter 4

Hot and Cold

As soon as her headache eased, Marie sat at her writing table to compose a letter to Susan Connors. She needed her old friend's sympathy but kept her account of the boat ride as humorous as possible.

Remembering Susan's childhood adoration of Lord Shelburne, Marie continued with news of him. She visualized the other girl sitting on a rug under their favorite beech tree and imagined they were talking.

> *Uncle Edward and Rebecca have set their wedding date for June, which he says is the perfect time for a honeymoon cruise on his yacht. I say better them than me! My honeymoon, when it comes, will be on dry land.*
>
> *Lord Beaufort continues to ignore me. In fact, he does not even know I exist. As a woman, I mean. He sees me as the daughter of his business acquaintance. I try to get his attention, but he looks right through me. He didn't even answer when I invited him to escort me to the Langfords' Venetian breakfast and the Buxteds' picnic.*
>
> *I can almost hear you ask if I'm truly interested or am I piqued because he does not respond. To that I can only say, yes, at first, it's true I only wanted his attention. After all, he has been on*

the Town for several Seasons, and no one has brought him up to scratch. Yet I realize more and more it is not only that. I want him to like me.

Having crossed and recrossed the single sheet of paper, Marie ended the letter with the hope her dear Susan was feeling more the thing and could soon join her in Town.

Placing the letter on the hall table to be franked and delivered to the post office, Marie wondered how soon she could expect a reply.

It came sooner than she had dared hope. Finding it on the breakfast table a few mornings later, she perused it and read the village news to her parents. As soon as she could excuse herself, she returned to her sitting room to consider the advice Susan had given about Lord Beaufort.

My dear Marie, I hesitate to sound censorious, but has it not occurred to you he sees your behavior as quite hoydenish? The way you lie in wait for him could spoil whatever chance you might have of attracting his notice. Perhaps you try too hard to gain his attention. I am not saying you should ignore him but treat him the way you treat the rest of your father's business associates. Think of Sir Julian's most gruesome acquaintance, and then treat Lord Beaufort half way between the way you normally treat him and the way you treat Sir Julian's other acquaintance.

Nevertheless, you know you have my constant support. I miss you more than mere words can convey. Home is so boring without you popping in and out to relieve the tedium. Even my brothers are subdued, and you know how rare that is!

Susan's admonition occupied Marie's attention for only a moment. She frowned over Susan's suggestion about Lord Beaufort for a moment. Her face cleared, and she chortled. "Mr. Sansbury! From now on, I shall look at Lord Beaufort and think of Mr. Sansbury. I will surely ruin everything by laughing at him."

Marie had her first opportunity to test this theory that evening.

Marie glanced around the gold and cream ballroom of the Claremont townhouse. A tremendous squeeze, indeed, with at least three hundred people present.

"Good evening, Miss Haverford."

Startled, Marie spilled lemonade down the front of her gown. She had been so engrossed watching the crowd that Lord Beaufort had caught her unawares.

As usual, he was neatly dressed, a modicum of starch used to stiffen his shirt points and his cravat tied in such a simple style it didn't merit a name. No one would ever mistake him for a member of the dandy set.

"Please forgive me for startling you. Is your gown quite ruined?" His worried face caused her to smile.

"No, no, my lord. Lemonade does not stain, as I often have reason to know. I'm a very clumsy person."

The mauve silk was new, and she hoped she was right about the staining. Nevertheless, it must be all right to prevaricate in a harmless way if it put someone at ease.

A slow smile crossed his face. "You are most considerate, Miss Haverford. Most ladies would be upset."

His smile was worth the wait, she decided, as she flashed her dimples at him. "I had a tantrum once, and my nanny turned me across her knee. I never tried it again."

Marie's father interrupted their laughter when he slipped his arm around her shoulder and smiled before turning to her companion. "Good evening, Beaufort, are you enjoying the ball?"

"I would not go so far as to say that, but I am enjoying this conversation." He turned his lazy smile toward Marie. "If there were room to dance, I'm sure I would enjoy that too."

She glanced toward her father, who squeezed her shoulder and moved away. Suddenly overcome with shyness, Marie gazed at the mauve slippers peeking out from beneath her gown. She was not sure how to respond to this new Beaufort.

A deep chuckle brought her eyes to her companion's face, alight with amusement. "I have never seen you at a loss for words before now."

She smiled, searching for a reply, but the arrival of her supper partner prevented her. She cast an appealing glance at Lord Beaufort, whose face became a mask before he bowed and strolled away.

She did not see him again that evening, although her gaze roved over the crowded room. Later she lay awake, staring at the canopy over her bed and musing over the evening. Lord Beaufort was different tonight, amiable, even teasing. She had been right about his face. A smile transformed it, even vied with his mahogany eyes for attention.

Mr. Sansbury had not entered her mind even once.

When Hannah brought her a morning cup of chocolate, Marie stood at the open window and listened to the chirping birds.

"Whatever are you doing out of your bed so early?"

"This is a glorious day, Hannah. No one could be a slug-a-bed on such a morning." Marie sipped her chocolate, while the maid put the room to rights. "Lay out my new lavender gown, Hannah. Mama and I are paying calls this morning."

A few moments later, Marie greeted her parents with a kiss when she joined them at the breakfast table and kept up a bubbling commentary on the Claremont ball, while she devoured an omelet filled with slivered ham and cheese, washed down with two cups of coffee.

Sighing with repletion, she met Lady Becca's twinkling eyes with a wry smile. "Yes, I know, Mama. If I continue eating the way I do, I shall someday be so heavy that I waddle instead of walk."

"I wonder how many other young ladies who nibble at dinner parties are this voracious while dining at home."

"Shall we ask them when we make our visits this morning?"

Sir Julian folded the newspaper and joined the conversation. "What are our plans for the evening, dear?"

Becca looked up from perusing her mail. "We plan a quiet evening at home. We're dining *en familie* with Mama and Edward, who will bring Rebecca."

"A *quiet* evening when Edward and Marie are in the same room? Surely you jest!" He pushed back his chair midst their laughter. "You must tell me the results of your questioning at dinner this evening, Poppet."

With a quick smile for his ladies, he quitted the room.

"Where are we going, Mama?"

"As yet this Season, I have spent too little time with the Duchess of Amesbury, so we must start there. After that, we shall call on two of Almack's patronesses, Mrs. Drummond-Burrell and Sarah, Lady Jersey."

"I must say I am no end relieved we don't have to fret ourselves about vouchers for Almack's this Season. Last Season was too much to bear, even though you seemed certain we would receive them."

When they entered Amesbury House, they rejoiced to see that they were the first visitors.

"You visit me at last, you naughty girl," the duchess chided Lady Becca in an affectionate tone, greeting her with an embrace, and directed a smile at Marie.

Marie dipped into a deep curtsy. "You must hold me accountable for Mama's dereliction of duty, Your Grace. You see, she finds chaperoning me requires all her time."

"You are as impertinent as your mama was at your age," the duchess told her.

"Oh, no, Your Grace, please do not recount my escapades to my daughter. I would not want her to get more ideas in her head."

As other visitors arrived, the conversation became general, and after the requisite half hour, the Haverford ladies went on to other houses, more cups of tea, and more *on dits*.

That afternoon, Marie and Deborah strolled in the park, their maids a few steps behind. Ignoring the chatter around them, they discussed the Claremont ball.

"I believe Lord Beaufort left at that point, because I didn't see him again." Marie shook her head. "I admit I do not understand him."

"Men really are beyond anything, are they not?" Deborah sympathized. "What in particular about Lord Beaufort puzzles you?"

"Everything! Well, not really, but sometimes it seems that way. He was friendly last evening, yet at other times he acts as though I am an absolute stranger. No one has ever treated me that way before. Why does he?"

Deborah shrugged in answer. "I don't have that problem with Mr. Anstey, I assure you. He is always most attentive, and I expect a declaration any day. I might be betrothed before you." She babbled on until she received a jab in the ribs, which made her jump away. "Why did you do that?"

Marie nodded to their left, where a pair of horsemen approached. "Lord Beaufort is on the black. I wonder if this will be a friendly encounter or if he will cut me."

She was not long in doubt.

As the gentlemen reached them, Marie smiled. "Good afternoon, my lord. Is it not a pleasant day?" Ignoring his silence, she continued to chatter. "That is a magnificent mount, sir."

Lifting his hat ever so slightly, Beaufort murmured, "Good afternoon, ladies," and rode away without a backward glance.

Deborah gasped. "Well, I never!"

Marie whispered in a broken voice, "Now, do you see what I mean? He runs hot and cold. I never know what to expect from him."

"He cut me! Whatever reason he thinks he may have for being rude to you, there is no reason to cut me. He doesn't even know me."

"I vow the next time I see him, I shall give him the cut direct." Marie tightened her lips and willed the heat to leave her face.

"Good afternoon, ladies."

At the sound of a deep masculine voice, the girls whirled around, and the frown left Marie's face.

"And a good afternoon to you, Mr. Abernathy," she said. "May I introduce my friend, Miss Langford?"

"My pleasure, Miss Langford," he assured her with a bow.

"Deborah, Mr. Abernathy is an acquaintance of my father, and I must in good faith warn you that he is a rogue of the first stare!"

"You wound me to the depth of my being, Miss Haverford." With a hand placed over his heart, he heaved a great sigh, bringing laughter from the girls. "Ah, just what I wanted to see, smiling faces on two beautiful young ladies. Now, I bid you both a good day."

With a bow, he sauntered away.

Deborah turned to Marie. "What a handsome gentleman! Do you know him well?"

"I only know what everyone does."

"Not everyone knows anything. I've never even heard of him before now."

Marie laughed. "He's the second son of a family in Oxfordshire—I've never met any of them—which means that he must make a life of his own because his elder brother inherited everything. That's the way of the world, as you must know from your own family. Most younger sons go either into the church or the military, even if they're not fitted for them."

"Yes, I do know that because our curate at home is the third son. The middle son chose the military. Mr. Abernathy hardly strikes me as being church-minded, and he is not in a military uniform, so how does he live?" In a mocking whisper she said, "Don't tell me he has gone into *trade*!"

"No, and he isn't a cardsharp either, in the event that's your next question, else he wouldn't be accepted by Society." Marie grinned at her. "However, he is a gambler. At least that was the *on dit* last year. It's amazing to me that gambling is acceptable but earning an honest living in trade is not."

"You said he doesn't cheat, but does he fleece people who don't know any better than to play with him?"

"Oh, no, that would put him beyond the pale too. The worst that Society says about him is that he is on the hunt for a rich wife."

"That leaves me out!"

On that laughing note, the girls separated.

For their family dinner, Marie chose a leaf-green gown with a single flounce edged with lace matching that around the square neck and puff sleeves. She presented herself in front of Shelburne the moment he strolled through the drawing room door.

She tucked her arm through his crooked elbow and twinkled up at him. "How do you like my gown, Uncle

Edward? I wore it to match your eyes so you won't feel abandoned amongst all the blue eyes."

He grinned down at her. "Good evening, Brat. I appreciate your thoughtfulness in making sure I do not feel like an outcast within the family."

Rebecca joined their conversation. "Marie, the green makes your eyes appear bluer."

"You weren't supposed to notice that. I'm trying to impress Uncle Edward so he will purchase me a diamond tiara, because Papa won't."

Symms interrupted the laughter to announce dinner.

With food in front of her, Marie left the conversation to the others.

Shelburne made a teasing remark to Rebecca. Turning to Becca, he said, "You will never guess what your namesake has convinced me to do."

With an indulgent smile toward their young guest, Becca said, "I'm sure she will get her way if she has the spunk her mother did. Tell us."

Shelburne smiled at his blushing betrothed. "She wants to rescue little girls who might otherwise end up on the streets."

"You see, Lady Becca, I would like to emulate the Duchess of Dorchester only in another county." She bit her quivering lip. "Last summer, a man pushed a little girl from a wagon into the street right in front of me. If God had not placed me in that spot at that precise time, who knows what would have happened to Miranda Abernathy? I believe that was God's instructions to me to help little girls the way the duchess helped me and so many others."

Shelburne lifted her hand to his lips, but before he could speak, Marie did.

"We talked just the other morning about doing that same thing, didn't we, Mama?"

"Yes, we did. My heart hurts to see so many children on the streets. Julian agrees and said we will talk to the Duchess of Dorchester as soon as he gets a couple of days away from his Whitehall duties."

"There are so many children who need help, a home in every county would not hold them, but we can make a further dent in the problem." Lady Olivia nodded to the footman to remove her plate. "However, Julian, if you wait until you've met your responsibilities at Whitehall, you will never make it to Hampshire."

He nodded. "That occurred to me, so I asked Colonel Hayes if I can be away while he and Beaufort confer on current problems."

"Elizabeth Dorchester and I made our come-out together, but I haven't seen her since she married. I'll write her that we are about to invade her household. We can set a date later."

They continued their discussion over a tea tray until Lady Olivia called for her carriage.

The young ladies were not the only people who commented on Beaufort's rude behavior in the park that afternoon. His companion, Mr. Brownlee, stared at him. "I never knew you to be ill-mannered to a young lady. You're often less than cordial but never rude."

Instead of answering the oblique question, Beaufort changed the subject, commenting on the coming races at Epsom Downs.

He could talk on other subjects, but he did not forget Marie Haverford. Late that night, sitting before an apple-wood scented fire in his study with the brandy decanter at his elbow, Beaufort berated himself. Why was he rude to her? She seemed to bring out the worst in him. No, that was not true. Last night at the Claremont ball, he was pleasant to her, yet this afternoon he embarrassed her in front of her friend. She was such a sprightly little thing too. So different from the usual missish behavior he encountered among the chits, which each Season produced and which bored him almost to tears. No one should be rude to little sprites, he scolded himself, especially ones with big blue eyes that looked so trustingly into his. Besides, had he not decided to be sociable with her because of his relationship with her father?

How would he react to her on their next encounter? He learned the answer to that question when he encountered her in Hyde Park the next morning.

Riding with Mr. Desmond, Marie glanced around the deserted park. "Race you to that stand of trees!"

He grinned and started after her, his huge roan outdistancing the smaller chestnut.

"You cheated! You know you did!" Her laughing words came out on gasps for breath when she reached him. As she raised her eyes, she noticed a rider approach and swallowed a groan when she met Beaufort's speculative gaze. In her embarrassment, she forgot her vow to cut him. She raised her chin and introduced the men.

"La, Lord Beaufort, what must you think of me, galloping *ventre á terre* in the park. Without my groom too! However, I assure you he is just behind . . . ."

Her affected voice faded when he answered in his usual bored tone, "No need to explain, Miss Haverford. Your behavior is of no concern to me."

Her mortification complete, she maintained an aloof silence until her groom joined them at the gate. Lord Beaufort tipped his hat and rode away without speaking.

Desmond had been quiet in the presence of the older man, his anxious gaze moving from face to face. Only when Beaufort rode away did he speak. "I say, Miss Haverford, who is he? I mean, is he related to you in some fashion? I don't recall ever seeing him."

Her brittle laughter assaulted his ears. "An associate of my father's. He's nothing to me."

"Perhaps I'm dense, but I fail to understand the strain between you."

With those words, they arrived back at Haverford House. Marie jumped from her horse without waiting for assistance and, bursting into tears, wailed, "Oh, I wish I were dead!"

His mouth agape, Mr. Desmond followed her up the steps as the butler opened the door.

Marie darted in without a word but could not avoid hearing the conversation behind her as she hurried up the stairs.

"Sir, do you feel an explanation to Sir Julian is indicated?" Symms inquired.

The younger man flushed. "I don't know what happened. She was all right until we met Lord Beaufort. I don't know why she changed, but I don't believe I insulted her in any way. Certainly, that is the furthest thing from my mind."

"I would not worry about it, sir. Young ladies can be difficult to understand."

Difficult to understand? Marie fumed. Her motives were clear to the meanest intelligence. She wanted pleasant attention from a gentleman who seemed capable of it only on rare occasions. She was polite to him despite his rude behavior, both yesterday and this morning.

"I deserve a reward for my magnanimity," she told her mirror image.

Chapter 5

Business and Pleasure

Almack's!

Even though Marie had attended balls here during her first Season, it still thrilled her to receive vouchers. If the rooms were less grand than one might expect, the magnificence of the company made up for its deficiencies. She gazed around the cavernous room, noticing how the brilliant colors of the ladies' gowns stood in high relief against the black and white of the gentlemen's formal evening wear.

She turned to Deborah and murmured behind her fan, "All this black and white is depressing. I wonder what would happen if just once a gentleman wore a flaming crimson waist coat?"

"The doorman would not admit him, but it would be fun if a dandy smuggled one into the rooms and then changed. Mrs. Drummond-Burrell would swoon without a doubt!"

Marie saw Beaufort enter the door with five minutes to spare before it closed for the evening. He circled the room toward her until an overblown dowager, sporting no less than six plumes in her orange turban, stopped him by grasping his sleeve.

"I vow, my lord, 'tis an age since you favored us with your presence. You remember my daughters, of course. Hortense, Gertrude, make your curtsies to Lord Beaufort."

The florid-faced girls giggled behind their fans, and their voices came in a high-pitched chorus. "Good evening, my lord. You should attend more balls."

Hortense nudged her mother, who chimed in, "Oh yes, my lord."

When he sketched a bow and turned away, his glance settled on Marie, who controlled her laughter with difficulty. A slow smile lit his face, softening his harsh features. "Good evening, Miss Haverford."

Marie again forgot her vow of indifference. Tonight, he was in an agreeable mood, and she would enjoy it. "My lord, are you acquainted with Miss Langford? Deborah, this is John, Viscount Beaufort."

Deborah's eyes widened as she acknowledged the introduction.

"It surprises me that beaux do not surround you ladies. How can the young bucks be so remiss?"

Marie saw the twinkle lurking deep in his eyes, and her dimples appeared, but it was Deborah who answered. "La, sir, we poor females must catch our breaths on occasion. Here is my partner, now, for the next dance." She swept the stammering young gentleman onto the dance floor, leaving Marie with Beaufort.

"You have no partner for this dance?"

She glanced around and swallowed a sigh of relief when she didn't see her would-be partner. "I did have, but it appears he forgot."

"Please allow me." Beaufort tucked her hand into the crook of his elbow and led her on to the dance floor, while Marie admonished her heart to behave.

"It's a pleasure to see you this evening, my lord." Marie breathed in the spicy scent emanating from his skin. Quite an improvement over the wine fumes she had encountered with her other dance partners.

"I seldom attend social functions, but perhaps now is the time to change my habits."

She seemed unable to pull her gaze from his, and her voice came out in a whisper. "Yes." Marie hardly heard the music end and seemed to float as he escorted her back to her mother. He chatted a few moments before taking his leave.

As Marie and her new partner joined a Scottish reel, she surreptitiously watched Beaufort make a tour of the room, speaking to a few people, before leaving. Her heart bounded when she realized he danced with no one else. *Why is he not always this affable?*

Too excited to sleep despite the maid's soothing use of a hairbrush, Marie decided to talk to Susan by way of the post.

> *My dearest Susan, I danced with him tonight! Of course, you know I mean Lord Beaufort. After seeing me galloping in Hyde Park this morning, I didn't expect him to acknowledge my existence, but he was most amiable at Almack's this evening. And he danced only with me! He did the same thing once before when he sought Father's whereabouts. He danced once, talked to a few people, and left. I didn't see him talking to Mama this evening, but I suppose he did. Still, he could have danced with someone else, yet he chose me. With that thought, I bid you pleasant dreams and desire the same for myself.*

Marie started to sign her name but then began writing again.

I wonder if you think of me even half as often as I think of you. Probably not, because you have such an active household. I'm envious of them! With that thought, I will stop this scribble. May God speed your recovery, my dearest of friends.

Marie settled against her pillows and waited for sleep to come. Feeling again the warm clasp of Beaufort's hands as they met in the dance, she closed her eyes and drifted into dreamland. There, she again danced with him, and with each turn of the minuet, she wore a different gown, gowns that were not in her closet.

She woke the following morning determined to have a serious discussion with her father. Those dream-gowns were a clear indication that she must visit the modiste. With that in mind, she went to his study soon after breakfast.

She paused outside the door and listened for a moment. She could distinguish an occasional word when the voices rose above a murmur. She had not realized her father had a visitor so early. Hearing a reference to a gold shipment, she realized it was a business meeting and decided this was not the time to request a larger clothing allowance. She moved away and went in search of her mother.

"Mama, who is in the study with Papa? I didn't hear anyone arrive."

Becca raised her gaze from the paper she held and smiled at her daughter. "Lord Beaufort, I believe." She shook her head at the wry expression on Marie's face. "Are you still trying to fix his attention?"

"Why is he so changeable, Mama? I never know how he will respond, and it confuses me. Sometimes I am sure he likes me, yet at others he acts as though I don't exist. He runs hot and cold!"

"There's no accounting for men, my dear, but please realize he has business on his mind." She smiled in sympathy and cautioned, "Possibly, he only sees you as the young daughter of his associate. You will recall I suggested this before."

Marie nodded and turned the subject. "What are your plans for today?"

"I stay at this desk until I get my correspondence done." Her determined expression caused Marie to break into laughter, which her mother soon joined.

"Are there any errands I can do for you after I exchange some books at Hatchard's?"

"I need to replace the ribbons on my favorite poke bonnet, so you might get some at the drapers. I want a deep pink shade this time."

Marie returned to her bedchamber where her maid waited. "Come on, Hannah, I need to walk off some energy before we reach the busy thoroughfare."

They stepped out briskly, yet when they neared the crowded streets, Marie slowed to a ladylike pace. They stopped to chat with several acquaintances as they made their way to Piccadilly. At Hatchard's, Hannah sat on a bench outside the door, while her mistress browsed through the shelves.

"Marie, how lovely to see you. Have you found anything interesting?" Rebecca's quiet voice pulled Marie's attention away from her perusal of a volume clutched in her hands.

"I understand there is a new book out by the lady who wrote *Sense and Sensibility*, but it isn't here,"

Marie replied. "I decided to read her first one again. I wonder if the new one is as entertaining."

"I have not yet read the new one either, but it could hardly be better than her first novel. I recently overheard an interesting conversation at a literary salon about the author who styles herself 'A Lady.' It seems that her brother revealed her name as 'Jane Austen,' but she does not acknowledge it."

"I suppose she does not want the attention such acknowledgement would bring. If she is, in fact, a lady, being a novelist could ruin her reputation, and society would never accept her."

Rebecca nodded. "I believe we pay too much attention to what society expects of us, yet as long as we live among the *ton*, how can we ignore its decrees on proper behavior?"

"I wish I knew. I'm torn between doing what I know God expects of me and what Society demands of me."

"I have the same problem, but I doubt that will comfort you."

They moved toward the desk, and Marie glanced at the book in Rebecca's hand. "What did you choose?"

"I admit to a fondness for Lord Byron's poetry," Rebecca confessed. "This is *Childe Harold's Pilgrimage*, which I want to read again."

Marie agreed with her choice and changed the subject. "I must go to the drapery shop. Will you join me?"

A smile spread across Rebecca's face. "Oh, by all means. I can never resist going there, and since my grandfather gives me such a generous allowance, I confess I spend more time there than I should."

They handed their books to their maids and strolled toward the draper's.

Marie's heart quickened, and her eyes widened. Was that Lord Beaufort ahead of them? The compact shape resembled his. She walked faster until the gentleman turned into a shop. She slowed her pace again. The profile was wrong. Had she glanced across the street, she would have seen Beaufort watching her, a slight smile on his face.

An hour later, with their maids carrying additional packages, Marie and Rebecca called a halt to their shopping and turned toward home.

Rebecca was in a reminiscent mood. "Last year when I lived in London, I used to visit the drapery shop often with Louise Mansfield. I should say Louise Stafford as she is now. We dreamed of the day when we could afford to make purchases."

Marie never considered how she spent her own pin money, nor could she visualize earning it. "Were you able to afford many treats?"

"Not a lot, but we did go to Gunter's whenever possible. Louise vowed that someday she would eat ices every day."

Marie envied their close friendship and had a yearning to see Susan. She hurried into speech. "Let us go there now."

Over their ices, Marie asked if Rebecca's evening plans included the Kendall ball.

"Yes, Shelburne and I will be there," replied Rebecca. "I gather you're going too?"

"We dine with the Carlisles first, I believe, and go to Lord Kendall's at some point during the evening. Now, I really must go, or Mama might think I absconded with the glover, or some such."

On that lighthearted note, they went their separate ways.

Several hours later, Marie wished it were the custom to speak across the dinner table rather than only to her immediate partners. The blushing youth on her left hardly spoke but spent a considerable amount of time staring at her with rapt eyes. Embarrassing to say the least. The older gentleman on her right relived his prowess on the hunting field, all the while helping himself to his wine glass. At this rate, he would be under the table before they finished dinner or else in her lap, because he leaned ever closer to her as he shouted into her ear. It was fortunate dinner was over before she took recourse to shoving him away. Otherwise, she would have created a scandal of unmatched portions.

"Marie, are you ready to leave?" Lady Becca materialized at her daughter's side after rising from the table.

"Oh, yes, please," Marie begged *sotto voce*. "I developed a headache and a strong desire to scream during the second course. If ever I cared about hunting, I would not after this dinner."

Her mother commiserated with her. "I know how you feel because Lord Wolfden has been my dinner partner on several occasions. He and the Carlisles are close friends of your Haverford grandparents, so we must strive to be pleasant, regardless of the toll on our patience. Perhaps your other dinner partner was an improvement?"

"He spent the entire meal staring at me instead of eating. If he does that at all dinner parties, it's no wonder to me that he is so thin."

Marie's headache eased somewhat during the carriage ride to the Kendall's soirée, and she scanned the ballroom in search of a certain patrician face. Her heart skipped a beat when she saw him standing a short distance to her left. She met his eyes and smiled before turning to Mr. Desmond for the first dance. He merely nodded. Couldn't he smile?

Throughout the evening, she went from one dance partner to another, yet Beaufort did not approach her. She fumed to Deborah but pretended indifference otherwise. She sat out one dance and hoped he would join her. Instead, her adoring swain from dinner begged a dance with her. It was a disaster. He stepped on her toes. He stumbled over his own feet, and in doing so, he stepped on the hem of her gown. She cut his apologies short by excusing herself to mend it.

Marie met her mother's amused smile and hurried to the ladies' withdrawing room. Using pins from her reticule, she pinned the flounce into place and seized the chance to relax a few moments in the quietness of the otherwise empty room. Her head now throbbed in earnest. She heard distant voices in the hallway and stepped to the mirror, where she patted her curls into place before turning to leave. When she heard masculine voices, she waited behind the slightly opened door until they passed.

"There must be another shipment in the next few days, and I need the gold more than old Hookey does," a stammering voice said.

A more high-pitched voice laughed. "And this one will go astray too!"

"Quiet, you ninnies, anyone might hear you."

Marie stood in the shadows, almost holding her breath as the voices receded. What should she do?

Old Hookey was the nickname people called Wellington, so they were talking about money going to the Peninsula, and her father had an interest in that, as did Lord Beaufort, she reminded herself. Her father was not at the ball, but his lordship was, so she would tell him.

Before she could leave the room, a group of chattering young ladies entered, and she joined their conversation. They made such a din that no one could believe they had overheard a conversation not meant for their ears, so she returned to the ballroom with them.

An hour later, which she deemed an appropriate time lapse, Marie stood at the entrance to the supper room and surveyed the ballroom. When she spotted Lord Beaufort near the door, she kept a slight smile on her face as she willed him to approach her. She emitted a quiet sigh of relief when he arrived at her side. "Good evening, my lord."

He nodded a brief greeting. "You are not dancing? It must be the first time tonight."

His stiff face and cold voice gave no hint of pleasure in her presence. His obvious boredom dismayed Marie, but she would not allow him to cut her this evening. She answered with a snap, "Lord Beaufort, I was not aware you keep track of my dances. In the future, I shall confer with you before accepting them."

He stared at her a long moment and then turned away.

Marie touched his hand, her own quivering at the contact. She withdrew hers and raised her fan to guard her lips. "I apologize, my lord. My abominable temper got away from me, but please don't walk away. There is something I should tell you."

His cold gaze rested on her face for a moment before he nodded.

"I overheard a conversation that might interest you." She could detect no change in his face but continued with determination. "Lord Stokely and Mr. Rayson, together with another man, spoke of a gold shipment being sent to 'Old Hookey,' and said it would *also* go astray."

He made no sound or movement, yet as she talked, he seemed to grow even quieter. "Tell me, Miss Haverford, what makes you think I am interested?" The steel undertones belied the casual question, and his dark gaze demanded an answer.

Must he be so wary? Couldn't he just admit his interest? No, she supposed not. Spies must not reveal curiosity. "I heard you and my father talking about a shipment being stolen."

"Have you told him you listened to our business meeting?"

She flinched, but met his eyes. "No."

"Had you not better find him now and tell him about that as well as what you overheard tonight?"

"He is not here, my lord. After he escorted us here, he went on to his club, as he so often does. That's why I told you."

"Did anyone else hear the conversation? Did anyone see you?"

"I am sure no one saw me. I was alone inside the ladies' withdrawing room with the door barely cracked open. I heard the voices passing, so I stayed there for several minutes. Then, when a group of girls came in, I joined them to return to the ballroom." She paused a moment. "As to your other question, I cannot know if there was anyone else who might have heard."

"Are you sure of the identity of the voices?"

"Certainly. I often hear both Lord Stokely and Mr. Rayson speak. Lord Stokely has a very cold voice even his laughter cannot conceal, and Mr. Rayson stammers."

"What about the third voice?"

"It was a young voice, high-pitched but masculine. I never heard it before, but I expect I would recognize it again."

"I recommend you do not meddle in things you cannot understand." His voice was like steel. "You tend to your needlework and leave the important matters to men."

Marie drew herself up to her full five feet, tilted her face upward, and stared him straight in the eyes. "My lord, I realize you consider me frivolous, and perhaps I am at times. However, you should know that I am also rational and far from stupid."

With quiet dignity, she walked away.

A bemused Lord Beaufort watched her until she disappeared from his view. Somehow, the small, rigid form didn't match the soft bit of femininity she most often portrayed. He preferred the softness. He strolled around the room for a few minutes and then left in search of Sir Julian. He at last ran Haverford to earth at Boodle's where he was one of a small group of men gathered around a card table.

"Ah, Beaufort, care to join us in a hand of whist?"

"I don't believe so at this hour. It might last all night. Whist isn't my game. However, I shall observe for a while if I may. I might learn something!"

After some desultory conversation, the gentlemen departed one by one. Sir Julian spoke when only he and Beaufort remained. "You are not a regular at this club. Is something amiss?"

Beaufort kept his voice low. "Your daughter is aware of our military problem. She overheard a conversation between Stokely and Rayson this evening in which they laughed about a shipment not getting through to Wellington and commented on another one."

"Stokely and Rayson?" Sir Julian shook his head in disbelief. "Do you realize they're close friends of the Duke of York? I thought he learned his lesson after the Clarke scandal."

"I never quite believed he didn't receive any part of the money she obtained from selling those military favors, so he's a possibility." Beaufort paused a moment. "However, I'm more inclined to suspect Kent than York because he wanted to be commander-in-chief so much that he connived behind York's back, even though authorities could not prove it. Or perhaps didn't investigate thoroughly. There's no question Kent was upset when Prinny's first act after becoming Regent was to give the post back to York."

"I dare say you're right, yet we remain where we were. How is the information getting to them? As far as I am aware, even York doesn't know when we ship funds."

They now had some names to consider, so there was progress at least. They parted, agreeing to meet with Colonel Hayes the following morning.

While Beaufort conferred with Sir Julian, Marie paced her bedchamber. *Tend to needlework, indeed*, she fumed. Typical arrogant man, that's what he was. Arrogant. I'll show him! I will learn who that third man is, and before he does, no matter what it takes.

Chapter 6

Rational Decisions

"Good morning, Papa, Mama." Marie's joyous voice preceded her into the breakfast parlor. She favored Symms with a smile when he handed her a plate containing buttered eggs and a kipper. "Hmmm, this smells delicious! It's great to be alive on such a beautiful morning, is it not? Have you ever known such delightful weather to continue for so long?"

Her father grunted his answer, but her mama agreed. "We must enjoy it now, because it surely cannot last."

Sir Julian studied his daughter's countenance until she wrinkled her pert little nose at him.

"Do I have a smudge, perhaps? Or is my nose shiny? It isn't chivalrous of you to notice, Papa."

He lay down his table napkin and muttered, "Excuse me," still with a thoughtful expression and left the room.

Marie stared after him for a moment before turning to her mother. "Mama, am I in disfavor?"

"I don't believe so, dear. He's probably thinking about a problem of some sort. I understand he has an engagement with Colonel Hayes and Lord Beaufort this morning, so his abstraction need not concern you."

Marie concentrated on her breakfast. She had a notion of the problem but chose not to divulge her knowledge. Instead, she changed the subject.

"Will you attend the Pattersons' musicale this afternoon, or do you have other plans? If you do, I can ask Deborah's mama to take me up in their carriage."

"That's unnecessary because I plan to go. Caroline Osborne, as she was then, made her come-out the same Season as I, although I did not know her well."

"Naturally," Marie teased her. "You were too busy helping your friends to elope. Admit it!"

Lady Becca smiled but refused the bait. "Caroline married Mr. Patterson early in that Season, and I didn't see her again until this year. I understand Mr. Patterson is somewhat reclusive. I believe you told me you met her daughter at the Buxteds' picnic."

A moue of chagrin crossed Marie's face. "Don't remind me of that day! However, yes, that's when I met Miss Patterson, and she struck me as being a demure sort of girl. Until, that is, she bested the gentlemen at skipping stones on the pond. I promised to introduce her to Susan, assuming, of course, that Susan comes before the Season ends. Both have brothers who play pranks on them, so they have much in common. I like her quite well and hope her musicale is a success."

The musical afternoon at the Patterson townhouse was, indeed, a resounding success, at least in the eyes of the hostess. The Italian soprano was in good voice, people occupied every chair at the beginning, and few slipped out during the first part of the program.

Marie held a different opinion. Listening to the caterwauling gave her a headache, so she slipped away in search of a quiet place. Seeing a door standing ajar, she peeped around it and, thinking the room empty, closed the door behind her and moved toward a chair near the window.

"Have you escaped that atrocious voice too?"

Marie whirled around with a gasp.

"I'm sorry! I didn't mean to startle you." A lady smiled at her from the depths of a long sofa.

Marie caught her breath. "You did startle me, but I'm quite recovered now. I'm Marie Haverford. I do not believe we've met?"

"I have been retired from society for a while, so perhaps not. I'm Lady Emily Cavanaugh."

Marie didn't understand the other's intent stare, but she acknowledged the introduction. "I'm pleased to make your acquaintance, my lady." She paused a moment. "Do you realize that Mrs. Patterson believes she found a rare treasure? I sing better, and I never had a singing lesson in my life."

Lady Emily's laughter filled the room. "I can't imagine anyone sounding worse! And if she's Italian, I'm a Chinaman!"

"Since you are neither a man nor yellow-skinned, you cannot be a Chinaman, so I suppose that means she is not Italian. Where do you think she originated?"

"Who knows? Probably an East End brothel. Doubtless a lover taught her how to speak like the upper classes, before he cast her aside. Singing is a better way to earn her keep than being on the tiles."

Marie's eyes widened. Ladies don't talk that way! Where does she hear such things?

A brittle laugh essayed from the sofa. "I see I shocked you."

"No, no," Marie protested.

However, Lady Emily swung her limbs off the sofa, sending a delicate scent swirling as she rose to her feet. "I'm forever doing that. I shall leave you in peace." Her bitter words lingered after she left the room.

Marie sat a few moments longer, thinking of this new acquaintance. Ladies don't recline on sofas either, at least only in their own homes. She eyed the sofa thinking how much better her head would feel if she lay down for a while. She resisted the temptation. For whatever reason, Lady Emily had free and easy ways, but Marie knew better than to emulate them no matter how freeing they would be. She shook out her skirts and left the room.

Marie saw Lord Beaufort when she neared the music room, and with head held high, she brushed past him. She heard him speak, but her heart was thumping so loudly she did not understand his words. So now he knows what it means to receive the cut direct. The thought gave her deep satisfaction.

Lord Beaufort heard a gasp from somewhere to his left but was too furious to identify the source. His countenance pale with rage, he strode out of the house, looking neither to the right nor to the left. He realized he collided with someone but didn't slow his pace and left Mr. Brownlee staring after him.

The chit would cut him, would she? He tried to be nice to the daughter of his friend, and this is what he got for his efforts. Snubbed in front of who knows how many of his friends by a schoolroom miss. It would serve her right if he never spoke to her again. A silly giggling child is all she is and without a serious thought in her head.

He still fumed when he arrived at his own front door without any recollection of how he got there. Why did he let that nonentity affect him this way? She was of no importance, and he would indicate that by his manner when he next saw her. She would probably attend the Fitzgeralds' rout tonight, and he would go just to show her exactly how unimportant he considered her.

His difficult morning accounted for most of his upset. Colonel Hayes had ridiculed the idea that either York or Kent was involved with the missing funds, although he did admit that both gentlemen often were short of ready cash. With King George permanently off the throne, Parliament did its best to control royal spending, not always succeeding. However, that was neither here nor there because they didn't have a shred of proof that Stokely and Rayson were involved either. Furthermore, just because they were York's friends, it did not follow he knew anything about their activities. So much for that. They should concentrate on finding the real culprits and leave the royal dukes out of it.

Beaufort spent the remainder of the afternoon in his study, brooding. That chit! How dare she? When light from the windows dwindled into evening, he left the study, informing his butler he would have dinner at Watier's and go to the Fitzgeralds' rout from there. He dressed for the evening with more care than usual, flinging away no less than four cravats before he tied one that satisfied him. That bit of conceit irritated him further, and he called for his carriage in a stormy frame of mind.

Meanwhile, Marie found a chair in the Pattersons' music room where she could watch the door from the corner of her eye. Beaufort didn't enter, but Deborah did. Marie quickly made eye contact and motioned toward the vacant chair next to her.

"You put his lordship in a miff." Deborah whispered. "He left so fast he bumped several people and didn't even apologize."

"Never mind him. Before the music begins again, tell me what you know about Lady Emily Cavanaugh."

Deborah glanced at her in surprise. "I only know what everyone knows."

"As you said to me some days ago, not everyone knows anything! I never even heard of her until a few minutes ago when we met in an anteroom."

Diverted, Deborah inquired, "What were you doing in an anteroom?"

"Trying to find a quiet place until my headache eased, but instead I found her. She stared at me when she said her name as though I should recognize it."

"That does not surprise me. The highest sticklers of the *ton* refuse to acknowledge her since she made a *mésalliance* a couple of years ago. She married a wealthy Cit to get her family out of debt, which was a sacrifice on her part, but they didn't appreciate her efforts. They even disowned her for disgracing their name, as I understand it. They preferred living in genteel poverty to having a Cit in the family. Anyhow, he died a few months later and left her a wealthy widow."

"I wager her family decided on the instant to 'own' her again," Marie commented with a sniff. "I hope she cast them out of her life."

"She did, according to the *on dits* and that added to her disfavor by the *ton*. I heard rumors she is Lord Stokely's mistress. Are you acquainted with him?"

"I know who he is. He is such a cold fish I'm surprised anyone is his mistress."

They dissolved into soft laughter, and Lady Becca had to shush them.

When the singer at last warbled the final aria, Marie heaved a sigh of relief and turned to Deborah. "I must go straight home and lie down for a while. If I don't get rid of this headache, I shall make a very poor partner at the Farnsworth whist party tonight. Will you be there?"

"No, I'm promised to the Fitzgeralds' rout."

"Then, perhaps we can meet tomorrow." With a smile, Marie turned to her mother and indicated her desire to leave.

A few hours later, Marie alighted from her family carriage in front of the Farnsworths' Portland Place residence. Her headache had abated somewhat, and she could face the card party with equanimity if not real enthusiasm. She followed Lady Becca through the doors and greeted Lord and Lady Farnsworth with becoming modesty. Her mood changed when she entered the card room.

"Mr. Desmond! I did not realize you would be here this evening."

He grinned. "Of course, I'm here. Did you forget Alice Farnsworth is my sister?"

"Yes, I did," Marie confessed and glanced around. "I feared I would be the only young person here, but I see Miss Patterson conversing with Mr. Buxted."

"Yes," he nodded with satisfaction. "Buxted asked me to be sure she received an invitation."

"Oh! I do remember he stayed close by her side at the picnic, but I did not realize he had formed a partiality for her. Does she return his admiration?"

"I believe she does. At least her eyes lit up when she saw him across the room a few moments ago."

"Shall we join them?"

"Miss Haverford, it is indeed a pleasure to see you this evening. I was not at all sure I would know anyone here."

"Likewise, Miss Patterson. Just seeing you and Mr. Buxted here improves my expectations of pleasure out of all proportion."

The gentlemen greeted this sally with laughter.

Marie forced herself into a falsehood. "And I must tell you how much I enjoyed the music your mother provided us this afternoon, Miss Patterson. I had not heard that singer previously. Is she new in Town, or am I admitting my ignorance of cultural attractions?"

Miss Patterson flushed with pleasure. "She is, indeed, new in Town this Season. I shall tell Mama how much you enjoyed hearing her. We believe our guests received her well, and Mama will be in alt that you agree."

Mr. Buxted's glance encompassed Mr. Desmond on its way to Miss Patterson. "I notice that Desmond does not comment on this glorious sensation. Was he not invited either?" A distinct twinkle in his dark blue eyes belied his hurt tone.

"You were invited, Mr. Buxted." Miss Patterson controlled her twitching lips with an effort. "I clearly recall you told me that you had an engagement with someone named Jackson."

Mr. Desmond gazed at her in awe. "*Someone named Jackson?* Do you tell me you are not familiar with the name of the greatest pugilist of all time?"

Marie intervened before Buxted could dispute him on that point. "We ladies know nothing about pugilists, nor do we care to learn about them. Therefore, gentlemen, we will talk of something important." Turning to the grinning Miss Patterson, she inquired,

"Have you seen that delicious straw bonnet in the window at Chlotilde's Millinery?"

Hoots of derision from the gentlemen drowned out Miss Patterson's answer. It was fortunate for the peaceful coexistence of the combatants that Lady Farnsworth interrupted.

"Children," she admonished. "You are here to play whist, remember. I see now I must place all of you at separate tables before you come to blows."

When they protested, she continued. "When we change tables later in the evening, perhaps the four of you can contest each other with cards instead of words."

Marie joined a table consisting of a dowager and two older gentlemen and realized they played with determination to win at all costs. Sir Julian had taught her to play whist several years before, and she believed she would not disgrace herself, even with these ferocious competitors. Partnered with one of the gentlemen, she concentrated on the bidding and believed she acquitted herself well.

"The chit takes after her sire," her partner informed the others. "Haverford is the most dedicated whist player I ever played against, and that is going some. He beats me all hollow every time I make the mistake of sitting down with him."

Marie smiled with pleasure. "Thank you, sir. My father taught me the game, and I'm never able to defeat him no matter how hard I try."

They exchanged partners for another hour of play. Her new partner scowled at her from beneath bushy eyebrows. "I hope you intend to play as well with me as you did with him, young lady, despite his overblown flattery."

With a slight chuckle, Marie reassured him on that point but admitted to herself a few moments later she was finding it difficult to follow his bids. Why would he throw away that card? Did he forget trumps? It relieved her to note they did win some points despite his erratic play, and she welcomed Lady Farnsworth's reminder of the supper laid out in the next room.

Marie and her friends sat down to heaping plates of cold chicken, asparagus with lemon sauce, fruit, and hot buttered rolls. She intended to nibble in a ladylike manner. She did at least manage not to lick her fingers, as she pointed out to her mother later. Nevertheless, she ate everything on the plate and accepted the apple Mr. Desmond pared and sliced for her. Wiping her fingers on a table napkin, she sighed with repletion. "I was famished."

"One would never have guessed it," Mr. Desmond told her, a twinkle lighting his eyes.

Marie grinned at him and turned her attention to Miss Patterson and Mr. Buxted. She watched them for a few moments, noting how absorbed they were in each other. When she turned back to Mr. Desmond, an expression of tenderness in his eyes made her blink.

She had known him forever, it seemed, and had never suspected him of warmth toward anything except his horse. Before she could speak, Lady Farnsworth approached their table.

"We are beginning play again, children, and this time you may share a table."

One could not in all honesty say the caliber of play at their table matched that of the early part of the evening. Animated conversation mixed with the bidding in the first hand, but soon Miss Patterson and Mr. Buxted began sharing glances more than the conversation. Marie turned to Mr. Desmond to comment on them and surprised another tender expression in his eyes. After a moment of stillness, her face became pensive, and she forced her gaze back to the cards in her hand.

However, her mind was not on them, and if she admitted the truth, she hardly knew what she held. Her thoughts were on Lord Beaufort. Why did he not look at her the way Mr. Desmond did? Would she ever surprise an expression of such tenderness in his eyes? She tended to doubt it.

His lordship gazed around the ballroom at the Fitzgeralds' townhouse, seeking yet again a glimpse of the Haverford chit. How could he dismiss her with cool politeness if she were not there?

He noted a young female standing to his left, watching him with amusement.

"Good evening, my lord. This is a famous squeeze, is it not?"

He knew he had met her but, for the life of him, couldn't remember her name.

She came to his rescue with twitching lips. "Deborah Langford, my lord. A friend of Miss Haverford. I dare say you remember her?"

"Ah, yes, Miss Langford." He gave her a perfunctory bow.

"I noticed you staring around the ballroom, my lord. Are you looking for someone in particular?"

"Ah, no, Miss Langford, no one in particular."

"I thought you might be searching for Miss Haverford. She told me she would be at the Farnsworth whist party this evening." She hesitated before continuing. "In the event you care to know, my lord."

"I do not care to know," he answered and, with an abrupt bow, left the grinning Miss Langford standing alone.

How dare she assume he was looking for the Haverford chit? They were as alike as two ha'pennies in a purse. Both were silly, chattering schoolgirls who didn't know how to treat their elders. Elders? Was he so much older than they? The thought appalled him. He accepted his hat and cane from the footman and hurried out into the night.

The walk home from the Fitzgerald rout calmed him considerably, but he could not ignore the knowing grin that was on the Langford chit's face when he left the ballroom. Was he so transparent? He decided on the instant he would guard his expressions with more care in the future and ignored the little voice that added, "And your heart, also, if you have good sense."

That stopped him in his tracks until the jostling crowd forced him to move. What put that idea in his head? His heart was not involved. Or was it? The question bounced around in his mind as he proceeded homeward.

Chapter 7

Country Pursuits

Deborah managed to be the first caller at Haverford House the following day and regaled Marie with her story before anyone else arrived.

"You should have seen how stiff his shoulders were as he walked away," Deborah chortled. "One would think he was attached to a backboard."

Marie shrugged. "Are you sure he was looking for me?" At her friend's affirmative nod, she continued, "He probably only wanted to give me a set-down. Another one, I should say."

She turned to greet other visitors, and their conversation lapsed, but Lord Beaufort continued in her thoughts. Had he intended to ignore her, or had he truly wanted to dance with her? A few moments later, a new subject occupied her mind.

"A house party? What a marvelous idea!" Marie told Mr. Desmond, who had extended the invitation to visit his parents in Hertfordshire. Only their usual group of young people occupied the drawing room at that moment, and Marie turned to her mother. "Oh, Mama, please say we may go. It will be beyond anything great!"

Before Lady Becca could reply, Deborah added her entreaties. "Oh, please, my lady, do say you approve! If *you* favor the idea, my mother will also, and I do so want to go. I'm sure Miss Patterson's mother will follow your lead too."

Miss Patterson nodded her agreement, and with the others she awaited Lady Becca's answer.

Lady Becca hesitated for a moment while she eyed Mr. Desmond closely. "Are you sure Sir Ambrose and Lady Desmond know about this invitation? Or are you collecting acceptances before telling them?"

He turned a shocked face toward her. "Oh, no, my lady, I would not do that! I asked if I might issue the invitations, and they assured me they would welcome anyone I care to bring. Still, if it eases your mind, I shall send a note off to my mother this very morning and ask her to be in touch with you directly."

Lady Becca smiled at his earnestness. "I realize you think me lacking in good manners for questioning your invitation, yet it would be uncivil of me to present your parents with a crowd of young people they did not expect."

Ignoring the murmurs of denial at such a thought, she continued. "I shall accept the invitation providing Mrs. Patterson and Mrs. Langford also agree to go. I warn you they might think a sennight out of London in the middle of the Season is not a sound idea."

"We must go immediately and tell them of the treat that's in store for us!" The Misses Langford and Patterson hurried toward the door with Mr. Buxted and Mr. Anstey close on their heels.

"And I shall send that note to my mother on the instant," Mr. Desmond promised as he, too, headed toward the door.

Left behind, Marie embraced her mother. "Mama, you are surely the best mother in all of England. Nay, in all the world!"

She must write the good news to Susan without delay! Thus, another letter winged its way to Kent. By way of reply, Susan wrote her congratulations by return post.

> *How fortunate you are to have a sennight in Hertfordshire with Mr. Desmond's parents. I remember him as being an amiable gentleman who showed signs of sitting in your pocket last Season. I look forward to hearing all about Desmond Park upon your return.*

Did Susan sound wistful? Marie perused the missive again. Yes, her dear friend did sound wistful. Probably boredom from remaining at home. With a deep sigh, she acknowledged there was nothing she could do, so put the matter out of her mind.

Plans proceeded apace but only after Becca inquired of her mother if she had received a reply from Elizabeth Dorchester. Lady Olivia shared the news some of the girls had thrown out a rash of unknown origins, possibly contagious, so it would be better to postpone their visit until the situation improved.

Sir Julian and the senior Mr. Buxted regretted they could not join their country sojourn but declared business interfered. However, Mr. Patterson and the senior Mr. Anstey leaped at the chance for a week out of London's noise. So it was that, in midmorning a week after Mr. Desmond issued the invitation, three carriages and a baggage wagon wound their way through London's traffic in a northwesterly direction.

The ladies were loud in their praise of the landscape as they traveled over the rolling hills and along the banks of the River Lea. Despite the slow travel, they reached their destination in time for luncheon.

"Sir Ambrose, Lady Desmond, it's good of you to allow us to invade your quietness," exclaimed Lady Becca.

"My lady, we must always find it a pleasure to entertain our son's friends. You honour us with your visit." Lady Desmond spoke in a soft voice accompanied by a gentle smile that encompassed the entire company. "You have time to freshen yourselves before luncheon is served on the terrace. You ladies come with me while Robert escorts the gentlemen to their rooms."

Half an hour later, they gathered around a table laden with sliced ham, cold chicken, chilled asparagus, boiled and sliced potatoes sprinkled with finely chopped shallots, and an assortment of fruit and cheese.

When Lady Becca found a moment alone with Marie, she warned her about her usual eating habits. "For if this meal is a good example of what we may expect throughout the week, neither of us will be able to wear our gowns by the time we leave."

"Oh, but think how much pleasure we would have in replacing them!"

"I seem to recall your father said something about your dress allowance just recently."

"Oh, I intended to use yours!" her irrepressible daughter replied with a saucy smile. However, they soon learned that there would be plenty of opportunity for exercise.

"Shall we stroll through the gardens or would you prefer a game of lawn croquet?" inquired Mr. Desmond of his guests.

"You have a croquet lawn?" The question came in a chorus from Mr. Buxted and Mr. Anstey, even as the girls gazed at him in surprise. They thought this pastime, which had come over from France only a few years before, was the prerogative of royalty.

Their host looked a trifle smug at his success in surprising his guests. "We set it up last autumn. Shall we play?"

The gentlemen were eager, the ladies less so, but they expressed their eagerness to learn after glancing to their mothers for approval.

Thus, while their elders sat in the shade and observed, the young people listened to the instructions. Soon the crack of mallet against ball resounded around the area, accompanied by much laughter.

"I say, Miss Haverford, for such a tiny person, you send the ball flying." Mr. Desmond gazed at her with obvious admiration.

Marie dimpled at him but confessed, "Miss Patterson is a better player than I. She always angles the ball correctly, and mine has a tendency to go off in the wrong direction."

The game continued until the players' shrieks became so loud their elders called them to order. The instant the young people laid down their mallets, the older gentlemen grabbed them and headed for the wickets.

"Aha!" Mr. Anstey exclaimed to his father. "You only wanted to play yourselves." With a grin across his shoulder, the senior Mr. Anstey acknowledged the hit and continued toward the croquet lawn.

A few hours later as Marie put the final touches on her evening toilette, the door opened, and Deborah slipped inside, followed by Miss Patterson. She greeted them with a smile and urged them to take chairs. "I declare this is a week to remember always.

Just think, we learned how to play croquet. We're the first ones in our circle to do so."

Deborah agreed in her usual exuberant voice. "Did you notice how quickly Mr. Anstey grasped the rules?"

"Miss Patterson . . . ," Marie turned toward the other young lady. "No, that's too formal. I realize our acquaintance is of short duration, but may we be on a first-name basis just as Deborah and I are?"

"I would like that," she answered. "My name is Grace."

"Grace it is, and you are to call me Marie and her Deborah. Now since we have settled that, I shall ask the question I started to ask earlier. Do you do everything well? I mean, you bested even the gentlemen at skipping stones at the Buxted picnic, and now you put Deborah and me to shame at croquet."

Grace flushed with pleasure at the compliment. "I suppose it comes from growing up with older brothers. I tagged along after them and attempted to do everything they did. I didn't always succeed, of course, but I did often enough for Mama to complain about my being less of a lady than I should be."

The bell for dinner sounded in the distance, and the ladies hurried down the stairs.

Later when Marie visited her mother's bedchamber, they agreed the day had been very pleasant and the morrow promised more of the same.

Marie arrived in the breakfast parlor to find the others already assembled. Although she normally saw only her parents this early in the day, the chatter amongst so many pleased her.

"We have a beautiful day already," the younger Desmond assured his guests. "If you're rested after your carriage ride yesterday, we might visit Hertford, which is a few miles north of here and an easy drive. Most of the Norman fortress fell into ruins a couple hundred years ago, but the gatehouse still stands. We can partake of luncheon at either the White Hart Inn or the Salisbury Arms, both of which date to the middle of the sixteenth century."

"Oh, I do enjoy visiting ruins," exclaimed Marie, turning to her mother. "Do say we may!"

"The drive sounds altogether delightful, unless Lady Desmond has other plans for us," Lady Becca agreed and turned to their hostess.

Lady Desmond put that idea to rest. "I have made no plans and will enjoy whatever pleases the rest of you. Do you other ladies care to join us?" She glanced impartially at Mrs. Patterson and Mrs. Langford, both of whom agreed.

There appeared to be silent communication between the older gentlemen, and Sir Ambrose spoke for all of them. "I believe we prefer to while away our time on the croquet lawn, right gentlemen?"

Amid teasing comments about their slothfulness, the remainder of the house party prepared for the drive to Hertford.

As the carriages wound their way northward, the travelers caught regular glimpses of the River Lea through stands of river birch and willows. Arriving at the Salisbury Arms, they alighted from the carriages and strolled around the area, while their host arranged food for themselves and the horses.

"Oh, look at this, Mama." Marie traced one finger along the trailing vines and clusters of flowers etched in the sides of the building across from the inn. "I don't recall seeing anything like this at other ruins."

"That type of plasterwork is called 'pargeting' and dates from the seventeenth century," Lady Desmond explained. "It's quite prevalent in this area."

Her son joined them, rubbing his hands together in satisfaction. "The proprietor promises us a meal in two hours, and there is much to see in the meantime. Shall we stroll around the town before going to the ruins?"

"By all means, Mr. Desmond. Lead the way." Marie smiled at him as he moved to her side.

"I say, Desmond, can that stream be the Lea? Seems to me it flows from the wrong direction," Mr. Anstey commented.

"There is yet another river on your left, Anstey," Desmond told him with a grin. "You're right, of course. Both are from the wrong direction to be the Lea. Three rivers flow into Hertford, these being the Lea, the Rib, and the Beane."

"I do hope they don't all flood at the same time," worried Lady Becca with a glance toward the cloudless sky. "That would be a disaster of major proportions, would it not?"

"I suppose the rivers must flood at times," he replied. "Do not all rivers? Yet many of these buildings have stood for more than 300 years."

"Are those the ruins just ahead of us?" Marie claimed his attention. "Somehow I expected more, parts of the fortress walls, perhaps, or piles of stones."

Mr. Desmond touched her elbow as he helped her over some stones. "Only the gatehouse stands, and it's in poor repair, so we must all take care," he warned in a louder voice. He used that excuse to retain his grasp on Marie's arm as they strolled around.

"I must warn everyone that I am famished and in danger of immediate collapse if I do not eat soon."

Deborah's words brought a general laugh, which dominated the remainder of their stay in Hertford as well as their drive back to Desmond Park.

Marie noticed her host's almost constant attention to her and wondered if anyone else saw it. Did she want his attention? She admitted she enjoyed his company, yet a somber face and mahogany eyes tended to intrude on her thoughts. Did he ever give her so much as a thought?

The following morning the house party woke to a slight mizzle that boded ill for any outdoor plans that day. Instead, Lady Desmond suggested their guests might enjoy a visit to their picture gallery.

Her son flashed a mischievous grin around the table. "I challenge each person here to produce ancestors who equal mine for both ugliness and ferociousness!"

Amid laughter the younger members of the party trooped up the staircase to stare at the long wall filled with portraits of various sizes and shapes.

Marie tried to be both discreet and polite as the group promenaded along the gallery, but truth to tell she didn't have even one ancestor who compared with these. For this, she tended to be grateful yet could not say as much.

When they viewed the last portrait, they glanced at their grinning host who leaned against the wall, his arms crossed over his chest. "Well? Are there any takers to my challenge?"

Into the silence that followed his query, Marie spoke. "You must take after your maternal family, sir. And either your father took after his maternal family or else his mother played his father false." She realized that her tongue had led her astray, and she popped her hand over her mouth, a fiery heat rising from the modest neckline of her morning gown.

Desmond threw back his head and roared with laughter. "Miss Haverford, you are a source of delight. Do not be embarrassed, I pray you, for you only said what I have said on several occasions."

"I am so sorry," she whispered.

He clasped her hand for a moment of comfort and then turned toward the stairs. "Now, I issue another challenge. Miss Haverford and I shall demonstrate our skills at spillikins and wager that none of you even come close."

His cheerful words loosened the tongues of his other guests as they vowed to show him the error of his words.

Thereafter, the day passed calmly, although Marie's thoughts persisted in returning to her earlier *faux pas*. When she visited her mother for a few quiet words at bedtime, she confessed what she said earlier.

"Marie Louise Rebecca Haverford, I am truly appalled that a daughter of mine would so far forget herself as to make such a statement!"

Tears stood on Marie's long lashes, but she could not speak.

"What's done cannot be undone, and Mr. Desmond did take it in good part. Wipe your tears and run along to bed."

Making good her escape, Marie snuggled against the pillows of her own bed and relived her agony of earlier in the day. What if Lord Beaufort had heard her? His somber face filled her mental vision. No, he was not ugly. Far from it. When his stern mouth softened into a smile, her knees wobbled. Perhaps he was thinking of her.

Against his better judgment, Marie did occupy Lord Beaufort's thoughts as he relaxed at the end of the day. He had been to Haverford House twice in the past few days to see Sir Julian and left each time with a vague feeling of disappointment.

This evening he didn't concentrate on the cards after dinner at White's and took some good-natured ribbing from Brownlee. With a wry grin, he threw his losing cards on the baize-covered table and rose to his feet. He lifted his hand in a casual salute to the comments of unlucky at cards, lucky in love and quitted the room.

His thoughts were in turmoil, and a fierce scowl marred his face as he strolled home among the revelers. Now he sat in his study, staring into the embers of the dying fire and tried to analyze his restlessness. It could be their lack of progress in the stolen funds matter. Very frustrating, that. Yet why would it make him restless at this time? Business must not be the problem.

Taking up the candelabra at his elbow, he climbed the stairs to his bedchamber where his valet was placing clothing in the armoire. Something clicked in Beaufort's mind. "What are you doing with that," he asked and pointed to a mauve silk waistcoat lying on a chair.

Smith cast a surprised glance toward him. "There was a stain on the waistcoat, my lord. I cleaned it and am now returning it to the armoire."

"What kind of stain?"

"Lemon sauce, my lord."

"And you were able to remove it?" Beaufort remembered lemonade spilled on mauve silk and the assurance lemonade would not stain.

"Certainly, my lord," Smith replied with a sniff.

"Very good." Beaufort nodded dismissal and prepared for bed. That could not be his problem, could it? Surely, he was not missing the Haverford chit. Her disgraceful gallop in the park a few days before had confirmed his suspicion she was beneath his notice, so why did she invade his thoughts so often?

He'd asked himself that question before without finding an answer and was afraid it would persist in bothering him until enlightenment came. Her blue eyes flashed into his mental vision. They were sometimes scornful but most often contained a twinkle. He cringed when he remembered the hurt which he had seen in them a few times. Hurt that he had caused, which he admitted with chagrin. Yes, he finally acknowledged, he missed Marie Haverford and wondered how soon she would return to town.

The object of his thoughts was not thinking of returning to town.

In the following days, Mr. Desmond was rarely far from Marie's side. He teased her until he was certain her embarrassment had passed and made a point of inquiring her thoughts on everything they did.

Marie managed to escape everyone's notice during the afternoon a few days into their visit and slipped into a garden, where she sat on a wrought-iron bench surrounded by sculpted shrubs. From an adjoining garden, the scent of roses reached her while she reflected on the previous days and Mr. Desmond's attention to her. He seemed always to be at her side. It occurred to her that perhaps he could not avoid it because Mr. Buxted paid close attention to Grace Patterson, and Mr. Anstey and Deborah Langford sat in each other's pockets. Yet she sensed it was more than mere proximity. Was he developing a *tendre* for her? What would she do if he offered for her?

Her thoughts turned yet again to Lord Beaufort in London. Why did he not seek her company more often? Should she end her efforts to attract him and accept Mr. Desmond? If he offered for her, that is. No. She could not accept an offer from one gentleman when another occupied her thoughts too often for her comfort.

Hearing voices approaching, she assumed a bright smile and went to meet them.

"Here you are." Desmond exclaimed. "We decided to take a walk along the Lea before dinnertime and hope you will join us."

"Oh, yes, I shall enjoy that above all things! This is such a nice day I cannot bear to be indoors, and a stroll is the perfect solution." She fell into step beside him, and they led the way.

On that evening, Lady Becca visited Marie in her bedchamber rather than wait for her daughter to come to her. Marie welcomed her with a smile and curled up on the sofa next to her.

"This is rather like our evenings at home, Mama."

"Are you enjoying your visit, dear?"

"Yes, I am," admitted Marie. "Yet I miss its being just you and Papa and me together. Especially in the mornings when we go over our plans for the day. Here, we must consider what others plan for us. Perhaps that's selfish of me."

"Not selfish, no. At times I feel the same way." Lady Becca held her gaze for a long moment. "Mr. Desmond appears to grow particular in his attentions to you. How do you feel about it?"

Marie sat in silence for a long moment. With a sigh, she answered. "I enjoy a gentleman's attention. You know that. Yet I am not comfortable about receiving so much from him. I truly don't want to offend Mr. Desmond, but I don't know how to discourage him without being presumptuous. I need your advice on this, Mama."

"Has he made you an offer, even tentatively?"

"Oh, no. It's just the way he looks at me sometimes. Has he spoken to you?"

"No, but it seems at times that he studies me with a questioning expression." She got to her feet and shook out the skirts of her dressing gown. "If you do not mean to have him, I suggest you spend less time at his side, although I don't know how you can manage that."

Marie nodded and gave her a good night kiss, enjoying the warm clasp of her arms.

Soon after Lady Becca left Marie's bedchamber, Deborah slipped through the door. Marie waved her to a small sofa and joined her there.

"We have not had a coze since we got here, and I miss talking to you," Deborah explained.

"We stay busy, do we not? And of course, your attention centers on Mr. Anstey."

Deborah looked conscious but was swift in her rebuttal. "Mr. Desmond stays at your side, so it is as well that Grace and I have our own beaux!"

A fleeting frown crossed Marie's face. The others had noticed.

Deborah hesitated a moment. "Mr. Desmond shows every sign of being smitten. Do you expect him to offer for you?"

Marie shook her head, not knowing how to answer that, but confessed her feelings. "I cannot be sure about that, and it would be unmaidenly of me to pretend otherwise. Yet I am not ready to receive an offer from him. Or anyone else."

Deborah declared she was ready just any time Mr. Anstey took the notion in his head.

Glancing at her and seeing only sympathy in her face, Marie made a request. "If you see that Mr. Desmond is too particular in his attentions while we're here, will you interrupt any *tête à tête* he might contrive? I assure you I shall avoid such a meeting if I can."

Deborah gave her a quick hug. "I shall if that's what you want. Are you sure you do?"

Marie answered that she was and ushered Deborah to the door. "It grows late, and we both need to get some sleep."

Yet Marie was unable to fall asleep. Instead, her thoughts bounced between Mr. Desmond and Lord Beaufort. She considered her reaction to Mr. Desmond's touch and admitted there had been none. No tingle. No warmth. Nothing. However, the simple thought of Lord Beaufort caused her to tingle all over. She pounded her pillow again. Why must life be so frustrating?

For the remainder of the visit, Marie managed to avoid private conversation with Mr. Desmond but knew that he stared at her with a peculiar expression in his eyes.

Although she had enjoyed most of the visit, it was with relief that Marie entered the family carriage for the return trip to London.

Chapter 8

Unwelcome Attention

"Symms, it's marvelous to be home again." Marie handed her bonnet and gloves to the butler. "Do I have a great many invitations?"

"Yes, Miss Marie. Several await your attention in your sitting room."

She blew him a kiss and ran up the stairs. From behind her, she heard the more subdued voice of her mother.

"Symms, give me half an hour to freshen myself and then serve tea in the morning room." She raised her voice. "Marie, do you care to join me?"

"Yes, Mama."

When Marie joined her mother somewhat later, she had engraved cards and invitations clutched in her hands. "Just look, Mama!"

"I can see it's just as well we spent a sennight in the quietness of the country because we surely won't have a tranquil moment again anytime soon."

They spent a few moments perusing their separate piles of invitations. Marie held up a folded sheet of paper. "Rebecca Blackwell wants me to walk with her to Green Park this afternoon. May I send her a note accepting her invitation?"

"Yes, that should be pleasant after the carriage ride. Her mother and I spent a considerable amount of time there, so she could see Captain Blackwell without her parents' knowledge."

Marie twinkled at her. "What would you do if I were considering an elopement like your friends did? I might even ask Rebecca to aid me, just as you aided her mother."

A dimpled hand reached out and tweaked her curls. "Under like circumstances I would almost expect it of you. Rebecca's grandparents did not treat their daughter at all well, you must understand." She studied her daughter's face before asking in a pleading tone. "We do welcome all your friends, do we not? Do you feel at all confined?"

Marie clung to her for a long moment. "You and Papa are the best parents anyone could wish, and I would no more consider an elopement than I would grow wings and fly to the moon. So there! You might as well accept the inevitable. I expect a huge wedding at St. George's in Hanover Square with at least a dozen bridesmaids and a trousseau that will put even royalty to shame."

"And you shall have it," her mother promised her, the anxiety leaving her voice. "Now send your *billet doux* to Rebecca."

Marie dispatched the note and turned back to her mother. "I would like to please you, but I fear I can never be as close to Rebecca and Louise as you were with their mothers. I believe, though, I am as close to Susan as you were to them, so I can understand your feelings."

"I've always been happy that you have Susan. As for being friends with Rebecca and Louise, when you are all married and dealing with nurseries and such, you might become closer. Right now, the three of you have little in common since one is married, one is betrothed, and one is still enjoying the single state. Don't fret about it, my dear. Closeness requires time and proximity."

"I find that letters keep me close to Susan and regret you didn't have a correspondence with your friends."

"So do I," Lady Becca agreed. "Their lives would have been much different if I had known of their difficulties."

"It was a miracle that Shelburne found their daughters last summer, was it not?"

"And a miracle that Rebecca and Louise grew up in the same orphanage," her mama murmured, finishing her cup of tea. "Their lives might have been unbearable under the machinations of people who did not have the same values as the Duchess of Devonshire. However, as both have said, they always had each other and that counted for a lot. Now, be off for your walk with Rebecca."

An hour later Marie met Rebecca in Piccadilly, and with their maids the requisite two steps behind them, they strolled toward Green Park.

"Tell me about your stay in Hertfordshire," Rebecca urged. "Did you enjoy it?"

"Oh yes, it was marvelous. Sir Ambrose even has a croquet lawn, and he allowed us to play on it several times. The weather was delightful, except for one day when it mizzled all day. Now tell me what happened in Town during my absence."

"Just the usual round of balls, soirées, and other such social activities," Rebecca replied, and they talked in a desultory fashion of who had attended what.

"Mr. Simon Abernathy has been much in evidence."

Marie scarcely knew how to respond. Had Rebecca developed an interest in him? Did Uncle Edward know or even suspect? She answered with a degree of caution, despite her desire to demand an answer to her suspicions. "I believe he attends most of Society's functions."

"That's my understanding too, and I make a point of speaking to him whenever possible in the hope of receiving news of his niece, Miranda. You will recall she stayed with Louise and me for a period last summer after her abduction."

"Now that you call it to my mind, I do remember, and I believe you told me of a visit to her parents' home in the country."

"That was a delightful fortnight and one I hope to repeat before too much time passes. I grew quite attached to Miranda in a very short space of time."

Marie wanted to inquire about Lord Beaufort's possible presence at any of these activities but restrained herself, and it did not occur to Rebecca to mention him.

Inside the park, they made their way amongst the playing children until they found a quieter area. The maids sat on a bench to rest their weary feet while remaining within sight of their ladies. Marie drew to a stop when she spotted Mr. Rayson looking furtively around before disappearing behind a clump of bushes. With a finger at her lips, she motioned the surprised Rebecca to silence as they approached that same shrubbery. They stood still for a moment when they heard two voices in a low murmur. One voice rose to a high pitch that caused Marie's eyes to widen. It was the same voice she had heard talking to Mr. Rayson and Lord Stokely. Motioning Rebecca to continued silence, she retraced her steps to a point where she could see anyone behind the bushes.

"I do have an explanation for my actions," she assured Rebecca in a soft voice. "However, I cannot reveal them at present, so I hope you will trust me and not inquire too closely into my behavior."

"Yes, of course, I shall respect your need for secrecy. Only promise me that you are not contemplating anything that might place you in danger." She stared at Marie, waiting for assurance.

"Oh no, nothing of that sort at all," Marie replied. She peeped around the taller Rebecca and spotted a gentleman walking toward them from behind the shrubs.

"Tell me if you recognize this gentleman coming toward us."

"Yes, I believe he is a Mr. Anderson, although I don't know anything about him. Someone introduced him at a soirée of some sort earlier in the Season."

"I would like for you to introduce us if you see him in close proximity to me."

Rebecca hesitated. "I understand that, even though a person is welcomed by polite society, he might not be a proper person for ladies to know. However, you know that better than I. I shall do as you ask and only remind you of your promise not to place yourself in danger."

"That's all I ask. Now, I promised Mama I would return home in time to rest before dressing for the evening. Do you attend the Ingraham dinner party?"

After Rebecca confirmed her intentions to be there, Marie hurried away.

She was in a flutter of excitement. She now had a name for the third person in what she believed was the conspiracy to steal government funds meant for Wellington. She did not know the extent of their actions, but she intended to learn whatever she could from this person regardless of Society dictates.

Success in that endeavor stared her in the face sooner than she could have hoped.

Stepping into the Ingraham drawing room a few hours later, Marie came face to face with the gentleman in question. She guessed his age at five and twenty and wondered about the faint color that invaded his cheeks as their hostess introduced them. In her experience, only very young gentlemen flushed in the presence of an attractive young lady.

"Mr. Anderson, it's a pleasure to make your acquaintance. I do not recall seeing you in Town before, so perhaps this is your first visit?"

"Ah, no, although it is my first time to participate in *ton* activities during the Season. My responsibilities on my estate usually require my attention at this time of the year."

"I have only a slight knowledge of estate requirements, sir, but I do know this time of year is a very busy one. Since you seldom come to Town in the spring, I suppose your estate is located some distance from London."

"Yorkshire," he acknowledged.

"Again, I possess little information but do realize Yorkshire is, indeed, a considerable distance from Town. You certainly could not come easily for any part of a Season's activities. I vow it is our loss, sir."

"Thank you, Miss Haverford." He swallowed hard. "You are most gracious to tell me."

Marie smiled at him and then turned to her other dinner partner. She told herself that she had made a good beginning. After dinner she managed to flirt with him discreetly and moved away, knowing he watched every move she made.

Someone else watched her every move. Mr. Desmond stood across the room when she entered the Ingrahams' drawing room and was unable to work his way toward her in time to escort her into dinner. He watched the *repartée* between her and the gentleman he did not recognize until his own dinner partners called him to attention. After the interminable meal ended, he again found her standing with the man whom he learned was a Mr. Anderson when he asked Lady Ingraham. When he at last wound his way to her side, she paid him little heed, instead moving from place to place like a butterfly sampling a flower. He clenched his jaws and forced himself to conceal his jealousy, which he was unable to do the following morning.

Desmond arrived at Haverford House indecently early, as the butler indicated by greeting him with raised brows when he demanded to see Sir Julian.

"Mr. Desmond, the family is still at breakfast." When the determined gentleman failed to excuse himself and leave, Symms continued in a dry monotone. "Perhaps you would care to wait in the morning room until he is free to see you."

"Yes," came the blunt reply as he handed his hat and gloves to Symms, who led him to a small room at the back of the house.

When the butler paused inside the breakfast parlor door, Sir Julian glanced toward him. "Yes, Symms, what is it?"

"You have a visitor in the morning room, sir."

Sir Julian raised surprised eyebrows. "So early? Who is it, Symms?"

"Mr. Robert Desmond. He appears agitated, if I may be so bold as to say so."

Marie turned toward her mother with a startled gasp, not missed by Sir Julian, who looked from one to the other.

When the butler left the room, Sir Julian asked, "Is there something happening here that I do not know about, but perhaps should?"

Marie swallowed hard but faced her father and admitted, "Mr. Desmond has paid close attention to me of late. I realized it when we were in Hertfordshire."

"I see. Have you encouraged him to think you might be open to an offer from him?"

"Not knowingly, Papa." She gazed into his somber face. "I do not want to receive an offer from him, and since I realized he was growing particular in his regard, I have tried to avoid a *tête-à-tête* with him. That has proved difficult."

Sir Julian turned to his wife. "This is what you wanted to discuss with me last night when we became, uh, distracted?"

"Exactly."

The tender smile he reserved for his wife alone crossed his countenance before he turned to their daughter.

"All right, Poppet. I will see him, and if he does, indeed, make an offer, I will send for you." He hesitated a moment. "You are sure you do not want to marry him?"

She gazed into his demanding eyes. "Yes, Papa, I am sure."

Accepting his nod as dismissal, Marie hurried to her bedchamber to await the summons. When it came, she entered the morning room accompanied by her maid. Standing just inside the door, Marie watched Mr. Desmond for a couple of moments before he realized her presence. The expressions crossing his face ranged from jealousy to hope to despair as his shoulders slumped. She could almost feel sorry for him.

"Good morning, Mr. Desmond. You are out and about at an early hour."

He held out his hand in greeting. "Miss Haverford. I felt I could not wait longer because others will doubtless surround you later in the day."

She might as well get it over with. She asked, "Did you want to see me about something in particular, sir?"

"Yes." Robert stared at her a moment after the bald statement. He walked a few steps away before taking a deep breath and turning to her. "Will you marry me?" He cringed at the bluntness he used. "I mean to say, I have come to care deeply for you and wish that you will do me the honour of becoming my wife. Your father gave me permission to approach you."

Marie sank into a chair for the simple reason her knees refused to sustain her any longer. In her heart she had known this was coming, yet the reality of it stunned her.

"Mr. Desmond, I don't know how to answer except to say that I'm honoured. However, I have given no thought to marriage." Marie watched a thundercloud gathering on his face and steeled herself for whatever came next.

"You gave me reason to hope in Hertfordshire," he reminded her with some heat. "I gather you met Mr.

Anderson since your return to Town, and he turned your head with his attentions."

Marie's mouth gaped open at that absurdity. "Mr. Anderson has not even attempted to turn my head with attention. He is much too shy to do anything of the sort."

"Oh, I saw you flirting with him last evening. You could hardly keep your eyes off him. And as for him! he knows a good thing when he sees it. He's a mere farmer, so his pockets are doubtless to let, and he came to Town to find himself a wealthy wife."

"Are you implying that my father's wealth is my only attraction?" The thought devastated Marie, but she kept her voice level.

"Wealth is the first thing any man considers if he has any sense of preservation."

That was too much to hear and especially from an old friend, one who was almost like a brother. "It appears that is the only thing about me that interests you. I do not care to be insulted further, Mr. Desmond, and insist that you leave this house on the instant and never return."

"I shall not," he retorted. "I shan't budge an inch until you listen to reason."

"I said, Get out!" Marie burst into tears when he stood there, an obstinate expression on his countenance.

The tears were his undoing. Before the maid could reach her, he sank to his knees in front of Marie, clasping her hands and pleading. "Ah, no, don't cry. Please don't cry. I am the biggest beast in nature for upsetting you so."

Her tears ended on a hiccup, and she groped for the scrap of lace-edged linen she carried in her sleeve.

She blew her nose and gazed at him through tear-drenched lashes. "Please let us not quarrel. I cannot marry you, but our friendship is of such long standing I cannot bear coming to cuffs with you."

He got to his feet and wandered across the room where he leaned his head against the mantelshelf. With a resolute smile, he turned in her direction. "I can only hope you change your mind about marrying me. Still, I cannot bear being at loggerheads with you either, so let us cry friends again."

They parted on amicable terms, and Marie hurried to her sitting room where she found her mother waiting for her.

Lady Becca didn't say a word. One glance at her daughter's face told the story, and she opened her arms.

Marie relaxed against her and, between gulps, whispered what had happened.

"At least you parted friends, and that is important. Now," Lady Becca continued, "wash your face and get ready for morning callers. Although I must admit crying does much less damage to your face than any I know."

With a shaky laugh, Marie agreed to join her in the drawing room. Upon entering that room a few moments later, the first person she saw was Mr. Anderson, and she remembered why she wanted to cultivate his friendship. She eased her way around the room, greeting the other guests, until she reached him.

"Good morning, Mr. Anderson, how nice of you to visit us."

"Good morning to you, Miss Haverford," he responded. He shifted from one foot to the other and blurted, "I wonder if you would care to drive with me in the park this afternoon? I have an open carriage."

"That would be delightful, Mr. Anderson. I shall look forward to it. At five o'clock?" Receiving his affirmative nod, she smiled again and turned to greet other guests. No one watching would have guessed her heart was racing with purpose. She would pursue this matter, regardless of what Lord Beaufort might think. Besides, could he not see she was being helpful?

When the last morning visitor left, Marie returned to her sitting room and poured out her heart to the one person who always understood.

> *My dearest Susan, I have received my first offer of marriage this Season. You will not be surprised to learn it came from Mr. Robert Desmond because I told you earlier of his marked attentions in Hertfordshire. I do not care to wed with him—he's too much like a brother—but to see him so downcast at my refusal severely discomposed me. We cried friends before he left, and I pray we can return to our old ease of manner. How I wish you were here! Your unhappy Marie.*

She folded the missive with a deep sigh and stretched out on the *chaise longue* to calm her renewed agitation.

At five o'clock, Marie and her maid were ready and waiting in Marie's sitting room when the footman advised them of Mr. Anderson's arrival. On the drive through the busy streets, she commented on the places of interest they passed and, upon entering the park gate, pointed out several important personages.

"Ah, I see someone I know. It's good to see a familiar face in such a crowd of strangers, do you not agree?"

"Yes, I do, Mr. Anderson. Who is it you recognize?" She followed his glance to the left and quaked inside when she saw Lord Stokely. Lady Emily Cavanaugh was with him, so perhaps Deborah had been right about her being his mistress.

"Lord Stokely, I just remarked to this lady what a pleasure it is to see a familiar face. Are you acquainted with Miss Haverford?"

Lord Stokely inclined his head toward Marie and gave her a cold stare. "Yes, we met on a previous occasion."

"Good afternoon, my lord. This is a pleasant day for a ride, is it not?" Turning to Lady Emily Cavanaugh, she gave her a wide smile. "My lady, I am pleased to see you again. At least this time, we are not consigned to the perdition of hearing any caterwauling masking as singing."

Lady Emily's throaty laughter surrounded them. "I agree that is a blessing, Miss Haverford."

Lord Stokely put his horse in motion, and Lady Emily perforce followed him, after flashing a smile in Marie's direction.

While Marie was explaining her reference to caterwauling, she glanced beyond Mr. Anderson and saw Lord Beaufort riding in their direction. She nodded her head when he tipped his hat but turned back to her escort. Suddenly very gay, she commented on her evening activities.

"Do you attend the Underwood soirée this evening, Mr. Anderson? Beyond doubt, it will be a delightful ball. I do so enjoy dancing, do not you, sir?"

"I fear I am not adept at that pastime, yet I do enjoy it. May I prevail upon you for a dance this evening? The supper dance, perhaps?"

Nothing could have suited her plans more, and she nodded her assent. "I look forward to it with a great deal of pleasure, Mr. Anderson."

The carriage circled the loop and turned out the gate. When they reached Haverford House, Mr. Anderson conscientiously assisted her out of the carriage and up the steps where Symms stood at the open door. With a last tip of the hat, Anderson took his leave.

The longer Marie was in Mr. Anderson's company the more convinced she was of his voice being the one she had heard earlier. She assured herself his acquaintance with Lord Stokely added evidence to her belief of their nefarious activities.

For the evening, she chose a new gown of ice blue gauze over a sheath of watered silk that was a darker shade of blue. Tiny pink embroidered rosebuds peeked from the folds of the gauze, and she threaded silk roses in the same shade in her hair. This should impress him. However, it was a patrician face with mahogany eyes that flashed into her mind, and not the shy countenance and gray eyes of Mr. Anderson. She shrugged away the vision. Well satisfied with her appearance, she joined her parents.

Entering the Underwood drawing room a short time later, Marie chatted with the young gentlemen sparring for a place on her dance card. When Mr. Desmond saw the name of her partner for the supper dance, he tightened his lips but did not comment. Instead, he placed his name beside two country dances and with a slight bow moved away. Marie drew a breath of relief that this first meeting since their tumultuous encounter was over, and she could relax and enjoy herself.

Waiting for the supper dance, Marie stood in the shelter of a large plant and watched Mr. Anderson following Lord Stokely out the door after a quick glance around the room. Avoiding her mother's eye, Marie began a slow stroll around the ballroom in the direction of the door, talking with friends until Lady Underwood demanded her attention.

"Come here, gel, and tell me about all those beaux you have dangling after you. Can't make up your mind, eh? Your grandmother was the same way. We came out together, you know."

Marie suppressed a sigh and flashed a smile at her grandmother's old friend. "La, Ma'am, from all I hear, the number of my beaux fades into nothing compared to yours and my grandmother's."

The old lady chortled. "Between us, we had all the gentlemen dangling after us. None of the other chits had a chance until we made our choices." Lost in memory, Lady Underwood continued to smile, and Marie rose and slipped out the door.

She moved on silent feet along the hallway, wondering where the gentlemen had gone. She was not going to miss this chance to help her father, and that dreadful Lord Beaufort had nothing to do with it. She traversed the length of the corridor, listening at each door until she heard the murmur of voices and discerned the words shipment and gold.

When one voice came closer to the door, she retraced several steps. Turning, she moved forward as the door opened. Fluttering her fan, she simpered, "Here you are, Mr. Anderson! Shame on you for forgetting our dance! Gentlemen, you must excuse Mr. Anderson. He is promised to me for the supper dance."

Lord Stokely, a smile not reaching his ice blue eyes, nodded to her. "Of course, Miss Haverford. It is remiss of us old men to keep young people from the gaiety."

Flashing a dazzling smile at him, she slipped her hand through Mr. Anderson's arm, and her bubbling voice chattering inanities floated back as they went toward the ballroom.

Marie kept up her chatter throughout supper and afterwards flirted with each of her dance partners, while searching the room for Lord Beaufort. She had seen Mr. Rayson return to the ballroom before supper and wondered about Lord Stokely, but now, standing beside her mother, she heard his voice.

"Lady Becca, how are you this evening?" Not waiting for her reply, he continued, "I admire your lovely daughter's gracefulness on the dance floor. May I have permission to dance with her?"

Marie knew her mother faced a dilemma. She didn't want her daughter within miles of this dissolute lord, yet he was accepted everywhere. There was no good reason to refuse him. "How thoughtful of you, Lord Stokely. Yes, she may dance with you."

With a smile that failed to reach his eyes, he offered Marie his arm. "Shall we join the others on the dance floor?"

Hiding her chagrin, she took his arm. At least it was a country dance, giving her some relief from his cold eyes as the steps separated them. Nonetheless, when they did meet, she babbled about the Season, referring to her beaux and the Venetian breakfast she had attended. But why was it called breakfast when it occurred in the afternoon? Could Lord Stokely tell her that? When he escorted her back to her mother, Marie admitted to herself that he had not been in the least improper. She simpered as she told her mother what an excellent dancer his lordship was and so smooth in the turns too.

Lord Stokely bowed himself away, and Marie sighed with relief. "Mama, I realize he gave you no choice, but I would rather not dance with him again. His smiles never reach his cold eyes."

The evening progressed with Marie standing up for every dance. She spotted Beaufort and looked in the other direction. Of course, were he to approach her, she would tell him that Mr. Anderson was the third man she had mentioned earlier. Just before the evening ended, Beaufort did approach her and Lady Becca.

"My lady, may I have this final dance with your daughter?" She acquiesced, and he offered his arm to Marie.

They were stiff and silent as they moved through the dance. At length, she spoke. "My father is not here, so I suppose I should tell you something."

"Eavesdropping again?" came the suave reply.

Her chin came up as she glared at him. "For your information, I do not eavesdrop all the time, my lord. I also use my eyes."

"And just what did you see that you consider so important?"

She glanced around and seeing Lord Stokely staring at her from a short distance away, she realized she could not explain. She returned a glib reply and changed the subject.

He followed her conversational lead, but when he returned her to her mother, he advised, "Whatever it was you saw, or thought you saw, you should tell Sir Julian at your first opportunity."

She cast him a glance of pure scorn. "Thank you for your advice, my lord. I shall give it my careful consideration." She kept a tight rein on her temper while he walked away.

Later that evening, she followed her father into his study and recounted the evening. "I realized yesterday that Mr. Anderson sounded like the third voice I heard talking with Lord Stokely and Mr. Rayson. Tonight, I verified it and also saw him with them again."

Sir Julian's gaze lingered on his daughter's face as she finished. His close attention mollified her. He appreciated her efforts, anyway.

His voice was grave when he spoke. "It pleases me that you're alert and realize the importance of what you hear and see. Nevertheless, you must not become involved. This situation is far over your head." He paused as she glared at him. "Yes, yes, my dear, I know you hide an intelligent brain behind your usual girlish smile. Yet this is much too dangerous for you. Promise me," he ordered.

"How else can I get Lord Beaufort's attention if I don't interest myself in what interests him? All he ever thinks about is business."

Her plaintive words brought a smile to her father's face, but they did not sway him. "Marie, I insist you do as I say. Trying to attract a man's attention is the worst reason for endangering yourself. Do I make myself clear?"

Sir Julian rarely used that tone with her, and she knew she had to pay heed.

"All right, I promise, but you will be sorry when I go into a decline!" She met his amused eyes with a frown and ran from the room.

Susan would understand.

. . . and there you have it, my dear friend, the latest obstacle in my pursuit of happiness. Even Papa refuses to realize I can be a help to him, although he did admit I have an intelligent brain. However, I promised him, so I will stop my endeavors in that regard. Please give me your counsel on my dilemma with Beaufort. I fear I am unable to withdraw my attention from him.

The object of Marie's attentions sat in his study and stared into space. Beaufort cupped a brandy snifter in one hand, taking an occasional sip and thinking of Marie. What had that chit seen? She was lovely that evening, but she always was. Her scornful glance had ruffled his feathers, and he admitted it with a wry grin.

Beaufort forced his mind back to the main point. What, or more probably who, had the chit seen, and doing what? He shook his head and rose to his feet. There was no point in speculating further. Sir Julian would contact him in the morning if he needed to know anything.

Across town Lord Stokely also pondered about Marie Haverford; however he was not thinking of her best interests. He wondered how close she'd been to the door of Underwood's library and whether she understood anything she might have heard. She gives the impression of being a pea brain, yet she would bear watching, considering her father's connections.

"I want you to cultivate the Haverford chit," Stokely told his companion.

"Pray, why on earth would I want to cultivate a simpering schoolgirl?" Lady Emily Cavanaugh stared at her lover in astonishment.

"Because I told you to do so," was his implacable reply. "I want to know what she knows about the military, and whether her father ever discusses his government work at home. I don't care how you do it, just do it."

She stared into his fathomless eyes for a moment. "If you say so, my lord, I will."

"I do say so. Now, my dear, I must take my leave of you." He sketched a slight bow and quitted the room.

Chapter 9

Danger on the Horizon

Lady Emily paced her bedchamber floor, frowning into the distance. What interest did Stokely have in the Haverford chit? More to the point, how could she cultivate her? On the few occasions she'd seen the girl, Marie had been with her own circle of friends. They were not likely to meet at any evening assembly. The wry thought crossed her mind as she considered that possibility. When had Lady Emily Cavanaugh last received an invitation to a *ton* gathering? She shrugged and finished her toilette.

During the day, anyone who cared to notice would have seen the beautiful Lady Emily Cavanaugh perusing books at both Hatchard's and Hookham's bookstores. She glanced through the windows of several modistes and milliners, but in the end, she found her quarry in Hyde Park.

"Good afternoon, ladies and gentlemen. The park is crowded as usual, I see."

"My lady, it is delightful to see you," responded Marie. "May I introduce my friends, Miss Langford, Miss Patterson, Mr. Desmond, Mr. Anstey, and Mr. Buxted?" Glancing at her friends, she continued, "This is Lady Emily Cavanaugh."

They talked for a few moments while Lady Emily searched her brain for a way to separate Marie from the others. Before she succeeded, the young people bid her a polite good-bye. In frustration, she watched the group stroll toward the exit amid a discussion of their various evening entertainments.

The following day, Lady Emily failed to get even a glimpse of Marie and hoped Lord Stokely would not put in an appearance that evening. He would have had an invitation to Carlton House, like everyone else. Except herself. A frown marred her face for several moments before she put the slight out of her mind and prepared to spend the evening at home, alone as usual.

No frown marred Marie's face as she prepared for the evening at Carlton House. She did grimace when she thought of how close she had been to staying at home.

After perusing their invitations over her breakfast coffee a few days before, Lady Becca had turned to her husband and exclaimed, "Oh, no! We're invited Carlton House!"

Sir Julian raised his brows at her consternation. "My dear, an invitation from Prinny has never caused so much alarm. Why now?"

"The invitation includes Marie," she almost wailed.

"Oh, Mama, am I to see the Prince Regent up close?"

"Not if I can help it," her mother stated. "We shall decline."

"Decline an invitation from the *Prince Regent*? Have you given any thought to the consequences?" Sir Julian studied his wife, not understanding her attitude.

"Not go, Mama? Oh, please, let us go. It will be exciting beyond anything. And just think, it's something interesting to write Susan. We didn't get even a glimpse of him last Season."

"I do not intend for my daughter to get within seeing distance of that disreputable old lecher!" Lady Becca pounded her small fist on the table, causing cups and saucers to rattle.

"Now, Becca," Sir Julian cautioned. "It's unwise to use such words to comment on our future sovereign, even in a family setting." Turning to his wide-eyed daughter, he said, "Marie, please forget what you just heard."

"Yes, Papa."

Lady Becca swallowed hard. "Can we not leave Marie at home?"

"No, my dear, we can't do that. If Marie's name is on the invitation, she must accompany us." He clasped his wife's hand. "We will keep her out of his reach, I promise. After all, I don't want our daughter close to him either."

So it was that Marie now stood in front of the cheval glass, studying her appearance. A halo of soft curls gave width to her narrow face and the sapphire clip perched over her left temple highlighted her shining blue eyes. Her gown of sky-blue satin with a white lace overdress reached from midway up her neck to the tops of her blue slippers. The loose sleeves extended below the top of her white lace gloves. Marie studied the effect. If the Regent tried to touch her, she doubted he would find an uncovered place.

Picking up her reticule, she joined her parents below stairs. Both studied her quite carefully before pronouncing themselves satisfied.

Marie was overjoyed. She had been a little disappointed the previous Season when she did not receive an invitation to Carlton House. Oh, she realized that the Regent's London residence did not compare to the pavilion in Brighton, about which she had heard volumes even though she had not been there. Still, Carlton House was not just any Town residence. It contained only the most exclusive furnishings and paintings. She especially wanted to see the Chinese drawing room, which she had heard contained dragons. If they were not artificial, she hoped there would be a St. George to slay one for her. She shook with silent laughter as she pictured that estimable saint with a patrician face, sculpted lips, and mahogany eyes.

The entire house lived up to Marie's expectations, as she gazed with wide-eyed wonder at the display of richness surrounding her. No live dragons of the four-legged variety attacked her, and her parents stood one on each side of her as Sir Julian presented her to the Regent. Marie curtsied to the sovereign and couldn't decide if she was happy when he gave her only the briefest nod. She'd heard about his reaction to Louise Mansfield the previous autumn and half feared drawing his unwanted attention. Mama would probably cause a scandal by punching him in the nose.

Marie saw the cold eyes of Lord Stokely watching her from a distance, but she stayed at her parents' side, and he did not approach her.

While she studied the small figures on the wallpaper in the Chinese drawing room, she heard a soft voice from above her head, causing a shiver of pleasure to engulf her.

"They are called Mandarins," Lord Beaufort told her. "Prinny has them painted on every conceivable object in this house as well as his pavilion in Brighton."

"Good evening, my lord. Is this not a marvelous place?"

"I'm not sure I would call it marvelous, but interesting, yes."

She grinned. "Do you mean to say you question the taste of our future sovereign? How audacious of you, to be sure."

He chuckled. "Have you met the large gentleman?"

"Oh, yes. He nodded at me after my curtsy. My lord, how did he get so huge?" she whispered after glancing around to be sure no one was listening. Most of the crowd gathered at the other end of the room, admiring some paintings, so she was safe from gossip. "Mama was in a real pucker about allowing me near him. But as large as he is, I daresay I could have dodged his grasp if he had been of a mind to reach for me."

His lips twitched, but he did not comment.

They stood in quiet conversation for a few moments, only a few steps from Lady Becca, but she did not approach them until it was time to leave. Smiling into his lordship's eyes, Marie said, "I'm happy to have seen you this evening, my lord."

Their gazes held for a moment, a slight smile on his face. "And I to see you," he replied. He bowed over her hand and strolled away.

Later, Marie snuggled into her pillows and thought how happy she was. Even such a brief touch from Lord Beaufort left her trembling long after they left Carlton House. She cuddled that hand next to her cheek. Life was almost perfect.

Almost but not completely perfect, she decided the following morning at the breakfast table.

"Mama, did you notice all those beautiful gowns at Carlton House last evening? I vow I don't have any gown that can rival those for elegance. My gown was childish by comparison."

Sir Julian lowered his newspaper and twinkled at his daughter. "My dear, if this is a prelude to asking for a larger dress allowance, you waste your breath."

"But, Papa, I need more gowns. This is my second Season, and I still look like a schoolroom miss," she said. How could she attract Lord Beaufort if he saw her only as a schoolgirl? She kept that thought to herself.

"Not quite," he answered. "I haven't seen any scraped knees and dirty fingernails in recent memory."

Lady Becca exchanged an amused glance with him. "Marie, you must remember the styles that appear elegant on taller females are not appropriate for us shorter ladies. You have a sufficient number of gowns, all of which Madame Bouchét designed for your stature. In addition, you have the deeper hues, which you requested. Or are you still thinking of that disgracefully short crimson satin gown?"

"What?" thundered Sir Julian. "I shall not permit my daughter . . . ."

Marie interrupted him by bursting into laughter that turned to hiccups as he spluttered, and Lady Becca grinned. "Papa, I was only teasing Mama, as I told her at the time."

Marie turned her mischievous face to her mother. "Now, Mama, just see how you have upset Papa. Are you not ashamed of yourself?"

Lady Becca squeezed her husband's hand. "Marie is correct, dear. She didn't ask for that gown, and I was only teasing her, not trying to upset you."

He glared at both his ladies a moment before a reluctant grin crossed his face. "Females! I shall never understand them."

Lord Beaufort had reached that same conclusion. How could anyone expect a mere male to understand a female who changed from one moment to the next? Or so it seemed to him. He had reached the definite conclusion Marie Haverford was a silly, giggling schoolgirl and much too young for his notice. Yet last evening at Carlton House, she seemed quite mature, both in her appearance and in her conversation. The blue and lace gown was an inspired creation for her daintiness. He must observe her again before he reached a final decision about her maturity.

With that determination made, he attacked the stack of papers awaiting him. Assisted by his secretary, he managed to clear the desk of most of the work before he called a halt for a late luncheon. Seated at a small table near the window, he perused a stack of invitations while he partook of a large slice of sirloin. Which of these engagements might Miss Haverford attend this evening? A ball? He visualized her gracefulness as she moved through a *contredanse,* her intent expression as she listened to a dowager, her bland expression when bored. Frustrated because he could not decide among so many possibilities, he decided he would ask her.

Calling to his butler that he would be in for dinner, he set his hat at an angle on his dark hair and strolled around to the mews for his curricle. Soon he was tooling along at a spanking pace in the direction of Haverford House.

"Do come in, my lord," Lady Becca greeted him. "May I serve you some tea, or would you prefer something stronger?"

"Tea will be perfect, my lady." He turned toward Marie with a slight smile and received a sedate smile in return.

"My lord, it is a pleasure to see you again." She kept her voice low, determined to be as un-schoolgirlish as she could manage. She wondered if her father had forgotten an appointment with his lordship, yet Beaufort did not appear impatient, and Symms did show him into the drawing room rather than the study. Marie decided she would simply enjoy this rare opportunity to be in his company.

They talked in a desultory fashion about the differences in Town life and that in the country. They even debated the merits of Shakespeare's dramas as opposed to his comedies.

"But, my lord, surely you would rather laugh than cry? Just think how crying mars one's face!" Marie's dimples peeped out as he burst into laughter after a moment of twitching lips.

"I had not thought of Shakespeare in quite those terms. I do agree, however, that I would rather laugh than cry."

On their note of laughter, Sir Julian entered the drawing room and greeted their guest before raising his wife's hand to his lips in a brief salute and smiling at his daughter. He settled down to talk with Beaufort, and Marie took the opportunity to change her seat to one closer to her mother.

"Mama, may we invite him to stay for dinner? It will be just us."

"He might have other plans," she cautioned. "But yes, we can ask him to stay." When there was a break in the gentlemen's conversation, she raised her voice. "Lord Beaufort, it will give us a great deal of pleasure if you will dine with us."

"Oh, I could not intrude without any notice, my lady. Besides, I am not dressed for dinner." Lord Beaufort made as if to rise, but Sir Julian stopped him with a hand on his arm.

"Nonsense, your presence could never be an intrusion, John. And, as I recall, we stay in this evening, so we won't dress either."

Beaufort glanced at Lady Becca and then met Marie's intent gaze. "If increasing your covers without more notice does not create a problem, I accept with pleasure. May I send a message to my butler?"

At the end of the evening, Marie gave both her parents a quick hug and danced her way up the stairs. She told herself she had done well. Not one giggle did she utter. She conversed on several adult subjects without stumbling over her choice of words. She had studied the changing expressions that flitted across Beaufort's countenance and the small smile that played around his mouth when they discussed Shakespeare. He most often appeared somber, but on this visit she had seen his lighter side.

She lay awake for several minutes reliving the evening and sent a heartfelt thank you heavenward. Yes, life was very nearly perfect.

"I was surprised to hear Beaufort's laughter when I returned from my meeting with Shelburne," Sir Julian told his wife, as they prepared for bed. "He sent his regards, by the way."

"Was he able to advise you on the horses at Tat's?"

"Yes, and after he pointed out their flaws, I decided not to purchase them."

"I dare say we don't truly need them at the present time anyway."

"To get back to Beaufort, I don't believe I ever heard him laugh so heartily. I had to ask Symms who was within."

"Lord Beaufort was here most of the afternoon, and I must admit I don't understand why," she told him. "He seemed intent on keeping Marie's attention focused on him, so I wonder if he feels something more for her than that she is your daughter."

"When I first heard him, it occurred to me I had missed an appointment, but Symms assured me I had not, and that John seemed intent on a simple visit. We won't try to analyze his feelings, and, of a certainty, we will not mention them to Marie."

"Oh, no, my dear. To do so might raise even higher her expectations, which could, in turn, cause her more heartache when nothing comes of it."

"I agree." He snuffed out the candle. "Come to bed now. We've discussed our daughter enough for the evening."

Perhaps life was not as perfect as she had thought, Marie decided the following morning when the first caller announced was Mr. Anderson. She remembered her father's injunction against involving herself in the gold shipment dilemma. However, she reasoned, just seeing Mr. Anderson did not constitute involvement in anything except simple enjoyment of a handsome young gentleman's company. Therefore, she greeted him with genuine pleasure and agreed to a drive with him that same afternoon.

When he arrived at five o'clock to take up her and her maid in his carriage, he turned toward Green Park, instead of the more fashionable Hyde Park. When she glanced at him in surprise, he explained, "Conversing in Hyde Park is so difficult I thought we might go elsewhere. I understand Green Park is more rural, and I must admit I miss being in the country. The heather on the moors is deep purple now, and you should hear the curlew's cries. Town birds, although musical, simply cannot compare."

"I miss being in the country too, although I admit to enjoying Town life. As I recall, you told me you are from Yorkshire. Are estates productive in that area in general?" Mr. Desmond's comment about farmers did not support success.

He shook his head. "I took over the management of the farms from my father only last year and must admit they are in worse shape than I realized. Sheep production can be very costly when weather is bad, as it was this past winter. However, I found a way to take care of the financial situation, so when I return home, I can put the estate on a successful basis again."

Her heart thundered against her ribs as she realized what he was telling her. She probed gently. "That is good news, indeed, sir. I suppose you have business speculations here in Town that will take care of the situation."

He nodded and changed the subject. "Have you heard of the balloon ascension tomorrow in Hyde Park?"

"I believe I did hear something about it," she answered, wondering if he was planning to ride in it, or was fly the correct word?

"I read a book about aeronautics, and I'm anxious to see a real balloon. Would you care to accompany me in my carriage? The seat is high enough that you can see over the crowds."

"I must admit I know nothing about balloons, but it might prove interesting, so I accept your invitation. What time is the ascension?"

"Midmorning, but we must be there early," he assured her. "We don't want to miss a thing."

He chattered about casks of hydrogen, speeds of up to fifty miles an hour when the wind was strong enough, and reaching heights of even a half mile.

When they reached the door at Haverford House, Marie's head was in a whirl, and she almost changed her mind. No, she must go. She might get him back to the subject of his expected windfall of funds. Her father's image flashed before her, but she pushed it away.

By the time they reached the park the following morning, she realized her mistake, because all Mr. Anderson would talk about was the balloon. Marie rolled her eyes at Hannah, who managed to keep a still face, although her eyes twinkled.

"See that pile of silk on the ground?" Mr. Anderson pointed toward a roped-off enclosure. "That is the balloon. They use the hosepipe to fill it with the hydrogen, and then you will be able to see the beauty of it. Is it not marvelous?"

Marie pasted an interested expression on her face and attempted an intelligent question. "Why do they use silk? I don't consider it a sturdy fabric."

"Appearances are deceiving. Aeronauts used linen in earlier years, but it ripped so easily they experimented with other fabrics and chose silk." His enthusiasm overflowed. "I can hardly credit that people can fly through the air."

Marie shuddered at the thought. A carriage seat was high enough off the ground to suit her. This one was higher than she was accustomed to occupying, but she conceded the height was exactly what she needed to view the entire area.

"Look! They're filling the balloon now. Is that not a beautiful sight?"

Marie had to agree. The alternating stripes of blue, yellow, and green silk billowed in the air and lifted the orange-painted basket slightly off the ground. She'd had no idea balloons were so large.

A shout rose from the crowd when a worker loosened the tethers, and the balloon slowly ascended into the atmosphere. Marie craned her neck backwards for a moment, only to bend forward to relieve the tension. When she gazed upward again, the balloon was out of sight. Oh, good. Perhaps they could leave now.

"Mr. Anderson, I believe it's time to leave now." She touched his sleeve as he continued to stare into space. She repeated herself.

"What? Yes, of course. That's all there is to see here. Was it not a wonderful sight? Oh, how I would like to fly, free as a bird!"

As they moved toward the gate, Marie spotted Lord Beaufort in close conversation with a dark-haired female she did not recognize. They were mounted, but their horses faced in opposite directions, so Marie assumed they had not arrived together. She watched the female reach out a hand and caress Beaufort's sleeve. Probably no better than she should be. With a sniff, Marie turned toward Mr. Anderson.

"Yesterday you mentioned your estate, sir, and how you plan to make it productive again. An admirable ambition. I do hope you soon receive good news about your investments."

"Investments? Oh, yes, investments." He flushed and turned the subject to her plans for the evening. "Do you attend the Amesbury ball?"

Marie admitted she was wasting her time trying to gather information from him this morning. Perhaps she would have more success another time.

"Yes, we plan to be at Amesbury House this evening. They're the grandparents of my close friend, Rebecca Blackwell, so we would not miss their ball under any circumstances. Perhaps I'm wrong, but I believe we can expect an interesting announcement this evening."

"Ah, sounds like a betrothal is in the works." He grinned at her. "I believe that's the usual meaning when a young lady mentions an interesting announcement. Am I correct?"

She chuckled in reply and alighted from his carriage at her door. "I hope to see you this evening, sir."

Marie entered the hall to hear the murmur of voices beyond the drawing room door. "Symms, who is with Mama?"

"Several of your friends are here."

Good. She needed her friends around her at this moment. They wouldn't bore her to tears about the wonders of balloons. She put Anderson out of her mind. Also, Beaufort and his female companion—his inamorata?—as she hurried up the stairs to remove her bonnet.

"There's a spot on your sleeve, Miss Marie. You must change before you go back downstairs," Hannah told her, pulling a sprigged muslin gown from the wardrobe.

When Marie entered the drawing room moments later, the noise rose to a crescendo as voices appealed to her for confirmation.

"You agree with me, I am sure you do, Miss Haverford," stated Mr. Anstey. "I say a pair of matched grays is better than a pair of matched chestnuts. What say you?"

Marie stared at him in amusement. "I have never given the matter my close attention, Mr. Anstey. Are there any differences in horses? Besides the color, that is."

That question brought the conversation to a sudden stop before the young ladies erupted into laughter. "Did I say something humorous?" Marie inquired with feigned surprise.

Even Mr. Desmond stared at her in stupefaction. "Come to think of it, I do not believe I ever saw you mounted on a horse in all the years I've known you."

"No, you have not, nor will you ever," she stated.

"Are you frightened of the beasts too?" Grace Patterson smiled at her in sympathy.

"Of course, I'm frightened of them! Any female in her right mind would be frightened of anything so much larger than she. Horses also have too many feet, and I dare say they bite."

"Ah, yes, just so," agreed the dazed Mr. Desmond.

Marie realized that she had found the perfect way to rid herself of an unwanted suitor, whether it was Mr. Desmond or any other horse-mad gentleman, which appeared to be all of them. While the discussion of horses went on around her, she moved to her mother's side.

"Mama, may we invite them to stay for luncheon?"

"Yes, of course. If you can tolerate the discussion of beasts while we consume sliced ham, I'm sure I can."

A soft gurgle of laughter escaped Marie's lips. "I tossed the cat amongst the pigeons that time, did I not?" With a quick hug for her mother, she went in search of Symms to give instructions for luncheon.

While these young people moved from one subject to another over the sliced ham and fruit, Lady Emily again searched for Marie in all the likely places. She thought Lord Stokely would surely want a progress report this evening, and she must have one. Otherwise, the consequences could be painful.

Indeed, he did want a progress report and was far from happy that she had not talked with the chit. "I do not understand what the problem, Emily. Why should it be so difficult to hold a simple conversation with her?"

She answered as quietly as she could, in contrast to his raised voice. "I must come across her in a casual way, and thus far, the only times I've found her has been in the park when a crowd of young people surrounded her. She attended the balloon ascension with Mr. Anderson but remained in his carriage, and I was unable to get close enough to speak."

"Mr. Anderson? I wonder what they find to discuss. I must ask him that. Have you seen her with Beaufort?"

"No, my lord, never. I don't recall ever seeing him with any young girl."

"All right. Now I remind you I want results from you, and I want them fast. Do you understand me?" His large hand gripped her lower face so hard she could not speak, but nodded. He squeezed her face hard enough to bring tears to her eyes before releasing his grip. "Good."

Why had she become involved with that brute? She knew the answer, of course. She'd hoped to use him as her entry back into the upper levels of polite society after her *mésalliance*. Well, no matter what she learned from Marie Haverford, she wouldn't tell Stokely the exact truth, but instead would prevaricate enough to throw him off her scent. The chit didn't deserve his callousness.

Stokely made his way to Anderson's rooms and soon reduced the young man to stammering incoherence.

"We don't talk about anything special, my lord, I assure you! I described Yorkshire to her because she has never been there. She talked a little bit about country life but told me she prefers life in Town. Stuff like that. Oh, and we talked about balloons."

"Has she asked you about your financial situation?"

Anderson appeared bewildered. "Why would she do that? They don't appear to be short of blunt, and she has Desmond sitting in her pocket if she wants a fortune."

"Have you seen her with Beaufort?"

"Yes, but only when they danced at some ball or other, my lord. She did not appear to pay him any more attention than any of her other dance partners."

"They seemed friendly enough at Carlton House the other evening."

Anderson shrugged. "I wouldn't know about that because I was not there. I've never spoken to the man, myself."

"You will do well to avoid him regardless of circumstances." Stokely started to take his leave, but turned back. "Have you had any conversation with your friend at Whitehall that you failed to tell me?"

"Of course, I didn't! He hasn't been in his usual haunts the last few evenings, and I hesitate to go to his home."

"No, wait for him to contact you, just as we agreed." Stokely strode out the door and to the street, a frown marring his brow. No footpads dared approach him, and he was soon sitting in his study, staring into space while he tried to decide what to do about the Haverford chit.

The chit in question was at that moment looking at the Duke of Amesbury, who stood in front of the orchestra in his ballroom. He cleared his throat drawing all attention toward himself.

"Ladies and gentlemen, most of you know that my granddaughter came to live with us late last summer after growing up in the orphanage patronized by the Duchess of Dorchester. Many of you have knowledge of the duchess, even if you are not personally acquainted with her. I hasten to assure you we did not know our granddaughter was in Hampshire but, in retrospect, realize and are thankful she was in the care of excellent people. We would prefer to keep her with us for a longer period, yet if we must lose her, it could not be to a finer gentleman."

He paused for the murmur of voices to recede. "Therefore, ladies and gentlemen, I present to you my granddaughter, Rebecca Marie Louise Blackwell, and her affianced husband, Edward John Cecil, the Earl of Shelburne."

Midst the loud applause, Rebecca and Shelburne joined hands and smiled into each other's eyes before Shelburne turned to the duke.

"Your Grace, thank you for the honour you do me. I promise to take good care of her."

Marie kept the smile fixed on her face, even as she wondered if she would ever stand in Rebecca's shoes. Not literally, of course, she admonished herself. After all, Shelburne was her uncle. No, she wanted a somber face highlighted with mahogany eyes across the breakfast table every morning for the rest of her life.

In the early dawn hours when she could not sleep, Marie lit a candle and settled at her writing desk. Susan would enjoy reading about Rebecca's betrothal ball. She concluded with,

> *I'm happy to tell you that Louise and Major Stafford were present. No one gave me details, of course, but I understand she is no longer increasing. That accounts for her wan appearance, I conjecture. Anyway, they have come to Town for the rest of the Season to*

raise her spirits. Perhaps I can now become acquainted with her, but I would rather have you here!

Chapter 10

Disobedience

While Shelburne gained his heart's desire, Lord Beaufort sat in his own study, staring into the small fire hissing in the grate, his thoughts on Marie Haverford. He had not spoken to her since the evening he joined them for dinner, having avoided her at the balloon ascension that morning. Seeing her with Anderson roused his curiosity. Did she disobey her father's specific orders? The man seemed innocent enough, yet she was positive he was the third man in the Stokely/Rayson triangle. He had made a point of asking Brownlee about Anderson after seeing them in the park. He had believed his question casual, yet Brownlee stared at him a moment before replying that he did not know the man. He probably thought Beaufort was jealous, and Beaufort left him unenlightened.

At Hatchard's the following morning, Marie kept her senses alert to any acquaintances who might be nearby. A familiar throaty voice spoke from behind her.

"Miss Haverford, have you found an interesting book?"

"Not yet, Lady Emily, although I'm considering this volume of poetry. I must confess I come here to find friends as much as to find books."

"I realize I am a mere acquaintance, but perhaps we can remedy that over a cup of tea at Gunter's Confectionery?"

"I would enjoy that above all things, my lady." Marie replaced the poetry book on the shelf.

Marie paused outside the door, where her maid waited on the servant's bench. "Hannah, I'm going to Gunter's for tea with Lady Emily. I suggest you go to the drapery shop and match the ribbons. Meet me at the confectionery in an hour's time."

"Yes, Miss Marie."

The ladies strolled to Gunter's, stopping to admire a bonnet in a millinery shop window. They chatted about the Season, as they sipped the hot brew and feasted on angel cakes. Rather, Marie feasted, while Lady Emily nibbled at one tiny cake.

Marie pushed the plate away, sighing with repletion. Darting a rueful grin toward her hostess, she confided, "Mama says if I keep on eating so much, I shall become a dumpling, but I don't see any signs of it as yet."

"You're so slender you need not worry about gaining weight. So different from me. I can glance at food, and my gowns become too tight."

With a chuckle, Marie nodded toward the door. "I see my maid is waiting, so I must take my leave now."

"Oh, pray, do not go yet. You see, I would love to have your company at the military review because I do dislike going alone. My friends who live next to the parade route told me I could view it from their balcony. Please say yes!"

"A military review?" Marie asked. "I've never attended one, but Mama has not told me it's improper, so I should think it is all right."

"And your maid is with us."

"Yes, to be sure, so I don't believe there is a problem." Gathering her reticule and gloves, she hurried to tell Hannah of the treat in store for them.

Lady Emily's open carriage waited in front of the confectionery with a groom there to assist them. Soon they were on a balcony high above a throng of milling people, watching for the uniformed men on horseback.

"I must admit I have no idea what to expect at this type of spectacle," Marie commented.

"Well, we might see Prinny, but his presence is not a sure thing by any means."

"The Prince Regent?" Marie glanced at her in surprise. "Would he inspect the troops, perhaps?"

"No, he will lead them, if he manages to get his uniform on and if his grooms manage to hoist him onto his horse."

"Surely you cannot mean he wears a military uniform. I'm not acquainted with him, but I have never heard that he is a member of the military."

Lady Emily chuckled. "Nor is he, but he tells people he served with Wellington in Spain."

Marie's eyes widened. She had a difficult time visualizing the obese regent in a military uniform. "By the way you say that, I gather that he did not?"

"No, but in all fairness, I must say he wanted to serve in the army, and the king refused to give his permission." Her hesitation was brief. "But I should think you would already know all this since your father is connected with the military."

"My father? My father is Sir Julian Haverford, and as far as I know has never been in the military." She met Lady Emily's speculative gaze with innocence.

"Then, I misunderstood something I heard," Lady Emily said as the volume of noise rose below them.

Marie turned to stare at the long column of uniformed soldiers passing below, but her thoughts were racing. What had Lady Emily heard and from whom? Lord Stokely, without doubt, which means she was probing Marie for information to pass on to him. A thrill of excitement passed through her at that thought. She would make certain they did not learn anything from her. With that determined thought, Marie turned her wide-eyed gaze toward Lady Emily. "I never saw so many red coats in one place. Are they not handsome? But why do some of them have so much gold trim while others have very little?"

"The braid indicates the difference in their ranks, I believe." She glanced sideways at Marie. "I sometimes think everyone working in an official capacity should wear uniforms. Just think of how elegant your father would appear when he goes out on his government business. Or do I have that wrong too?"

"Oh, no," Marie replied. "My father is connected with the government in some capacity. I doubt he would be more elegant in a uniform than in his regular clothing. He's a very handsome gentleman," she commented with obvious pride and turned back to the parade.

"Government work fascinates me. Just what is it that Sir Julian does?"

"I have no idea," Marie replied. "He never mentions it, and I admit it hasn't occurred to me to inquire. Oh, did you see that?" Marie managed a slight flush and fluttered her fan in front of her face. "That gentleman winked at me, I'm sure he did!"

Lady Emily returned a light answer to Marie's exclamation and indicated it was time to leave.

"Oh, is it over? This has been beyond anything great, Lady Emily. I thank you for inviting me because, otherwise, think what I would have missed. All those crimson coats!" Marie bubbled as she gathered her reticule preparatory to leaving.

"I enjoyed your company," the lady assured her. "May I take you someplace in my carriage? No? Then, I shall say good-bye and hope we meet again soon."

Marie nodded and turned toward her own home. Oh, yes, she intended to see Lady Emily again. It would be her turn to ask questions, and she intended to learn all she could. First, however, she looked forward to an evening at Almack's.

It was fortunate the Haverfords dined at home that evening. As Marie pointed out to Lady Becca, "Mama, you know how terrible the food is at Almack's. I shall starve if I must depend on the stale cake they serve."

Sir Julian stared at his daughter's heaping plate. "I see no evidence you're in danger of starvation."

Marie tossed him a saucy grin and delved into the plate of sirloin with roasted potatoes removed with asparagus in lemon sauce and tiny peas. She finished with sliced apples and cheese and sighed with repletion. "I believe I may survive the evening."

"I should hope so," Sir Julian replied. "The carriage will be here in fifteen minutes, ladies."

When she stepped inside the hallowed doors of the Marriage Mart, Marie found herself surrounded by young bucks seeking her hand in a dance or even two. She twinkled, but allowed only one dance to each.

About midway of the evening, Marie perched on a gilt chair next to her mother and wafted a fan before her face. She had a partner for every dance, just as she always did, yet the one person she most wanted to see was not there. At least, she had not seen Beaufort, although it was possible he was in the card room. A few moments later, she saw him stroll through the doorway with a beautiful dark-haired lady on his arm, the same female who accompanied him in the park, and realized she had misjudged the lady's quality.

Marie managed a brilliant smile as Mr. Desmond bowed before her and claimed his dance. She moved down the dance line, her eyes straying toward Lord Beaufort often enough for her partner to call her to task.

"If you don't care to dance with me, you have only to tell me."

Marie apologized for not paying attention.

"Who has captured your attention, anyway?"

"Oh, no one," she answered and began her usual merry chatter until he returned her to Lady Becca's side. He bowed and walked away, and Marie turned to her mother. With her fan guarding her lips, she inquired if Lady Becca recognized the lady with Beaufort.

"No, my dear. I don't recall ever seeing her before, which isn't surprising since she is some years younger than I am. Did you ask for a particular reason?"

"Oh, no, Mama, I was only curious about an unfamiliar face," Marie replied and accepted the arm of her next dance partner.

When she held much the same conversation with Deborah Langford and Grace Patterson a short while later, they knew no more than she did. Marie hesitated to display her interest to anyone else, so she left Almack's with the vision of her heart's desire, his head leaning toward another female.

"He didn't even approach me all evening," she muttered sadly as she prepared for bed a while later.

Hannah heard Marie's account of the evening in complete detail. "I imagine he will tell you about her the next time you see him. Now, get into bed," she cajoled.

A few mornings later, Marie wandered through the gardens, occasionally bending her head to sniff a rose. She did not know why she sought the solitude, still the quietness proved a balm. Perhaps she needed another respite from Town life. Her schedule left little time for introspection, and this morning she felt the lack of it.

She sat on a bench and allowed her thoughts to return to her conversation with Lady Emily yesterday. She was almost sure the questions were an effort to elicit what Marie knew about the gold shipments. It could not be coincidence. Marie was not sure she believed in coincidence, even about the smallest of things. What questions should she ask Lady Emily when next they met? A twinge of conscience made her chew her inner lip for a moment. Papa had told her not to become involved. Even more difficult to ignore was the fact she had agreed to abide by his wishes. She had not only agreed, she had promised. She turned when she heard footsteps on the graveled path.

Moments earlier, Lord Beaufort had entered Sir Julian's study to await his return. He glanced at the portrait over the mantelshelf, a gentleman holding a gun across his arm and a spotted dog standing to heel. Must be Sir Julian's father, because Sir Julian was not a hunter, nor did he pretend to be. Beaufort sauntered to the French window overlooking the small back garden with immaculate flower borders. When his gaze lighted on the figure occupying the wrought-iron bench, he hesitated only a moment before opening the window and stepping outside.

"Good morning, Miss Haverford. Am I intruding?"

"Not at all, my lord. Please join me." She smiled her welcome and moved over on the bench, making room for him.

A moment of stiffness passed when he commented on the quietness of the garden. "This is as peaceful as Hyde Park in the early morning."

"The high walls keep much of the sound out, my lord. At times it's almost like being in the country."

They sat in hushed silence as the chaffinches warbled in the high branches of a gnarled old tree they could not identify. "Tell me, do you enjoy living in the country, or do rural pursuits bore you?"

"Oh, I am never bored, sir! My father taught me long ago boredom is the result of an idle mind, and mine is too active ever to be idle."

"I must admit I never thought of boredom in just that way. I thought boredom was the result of idle hands."

"My lord, living in the country does not produce idle hands either. At least it does not if one attends to estate responsibilities, as Mama taught me to do."

"I notice you do not mention rural entertainment."

"My thoughts are not centered on entertainment," she assured him with a chuckle. "However, we do have many dinner parties and dances as well as card parties and all sorts of al fresco excursions."

"Do you live near any body of water?"

She gave him a questioning glance. "No, my lord. Why do you think we might?"

"I remember your enthusiasm about the boat ride at a picnic someone or other gave."

"That was not the most pleasant day of my life, sir." She answered his raised eyebrows. *"Mal de mer."*

He controlled his quivering lips with an effort. "Ah, yes, I imagine that might be a problem. Since my experience does not include a boat ride, I have no way of knowing, and I don't care to find out either. I shall keep my feet on dry land."

She gave him a speaking glance and changed the subject. "I believe you're from Yorkshire, my lord. I'm aware that county is in the extreme northern part of England, but that's the limit of my knowledge. Is your area very different from Kent?"

"Quite different. Kent is known for gardens and rolling inclines. Two hundred miles north, Yorkshire is almost the opposite. The clime is much less salubrious for growing flowers, as you know it in Kent."

She listened in fascinated silence as he described the dales, the high winds whistling over the moors, and the medieval city of York.

"You must love your home county very much, my lord, yet you spend much of your time in London."

"Business keeps me here more than I prefer, but I do spend a considerable amount of time at my estate near Middleham."

"I would like to see it sometime."

"Perhaps we can arrange that," he murmured. A moment later, he blinked and nodded toward the house. "I imagine Sir Julian is here by now, and I need to discuss some matters with him." He stood and bowed almost formally. "I enjoyed our conversation."

"As have I, my lord," she replied, her intent gaze fixed on his eyes, willing him to recognize her seriousness.

Marie sat for a few moments after he left, reliving their time together, the feel of his arm so close to hers. Even their minds seemed tuned. This visit was even better than the evening he dined with them. She had displayed interest in what he said and had not mentioned the *ton* even once. He appeared to be comfortable in her company this time, so perhaps Susan was right when she counseled against giggling and flirting. He didn't mention the dark-haired lady, yet it mattered not while he was here. She rose and went indoors, her earlier thoughts of Lady Emily forgotten.

However, Lady Emily had not forgotten Marie. That was because Lord Stokely, at that moment, stared into her eyes with icy calm and demanded an answer. A call from his lordship this early in the day was unprecedented. She struggled to gather her thoughts.

"What did you learn from the Haverford chit yesterday? What does she know about her father's government work?"

"As far as I could ascertain, she knows nothing. Oh, she knows he works for the government but said he never discusses his work at home, and she was not interested enough to inquire. Really, Stokely, the chit thinks of little other than the glories of the Season. You should have seen her eat angel cakes with her tea. She hasn't outgrown her schoolgirl tendencies yet. She's still self-centered."

"Did you question her? Ask about military matters?"

"Yes, my lord, I did. We watched the military review from the Hansons' balcony. She was very clear in her opinion her father has no interest in the military. All she could think about were the pretty red coats. Stokely, I do think she is a complete innocent about whatever it is you want to know."

"I didn't tell you to think. I told you to get me some answers. Now do it!"

"I think you are mistaken—"

He gave her a sharp blow across her face, sending her reeling across the room until she landed against a high-backed chair that bruised her ribs.

"You will do what I say, jade, or that's just a small sample of what you can expect." He slammed the door after him.

Lady Emily moved to the mirror over the mantelshelf and inspected her face. This was the first time he'd struck her. What he might do next sent a shudder down her spine. She must get away from him, but how? She pondered for several minutes.

England was not big enough to hide from him, but he would not be able to reach her out in the middle of the ocean. She nodded in satisfaction, remembering the merchant ship captain whom she met a few days before. He showed his interest at that time, and she knew she could persuade him to take her out of Stokely's reach, perhaps to the United States, as the former colonies now called themselves. No, that was out of the question because of the war, but there were other places. It was a big world, after all.

Emily stopped her pacing long enough to inspect her face once more. It was already misshapen and changing color. She should not go out looking like this, yet she must. With tightened lips, she sat at the small desk and pulled forward a sheet of hot-pressed paper. Her maid, who was trustworthy beyond doubt, would deliver a note to the captain. After that, Emily would go shopping.

Several hours later, the butler opened the door in answer to a thunderous banging and advised the caller that Lady Emily was not at home.

"What do you mean, she's not here?" Stokely demanded. "She knew I would be calling this evening, so naturally she's here." He forced his way past the butler and went from room to room, bellowing Lady Emily's name. When he returned to the hall where the butler waited, he spoke with a deadly calm that left the elderly butler shaking in his shoes. "When do you expect her back?"

"She did not say, my lord," the old man quavered.

"Send me word the instant she returns. Is that clear?"

"Yes, my lord."

Lord Stokely shoved the old man out of his way and jerked the door open, slamming it after him.

The butler pushed himself away from the wall where he had landed and straightened his clothing. He bolted the door and retreated to the kitchen where the other servants waited. They were few in number and decidedly in support of Lady Emily, whose face they had seen earlier when she made an unprecedented visit to the kitchen region.

Smiling as well as she could, she had ignored their gasps at the spectacle her face presented and spoke first to the young footman, who was her newest employee. "Henry, I recall you have not had a free day as yet, and I believe this is an appropriate time for you to take one." She had pointed to her face and continued, "I must stay indoors and shall not need your escort for a few days."

He had stuttered his thanks and left the room. Silence reigned in the kitchen until the noise of his leaving the house had faded to nothing.

Lady Emily sat at the table and motioned for the others to do the same. "You have all worked for me for many years. It's only fair to tell you I leave London tonight. I cannot take any of you with me, and for your protection, I shall not divulge my destination. I intend to leave the instant night falls, and I recommend you leave as soon thereafter as you can manage."

She had waved away their murmurs of concern. "I wrote letters of reference for you in my late husband's name, and I suggest you keep them on your person. Johnson and I must run some errands, and when we return, I shall give you funds to subsist on until you find employment."

Lady Emily had risen to her feet and gazed at each of her old retainers. "You have served me well, and I wish each of you much good fortune in the future."

The butler had watched her and her personal maid leave soon after darkness fell, taking with them all the valuables they could carry.

Lady Emily had smiled when she told him of the purchases she had made that day in Lord Stokely's name and his probable reaction in a few days when he received the bills. He would pay handsomely for damaging her face. She confessed only thoughts of revenge had allowed her to reveal her countenance to shopkeepers, because she must identify herself as the female who often accompanied Lord Stokely. They hid their reactions to her bruised face and didn't question her purchases.

Now, the butler spoke to the other servants. "He left, and we must do the same before he decides to return."

Within the hour, the servants slipped into the night, leaving behind no evidence they had ever been there.

Chapter 11

Consequences

"Stokely is on a rampage, I understand. Do you happen to know the particulars?"

Her father's voice came to Marie, who strolled in the garden outside the study window. Earlier, she had heard him and a visitor enter the room but paid little attention, her thoughts on Lord Beaufort. The sound of his voice caught her attention.

"The word around the clubs is that his ladybird has flown the nest, destination unknown, leaving behind a mass of unpaid bills. Despite her wealth, mind you."

"Sounds like spite to me. I doubt he cared for her overmuch; hence, there must be a different reason for his temper."

"Well, I got this thirdhand through my servants, so I cannot be sure how reliable it is. It seems my footman saw Lady Emily's footman at their club last evening. He complained that she gave him the day off, and when he came back after a night on the tiles, he found the house locked, and no one answered the door. He went to Stokely's to find out what happened, and that was when Stokely learned she was missing."

"I daresay Stokely took out his temper on him."

"I understand he tried, but the footman ducked and ran. He did tell his cronies Lady Emily's face carried a large bruise, when she gave him the day off, and that Stokely had visited her earlier."

"Adding two and two together gives us the answer that he roughed her up when she didn't do something he told her to do. I wonder what it was."

"This confirms all we have heard about his being dangerous when his temper is roused."

Marie's eyes dilated with horror as she listened. She believed she knew what had made Lord Stokely angry. Should she tell her father about her meeting with Lady Emily? She stared into the distance for a moment before, with a resolute air, she straightened her shoulders and marched through the study door.

"Papa, I did not mean to eavesdrop," she began, a plea in her voice. "I was in the garden and didn't realize you had a visitor until I neared the house." She made herself meet Lord Beaufort's gaze.

"How much did you hear, Marie?" Sir Julian's voice was quiet but demanded an answer nonetheless.

"Not much, sir. Only that Lord Stokely is angry because Lady Emily disappeared." Marie swallowed around the lump in her throat. "I know what he wanted her to do. At least, I believe I do."

"Tell us."

"He wanted her to get information from me about your military connections. She approached me in Hatchard's a few days ago and invited me to have tea at Gunter's Confectionary. When I started to leave, she invited me to watch the military review with her." Marie continued the story, her anxious gaze never leaving her father's face.

"It appears she didn't tell him what he wanted to know, but was it because she chose not to or because you didn't reveal any knowledge?"

"I never told her anything, I promise you, Papa," Marie assured him. "I knew she was probing, because she would not have approached me otherwise, so I was on guard. In truth, I chattered about the Season all through tea until she must have been bored to tears.

During the parade, I talked about the pretty red coats and gold braid until I almost sickened myself."

Sir Julian's perfunctory smile did not reach his eyes. "Very well, Marie. However, do you recall I told you not to become involved in this matter, and you promised me you would not?"

Marie nodded after a fleeting glance toward Lord Beaufort, who stared at her with harsh eyes.

"You disobeyed me. You not only permitted Lady Emily to question you, you also have been in company with the gentleman whom you believe to be involved. I find. it improbable you did not attempt to obtain information from him."

She tightened her lips but did not reply.

"We will discuss this later. In the meantime, go to your bedchamber and reflect on what happened to Lady Emily when Stokely became angry with her."

"Yes, Papa," she whispered and fled the room with her head lowered, closing the door quietly behind her.

After Sir Julian watched her leave, he turned to Beaufort. "Stokely suspects my daughter of having knowledge about his involvement in our problem. I fear that places her in danger."

Beaufort nodded his agreement. "What will you do? Send her back to Kent?"

"My first inclination, yes. However, is that the answer? It might serve to convince him she does have information he wants. In that event, what is to keep him from following her there?"

"Yes, there is that to be considered. What do you propose?"

"I simply do not know," Sir Julian conceded. "I must discuss the matter with her mother before I confront Marie. In the meantime, please advise Colonel Hayes of Stokely's latest actions and assure him that, to the best of your knowledge, Marie has no information helpful to Stokely. I shall talk with Hayes later today when my thoughts are clearer."

With a brief nod, Beaufort left the room, and Sir Julian went in search of Lady Becca, whom he found in the morning room. Half an hour later, the white-faced Becca accompanied her husband to their daughter's sitting room.

Marie could not sit still. She deserved whatever punishment her father chose. The longer she waited, the more intense became her self-castigation. Why did she continue to disobey him? When the door of her sitting room opened, it was all she could do not to rush into her mother's arms. Her lips trembled as she gazed at her father, but she did not speak.

"Sit down, Marie." Sir Julian seated Lady Becca on a small sofa and sat beside her, while Marie perched on the edge of a low, armless chair. "Do you have a reason for disobeying me?"

She opened and closed her lips but shook her head.

"Do you have a reason for going back on your own word?"

Again, Marie shook her head.

"Do you have anything to say for yourself?"

Salty tears slid down her face and into her mouth, but again Marie only shook her head.

"Allow me to explain the situation to you as simply as I can. Our only reason to suspect Stokely is that you told us of the snippets of conversation you overheard. He believes he is a suspect and you are the reason for his suspicion. That places you in danger from him and whoever works with him."

Marie listened with close attention. "Does that not prove that he is, indeed, responsible for the robberies?"

Her father closed his eyes in frustration for a long moment. When he opened them, he stared her straight in the face and spoke with deadly calm. "At this moment, Marie, I do not care if he is responsible for the robberies. I do not care if he is Napoleon's spy. I do not care if he is Napoleon's right-hand man. I don't care if he is Napoleon in disguise. My only concern is keeping you safe. Can you manage to focus on that point?"

Marie clamped her lips shut and nodded.

"Lord Beaufort suggested I might send you back to Kent . . . don't interrupt me, Marie," he ordered when she started up from her chair in protest. "I decided, and your mother agrees with me, that sending you away will confirm Stokely in his beliefs. Therefore, you must stay in Town and go about the Season in your usual manner with one exception. Do you understand me?"

"Yes, Papa." She cast a quick glance at her mother and flinched before the fear in her eyes.

"That one exception is this. You will not leave this house without a footman in attendance as well as your maid. At every soirée, you will surround yourself with people, preferably several males, and you will not be out of your mother's sight for even a moment, not even in the ladies' retiring room. Is that clear?"

"Yes, Papa," she answered.

"Do you have anything further to say?"

Marie moistened her lips before answering. "Only to apologize for the trouble I caused. I did not mean to do that, and I truly am sorry."

Sir Julian gave her the briefest of nods. "I must consult with Colonel Hayes. I shall return to dinner."

"Papa?" Marie bit her lip and stared beseechingly into his stern face. "Did you tell Lord Beaufort why I became involved in this matter?"

"No, of course not." He closed the door behind him.

"Perhaps you should tell me, Marie, for I am at a loss to understand your behavior."

"I was trying to attract Lord Beaufort's notice, Mama. He's so involved in business I believed that was the route to his heart."

"I told you he sees you only as the daughter of his business acquaintance. Although I must admit that just lately . . . however, never mind that."

Marie took her up on the cryptic comment. "Yes, Mama, what did you start to say?"

Lady Becca shook her head. "Never mind, Marie. Promise me, though, you will not again disobey your father. It is the only way to keep you safe, and I cannot bear the thought of your being in danger."

"Yes, Mama, I learned my lesson. I shan't disobey him again. Besides, beyond doubt Lord Beaufort is so disgusted with me I have lost whatever chance to attract him I might have had."

"Marie, I repeat, please put him out of your mind! Now, we must discuss our ball, which is this Friday night. How many more fittings does Madame Bouchét need to finish your gown?"

"Only one, I believe, and that is this afternoon." Marie perked up at the thought of the coming ball. "Have we received replies to all the invitations?"

"To be sure we have, and we may expect upwards of three hundred people." Lady Becca's voice oozed with satisfaction. "A veritable squeeze!"

The ladies continued the discussion, agreeing the numerous baskets of flowers they planned would keep the air fresh in the crowded ballroom. In addition, the silk butterflies suspended over them would offer a measure of charm not yet seen this Season.

While the ladies discussed social matters, Sir Julian met with Colonel Hayes and discussed affairs of state. "My daughter does not have any information Stokely needs, yet I believe she's in danger from him."

"In a negative kind of way, she does have information he needs, if he is, indeed, the culprit. And I must remind you that we still have no proof of that."

Sir Julian grasped what, for him, was the essential point. "What did you mean, sir, about her lack of information being useful to Stokely?"

"He could proceed more easily if he knew she didn't overhear anything crucial to his plans. Thus, it still behooves him to obtain information from her."

"I had not thought of the matter in that light, sir. Yet you are correct, so he must continue his pursuit of her."

"It seems to me you plan the correct route to protect her, so she should be safe enough," the colonel assured him. "Now if there is nothing further, I need to return to the everlasting paperwork." They briefly clasped hands, and Sir Julian left with his mind centered on his daughter's safety.

The few days before the Haverford ball passed quietly enough, and Marie stood with her parents in the receiving line that evening as they greeted their guests. There were even more people than there had been last Season at her presentation ball. Marie expressed this thought to her mother in a moment free of guests.

"Yes, I believe there are, dear. I doubt if many more arrive, so the dancing can begin now."

Marie managed to locate Beaufort from the corner of her eye but never looked directly at him. When he failed to approach her by the supper dance, she accepted Mr. Desmond's arm and adjured herself to pay strict attention to him. He, too, had avoided her that evening, although she saw him in conversation with a demure young lady with dark curls. Miss Helen Griswall was the goddaughter of someone or other of Lady Becca's friends, although Marie could not remember whom. A brisk recital of the Season to date carried them through the dance and into the supper room.

"Miss Haverford, do you mind if Miss Griswall sits at table with us?" Mr. Desmond asked. "She is shy and hardly knows anyone."

Thus, Marie consumed her supper with her old gallant giving all his attention to Miss Griswall. It did not help matters that Deborah Langford talked only to Mr. Anstey and that Grace Patterson seldom took her eyes off Mr. Buxted. Marie had only her thoughts, which were not happy at that moment.

When she returned to the ballroom, Lord Beaufort materialized beside her. "I've been unable to get near you. Do you have a free dance I might beg?"

Marie turned a dazzling smile on him. Her evening was improving by the moment. She glanced at her dance card and reported the next dance free.

The musicians struck up a *contredanse,* and Marie floated through the next half hour wishing the music would never end. Not a word sounded between them, yet Marie did not feel the need to chatter. Beaufort's slow smile, the feel of his warm hands touching hers were enough. She was starry-eyed when he escorted her back to her mother's side and bowed before going in search of his next dance partner.

Marie linked arms with her mother. "This is a marvelous evening, Mama."

Before Lady Becca could agree, a masculine voice greeted them. "Good evening, ladies."

Marie turned with a smile toward Beau Brummell, that arbiter of fashion for the masculine world. She had first met him during her previous Season and felt at ease with him, despite the ever-existing possibility he might slight her. "I trust you're enjoying the evening."

"How could I not?" he drawled. "I'm in such exalted company."

"La, sir, have you become a flatterer to add to your other illustrious traits?"

He raised supercilious eyebrows over eyes that twinkled. "Flattery is beneath my dignity. You should know that."

"I do, sir," she assured him with an answering twinkle. "But some day, I will catch you out on that!"

With a brief unfathomable smile, he rose from the gilt chair and bowed himself away.

Behind him, Marie transferred her smile to her mother. "If I had not already taken, I would now since he condescended to sit with us for quite five minutes!"

With a slight smile, Lady Becca agreed and nodded her approval for Marie's next dance partner. The evening progressed with Marie unaware her father had posted guards at the door to assure her safety.

She didn't even think about safety and, in fact, had forced from her thoughts the contretemps of a few days earlier. She danced every dance, smiled, and chatted without a care in the world, neither knowing nor caring about others' thoughts. She only knew she'd had the attention of the one gentleman from whom she craved it and was happy with that.

When the last guest left, she turned to her parents. "The evening was a success, was it not?" With their agreement ringing in her ears, she kissed them good night and slowly climbed the stairs to her bedchamber, where Hannah waited.

The maid got her ready for bed in silence, and still in silence, she left to seek her own.

Marie reviewed the evening. She was pleased, no ecstatic, Beaufort had danced with her but admitted she had enjoyed simply standing beside him in conversation. A quiet interlude was the perfect way to spend time with the one you loved.

Loved? She thought a moment as her heartbeat quickened. This was the first time she had used that word in relation to Lord Beaufort, but she rejoiced in it. She dwelled on it for a moment's pleasure before Mr. Desmond's face intervened. She remembered feeling chagrin when her old beau showed his preference for Miss Griswall. Goodness, was she selfish? She did not want him, but did she resent his turning to someone else? If so, shame on her.

The following morning, she woke to the sound of drapes moving on their rods. "Hannah?"

"It is almost noon, and her ladyship said to wake you." She busied herself around the room, while her mistress drank a cup of chocolate. "The bouquets that have arrived already this morning are a sight to behold, Miss."

"Oh, I must see them on the instant, Hannah." After scrambling into a morning gown of sprigged muslin, Marie hurried down the stairs and into the drawing room. Bouquets sat on every available surface, including some on the floor. She carefully inspected every card attached to the flowers but did not find the one she sought. She concealed her disappointment from the hovering footman and went in search of her mother.

"Good morning, Mama. To gaze upon your beautiful countenance, one would never know that you did not reach your bed until the wee hours!"

Lady Becca controlled her twitching lips at this outrageous greeting. "Good morning, dear, or perhaps I should say good afternoon."

Marie laughed, helping herself to a cup of tea while they reminisced about their ball until Symms tapped at the door.

"Miss Langford has arrived and desires to see you."

"Thank you, Symms. Will you send a tea tray to my sitting room, please?" She turned to her mother. "I shall take her up there for a coze."

The instant the sitting room door shut them inside, Deborah threw herself onto a small sofa and exclaimed, "You will never guess what happened last night!"

"My, you are excited. Tell me on the instant," Marie ordered.

"I am betrothed!" Deborah paused. "To Mr. Anstey, of course. I never thought I would bring him up to scratch and be betrothed before you, but I did it," she chortled.

Marie concealed the twinge of hurt at the callous words. "Do tell me all about it. Every detail."

Nothing loath, Deborah bounced around the room as she talked. "He offered for me while we sat out the first dance after supper last evening. Of course, I said yes, so this morning he waited upon my father practically at daybreak!"

Before Marie could comment, the door opened, and Grace Patterson rushed into the room. "You will never guess what happened last night," she breathed with a broad smile. Not giving them time to speak, she continued, "I am betrothed to Mr. Buxted! Is that not the most wonderful news you ever heard?"

Deborah grabbed her in a tight embrace. "So am I betrothed! When did it happen with you? Tell us all about it."

"It was right after supper last night . . . ."

"For me, too," exclaimed Deborah.

They talked and exclaimed together, ignoring Marie, who made an effort to hide her chagrin. Rebecca Blackwell would soon marry, and now both these friends were betrothed and would marry before she herself did. She must announce her betrothal by the end of this Season, her second, or she would well and truly be on the shelf. If Beaufort didn't come up to scratch, she could always marry Mr. Desmond.

The thought comforted her until the vision of dark curls and timid brown eyes gazing adoringly into his face last evening crossed her mind, and she winced. He probably found Miss Griswall more to his liking, and Marie questioned whether she should have declined his offer in such a final way. She became aware of stillness in the room and looked at her guests.

They stood in silence and watched her, anxious expressions on their faces. Deborah cleared her throat and asked, "Is this not amazing, Marie? That Grace and I became betrothed at almost the same instant?"

Marie forced a smile to her face and rushed to hug them. "To be sure it is. I only waited for you to stop chattering long enough for me to congratulate you! I do hope both gentlemen realize how fortunate they are to have captured two of my best friends."

Marie must have convinced them of her sincerity because they started chattering again. She joined their conversation but sighed with relief when they decided it was time to leave. She saw them to the door and then returned to her sitting room for some quiet reflection. Clinging to the memory of Beaufort's attention, Marie decided the first dance after supper was memorable for all of them but more momentous for the others. She rang for Hannah, who hurried into the room.

"I want to get some exercise and need you to accompany me."

They stepped outside the door side by side followed by a burly footman.

A babble of voices and the rattle of carriage wheels met them as they entered the park. Marie scanned the immediate area and moved to the edge of the long avenue, where she stood unnoticed in the shade of a large oak. Everywhere she looked she saw couples, walking or riding and absorbed with each other. She did not see even one female accompanied by only a maid and footman. She retraced her steps through the gate and turned toward home.

Marie returned to her sitting room without having uttered one word since she left it. She stared out the window for several minutes. Then, with a shrug for her thoughts, she went in search of her mother to discuss the evening's activities.

She sat through a dreary dinner with friends of her parents and tried to concentrate on her cards at the whist tables later. Her mother glanced at her a couple of times but didn't reprimand her for her inattention.

The interminable day finally ended, and Marie stood at the window of her bedchamber gazing into the starry night. Even a letter to Susan would not help now. With a deep sigh, she shook her head at her thoughts and crawled between the sheets. She managed to fall asleep as dawn broke through the haze.

Chapter 12

Now We Know

When Marie entered the breakfast parlor, the evidence of a sleepless night showed in the dark circles around her eyes. Sir Julian had departed earlier for an appointment, and when the footman had served Marie a plate of coddled eggs and left the room, Lady Becca probed.

"You appear to have had a poor night's rest. Is something bothering you?" When she didn't receive an answer, she said, "If I did not know you better, I would think you were moping."

Marie chewed and swallowed toast before blurting, "Deborah and Grace are betrothed."

Lady Becca sat in silence for a moment. "Are you surprised? It seems to me they spend considerable time in the company of Mr. Anstey and Mr. Buxted. I presume they are betrothed to those gentlemen?"

"Oh, I know they do, and Deborah even mentioned once that she believed she would bring Mr. Anstey up to scratch and become betrothed before I did."

"Is that what bothers you? They're betrothed, and you're not?"

Marie pushed the eggs around on her plate.

"If that is the problem, you must remember you had the opportunity to become betrothed some time back, and you declined."

"Mr. Desmond is just a boy, and I don't want to marry anyone so young."

"You still hope to attach Lord Beaufort, do you? We talked about this before, Marie, and on more than one occasion. He has avoided parson's mousetrap, if I may use such a crude phrase, for many years, and as he gets older, he's more likely to look toward older ladies if he ever decides to marry."

"Like the one he escorted to Almack's, you mean."

"I didn't speak of her in particular, but yes, she is nearer to him in age than are you."

Marie shrugged again and excused herself from the table. Returning upstairs, she stared out the window of her sitting room, although she did not see the glorious array of flowers, nor did she notice the scent of roses wafting on the breeze. She saw, instead, a pair of mahogany eyes and chiseled lips that rarely parted in a genuine smile, although when they did, it was a sight that made her heart sing. When they smiled at her, that is. She would win him, one way or another. On that she was determined.

Mama had not been encouraging, so there was no need to consult her further.

She had tried Susan's way. She had not flirted with him; she had not gushed at him; she had carried on rational conversations with him. They had not worked either, so she must try something else.

Louise Mansfield, now Mrs. Stafford, got what she wanted when she defied her grandparents last autumn and ran away. Maybe Marie should ask her advice. The idea of following in Louise's footsteps made her shudder. That would surely turn Lord Beaufort against her forever, but would it not be wonderful to do just as one wanted?

How she longed for Susan. If she were here, she would know how to help. Susan always knew what to do, even on that long ago afternoon when Marie fell off the bare-backed pony, she had managed to mount, despite his reluctance to be disturbed. Marie chuckled at the memory, but grew somber again. Susan had tugged her to her feet, dusted off her gown, and promised never to mention the episode to anyone. She had kept her promise.

She would have to depend on Deborah for advice. After all, she brought Mr. Anstey up to scratch, so she should be able to help Marie. She penned a note and hurried in search of a footman to deliver it by hand, and then she turned to the butler. "Symms, when Miss Langford arrives, send her up to my sitting room, and order a tea tray, please."

"Yes, Miss Marie."

"What is it, Marie?" It took Deborah only a few minutes to arrive. "Why did you want me to rush right over? I am always happy to come, of course, but why now?"

Before Marie could answer, Hannah entered with the tea tray. Waiting only for the maid to leave the room, Marie replied, "I need help. Mama does not enter into my sentiments on this, so I must turn to you."

"Naturally I shall help you. That's what best friends do for each other. Tell me all about it."

Marie bit into a macaroon. "Lord Beaufort."

"Has he been rude to you again? You need to give him a sharp set down."

"I don't want to give him a set down," Marie wailed. "I want him!"

Deborah stared, her cup halfway to her mouth. During an instant of silence, she put it down, her gaze never leaving Marie's face. "You want him? Why?"

"I want to marry him, you ninny!"

"Marry him? Are you sure you would not just as soon marry Mr. Desmond?"

"He is such a child," Marie protested. "Now, think. What can I do?"

Deborah sat in thought for a few moments. "I know. If you get Beaufort into a compromising position, he will have to offer for you. That is mandatory for a gentleman, you must realize, and he is a gentleman. Rude, to be sure, but a gentleman nonetheless."

"How would I do that?"

"You said he comes here most days. Waylay him, and throw yourself into his arms when you hear your father coming."

"I don't believe that would work. My father gets to the study so quickly there would not be enough time. What else can I do?"

Deborah gazed into the distance. After a moment of silence, she nodded her head. "Pretend you're eloping to Gretna Green with an undesirable person when Sir Julian is out of town. Lord Beaufort will come after you. You will be well on your way to the border and can convince him to go on with you."

Marie listened to her in horrified silence. "I refuse to get married over the anvil, do you hear me? I intend to have a proper wedding at St. George's in Hanover Square. I will have twelve attendants, and little girls will strew rose petals down the aisle in front of me. Think of something else."

"You can pretend someone kidnapped you. Lord Beaufort will realize he is madly in love with you and make a mad dash after you with his sword drawn."

"It would be my father who made a mad dash after me. He would make sure I regretted my foolishness. Probably lock me in my bedchamber and allow me only bread and water. Of course, if I declined to a mere skeleton, he might repent. Not otherwise though."

The longer they talked, the more extreme Deborah's suggestions became, until Marie escorted her guest down the stairs, both in spasms of laughter. As they reached the entrance hall, Symms opened the door to admit Lord Beaufort. Meeting his eyes, Marie's embarrassment caused her to push Deborah out the door.

He bowed, directing a sardonic glance toward Marie, and turned away without speaking.

Mortification caused Marie to rush up the stairs to her sitting room.

Hannah followed her into the room. "Your cheeks are flushed. Are you ill?"

Marie collapsed onto a small sofa and announced, "I am embarrassed beyond belief. I may never show my face outside this room again!"

"It's been a while since you treated me to such dramatics. Do you want to tell me about it?"

"Deborah and I were talking nonsense and were in a fit of giggles when Symms opened the door to Lord Beaufort. He must have thought we were discussing him."

"Were you?"

"Not at that moment."

Hannah laughed. "It may do nothing for your embarrassment, but I know how to get you out of this room."

"How?"

"As I recall, you mentioned wanting new ribbons for your straw bonnet."

"Shopping!" Marie dimpled at her. "The cure-all for every ailment. Let us go immediately!"

Downstairs in the study, Beaufort tried to order his thoughts, but Marie's self-conscious features persisted in intruding.

Why would simply the sight of him be an embarrassment to her? Awkwardness had never been evident in her before. Except perhaps on the morning when she confessed her meeting with Lady Emily to her father, his own presence may have embarrassed her. Is she involved in that situation again? No, those giggles did not portend anything of a clandestine nature. Had they been discussing *him*? Heat rose in his face at the thought of being the subject of schoolgirl conversation. That didn't bear thinking on.

"I apologize for being late, John. I got involved in a discussion at Parliament and was unable to get away."

Sir Julian's entrance forced Beaufort to push aside his puzzle over Marie's blushes. "Are they making any progress toward obtaining more funds for Wellington? Dare we hope?"

Sir Julian shook his head. "The Minister knows about the robberies, of course, and believes we will catch the culprits faster if the general populous does not know about them. Therefore, he advises against telling Members, who are reluctant to commit more funds to Spain so soon and who might discuss the matter at injudicious moments."

"I admit I was less than enthusiastic when Liverpool became Prime Minister after Perceval's death last summer, but he's doing a creditable job. After serving as Lord of the Treasury as well as Secretary of War, he understands both sides of our dilemma."

"Perceval's assassination left the government in a mess." Haverford laughed. "With your seat in Lords, you were aware of that even more than I, of course."

Beaufort nodded. "I liked Perceval, both as a man and as the Minister, but others didn't. I knew his death would cause controversy in Parliament, but the extent of discord surprised me. It was a relief when Prinny took a stand and confirmed him in the face of considerable opposition."

"To say truth, *that* surprised me. Between ourselves, our future king is not known for taking a stand on anything."

"I've noticed," Beaufort replied. "But back to your conversation with Liverpool. The fact that he is in agreement with Wilberforce should help our cause in the long run. Did you hear any recent news from the Peninsula?"

"Only that Wellington is marching toward Vittoria. I tell you, again between ourselves, if he is not successful in ridding Spain of the French presence this year, the war might continue for several more years."

Beaufort shook his head. "How can we supply the army for several more years when we are unable to get funds through to Wellington now?"

"We cannot, and the problems in America are not helping matters either." He shook his head. "I dare say our navy didn't consider the consequences when they raided the American merchant ships and pressed their sailors into our battles against Napoleon."

"I agree. It didn't occur to anyone war would follow."

"We're spreading our troops too thinly. I don't see how Britain can win in the Americas. That area is too distant and too vast to undertake. Our previous efforts there prove my point."

"Parliament would do well to back off from encounters with former colonies. They earned their independence at a great cost, both to them and to us, and we should leave them alone to sink or swim on their own."

With those words, Beaufort took his leave, a sense of desolation enveloping him.

Sir Julian stared into space trying to think of a solution to the present problem. They must know how the information about funds bound for Spain reached the villains, who, in turn, made sure it did not get there. Was Stokely involved? A couple of hours later, voices from the hall penetrated the study door, and he strolled out to greet his daughter, whom he had not seen that day.

"Hello, Poppet. You appear to be in excellent spirits." He nodded to the footman and Hannah, who carried packages. "Something tells me merchants had a successful day."

Marie dimpled at him. "Papa, you cannot expect me to resist new ribbons. And you should see the petit point reticule I spied quite by accident."

"I can hardly wait," he returned. "Now, I believe it is time for luncheon, so let us join your Mama. She might have a better appreciation of your purchases than I since I don't even know what petit point is. However, I'm willing to be educated."

Well satisfied with each other, father and daughter entered the dining room, where Lady Becca greeted them with a smile. "I had almost reached the conclusion I would enjoy this meal by myself."

"Oh, no," retorted her daughter, as she accepted a plate of fruit and cold chicken from the footman. "When did I ever miss a meal?"

After their laughter ended, they enjoyed their repast for several moments until Sir Julian inquired about their evening plans.

"Papa, have you forgotten you promised to escort us to Vauxhall this evening?"

"Oh, is that this evening?" He turned his teasing smile toward her and asked, "Do we plan to go by water, perhaps?"

Lady Becca allowed an unladylike hoot to pass her dainty lips.

"Papa is in a funning mood today. However, I shall come about, never fear."

They did not go to the famed gardens by the water route, thereby missing the reflected lights shining on the water. They strolled along the Grand Walk until they reached the Grove where Sir Julian arranged for a supper box, leaving a footman to assure it would be theirs when they were ready for it.

"Good evening, ladies, Sir Julian." Lord Beaufort attracted their attention as they turned onto the South Walk.

Marie turned at the sound of his voice, but her smile dimmed somewhat when she noticed his companion, the dark-haired beauty she had seen with him on two previous occasions. However, she joined the others in their greetings.

"Good evening, my lord."

"May I introduce Lady Arabella Sunningham, a friend from Yorkshire? This is Sir Julian, Lady Rebecca, and their daughter Marie Haverford," he told his friend.

When they had acknowledged the introduction, Sir Julian invited them to join his group. "We're admiring the Chinese lanterns, Lady Arabella. Have you seen them before?"

"No, Sir Julian, I haven't had that pleasure. This is my first visit to Vauxhall, and I admit to being most impressed."

He offered his arm and undertook to show her the famed painted archways. Behind them, Lord Beaufort offered an arm to each of the other ladies, and they strolled along, acknowledging an occasional passing acquaintance.

"Dear, I believe it's about time for the concert to begin. Shall we return to the supper box?" Lady Becca's raised voice drew her husband's attention away from his discourse on Palmyran ruins, as depicted on the archways.

Sir Julian turned back, and as he joined the others, he slipped his hand under Lady Becca's arm and left Lord Beaufort to escort both younger ladies.

Marie was silent for the most part. While Sir Julian escorted Lady Arabella, Marie had fastened her gaze on the back of Lady Arabella's head and willed her to do something outrageous. It didn't work. She now commanded a smile to appear on her own face and pretended she enjoyed being ignored while his lordship conversed with the lady on his right.

She saw Mr. Anderson in the distance and debated signaling to him but thought better of it since she did not want to upset her father. Oh, why had she not invited others and made a party of the evening? She knew why, of course. She did not want to watch the billing and cooing of her friends with their betrotheds. As they neared their supper box, she spied Mr.

Desmond standing alone, looking unhappy, so she waved gaily to him. The solution to her problem was at hand.

Marie removed her hand from Lord Beaufort's arm and turned to the newcomer. "Mr. Desmond, how delightful it is to see you this evening."

Lady Becca greeted him with a smile. "You must join us in our box for the concert, Mr. Desmond, unless you have other friends waiting for you."

He denied the presence of other friends and attached himself to their group. They enjoyed hearing Mr. James Hook play some of Handel's music on the organ, despite the fact people in the adjoining boxes chattered throughout.

Lady Arabella jumped and gazed around in consternation when a loud bell sounded nearby at the beginning of the intermission. "Whatever is that racket?"

Beaufort explained the bell signified it was time to view the Cascade before the second half of the program started.

Marie alternately prattled with Mr. Desmond and maintained a dignified silence, while watching Beaufort from beneath her lashes. She intended Lord Beaufort to know she did not care that he had another lady on his arm, yet admitted he had not noticed. They returned to their box where a light supper consisting of slivered ham and pastry awaited them while they enjoyed the remainder of the concert.

The Haverford party had a silent observer as they watched the fireworks display after the concert.

Lord Stokely stood in the shadows of a large elm only a few feet from them and watched the lights from the fireworks play across Marie's face. She stood with her father on one side and the Desmond cub on the other, so he had no hope of detaching her from her party. Somehow, he must learn what she knew of his activities. He played with the thought that perhaps she knew nothing yet could not be content until he knew for sure. Would questioning her reveal his hand? Possibly, which is why he had told Emily Cavanaugh to question her. If he could get his hands on that conniving female, he would make her sorry she'd ever crossed him. He cursed anew every time he remembered the unpaid bills she left in his name. He knew people were snickering behind their hands at him for letting the wealthy widow get away from him.

He stepped deeper into the shadows when the Haverfords began their trek back to their carriage. He must figure a way out of this mess and before much more time passed. He needed to know how soon Parliament would release more funds for Wellington. That was imperative, but so far, according to his contact, there hadn't been even a hint that Whitehall had requested some. Little time would pass before his creditors demanded his attention; of that predicament, he was sure. Why had he not married the Cavanaugh widow immediately? He berated himself for his stupidity.

Sir Julian held Beaufort back allowing the ladies to precede them into Haverford House. "Stokely was at Vauxhall, standing back in the shadows."

"Yes, I watched him from the corner of my eye. I don't believe he took his gaze off your daughter."

"He didn't. I need to discuss this with her mother again. Earlier today, I received a note from a friend of Lady Olivia Shelburne, inviting us to visit her in Hampshire for a few days. I dislike leaving the problems in your hands, but this may be the opportune time to remove my daughter from Town, even if only for a few days. Shall we meet with Colonel Hayes first thing in the morning?"

With a nod, Beaufort took his leave and Sir Julian went indoors. After handing his hat and cane to Symms, he asked for a tea tray in the small back parlor.

Becca and Marie entered the room to find tea already poured. Marie couldn't resist. With a droll glance toward her father, she said, "Mama, you have trained Papa well."

"Poppet, you don't know how well!" He winked at his wife. "However, after that impertinence, I am of a mind to leave you here when we go to Hampshire in three days!"

"Hampshire? Why are . . . oh, you've heard from the Duchess!" Becca cradled her teacup into its saucer. "Tell us, do!"

He obliged. "I neglected to mention that Lady Olivia sent round a note this afternoon. We are to be guests at Dorchester Park for a few days, if Colonel Hayes agrees I can be gone that long."

Marie rushed to embrace her father. "You're going too? We shall have such fun with you there, won't we, Mama? We truly missed you at the Desmond house party."

"I missed you and your Mama, too, Poppet. Now, off to bed with you."

When Marie's footsteps faded at the top of the stairs, Julian moved to sit beside his wife on the sofa. He cradled her against his shoulder. "Stokely was at Vauxhall this evening and didn't take his gaze off Marie."

Becca stared at him, her fingers touching her lips. "I know you and the others at Whitehall are doing everything possible, but can we not do something ourselves to protect our daughter?"

Julian shook his head. "We can only hope Beaufort and the colonel concoct a plan while we're in Hampshire." He rose to his feet and gently pulled her up beside him. "It's time for us to retire also."

The following days passed quickly. Early on the third day, Sir Julian raised his eyelids at the amount of baggage heaped inside and on top of Shelburne's second coach. "I always forget Lady Olivia carries everything she owns when she embarks on any visit that lasts more than one day."

"Always!" Shelburne shook his head in amusement at the countess's foibles and then followed his mother and his betrothed into the carriage. Their maids occupied the third coach with the Haverford maids.

Sir Julian contented himself with only two coaches, the second one carrying their baggage. He murmured to Becca, "Without doubt, the duchess will think we have come to stay permanently."

They received a rousing welcome upon their arrival at Dorchester Park. When Shelburne handed Rebecca out of the carriage, several little girls ran toward her, arms outstretched, screaming her name. Chaos reigned for a few minutes until the duchess appeared at the door. The girls sensed she was there, because they quieted immediately but still clung to Rebecca.

"Olivia, it has been a long time since last we met." The duchess stood back and frankly stared at her old friend. "The years have been kind to us, have they not?"

Lady Olivia twinkled at her. "I agree, Elizabeth. Neither of us looks a day older than the day I served as an honour attendant at your wedding."

"On that bit of absurdity, I invite all of you to join me inside."

Rebecca stood quietly until the duchess turned toward her, but then she rushed into the outstretched arms and whispered, "I'm happy to be home."

"I'm happy to have you here, my dear. Your happiness shines from your eyes, and the shadows are gone."

Over teacups, the duchess brought up the reason her visitors were there. "Shelburne, I understand you and Rebecca want to open a home for girls. It's an excellent idea. How may I be of assistance?"

Shelburne smiled at his betrothed. "Rebecca wants to follow in your footsteps. She rescued a child last summer and reunited her with her parents."

The duchess nodded. "I heard about that."

"My first thought was to keep Miranda Abernathy," Rebecca confessed. "However, Louise helped me see that was not the right thing to do, so I decided to bring her to you, if we couldn't find her parents."

"I would have welcomed her, but it's better she's with her parents. I was acquainted with the senior Abernathies years ago. They're an upstanding family, although there is some question about how the younger son, Simon, obtains funds to live. However, that's of no importance. Let us get details of opening a home for girls out of the way, so we can enjoy our visit."

The duchess began with the legalities involved for removing children from unhealthy situations.

Shelburne confessed, "We hadn't realized there *are* legalities."

"You were going to pick them up off the street? My dear boy, some needy children have families."

"You're right, of course, Your Grace. Please tell us what else we need to know."

After directing them to consult the vicar serving the area, she moved on to a discussion of location. "Is it your intention to house them at Shelburne Park, or do you have a different place in mind?"

"I believe our manor house is ideal for this purpose. The building isn't located on the original Shelburne Park property but on the adjoining property my father purchased many years ago."

Lady Olivia joined the discussion. "We have maintained the house, so it will require little renovation to make it suitable. I've given the matter some thought and believe we can comfortably house up to four and twenty children with all the amenities they will need."

"Education will be a top priority," Rebecca stated. "Please tell us how we can locate the best tutors."

The duchess talked for another half hour but then looked at the ormolu clock on the mantle and rose. "We will go into this matter, perhaps over dinner, after we have had a chance to rest. In the meantime, my housekeeper will show you to your rooms."

Marie asked, "Your Grace, may I walk around the grounds and perhaps meet some of the girls?"

"Yes, of course you may. I doubt you young people need to rest." The duchess turned a smile toward Rebecca. "Perhaps you would like to show Shelburne your favorite place."

"Thank you, Your Grace. I would."

As Rebecca slipped her arm through the crook of Shelburne's elbow, she heard Lady Becca say, "Your Grace, I want to thank you for taking such good care of Rebecca and Louise. They're the daughters of my . . . ." Her words faded when Rebecca stepped out the long windows onto the terrace.

"I wager I know where you're taking me," Shelburne told her. "The rose garden."

Rebecca dimpled, but didn't answer. A few steps took them around the side of the house and into a sight that took away his breath. Rose blooms from all shades of white to pink to deep red lifted their faces to the sun. A little further, blooms ranging from cream to deep yellow met his eyes.

"This helps me understand your love for roses. The aroma is as amazing as the colors."

Rebecca led him to a narrow, wrought-iron bench out of sight of the house. A sob broke her voice. "This is where I came to be alone to cry for Mama. No one bothered me. In later years, I realized Matron knew, because all the staff kept a close eye on the children, but she allowed me that time to grieve."

Shelburne slipped an arm around her and brought her head to his shoulder. Silent tears slid down her cheeks until she straightened and flicked them away. "I apologize for being a watering pot. Mama died when I was six years old, but I still think of her and wish she could know my happiness."

"I imagine she's looking down from heaven this minute," Shelburne comforted her. "She knows. I'm sure she also knows you will help other little girls. If she could be here, she would tell you how proud she is of you."

Rebecca pulled a handkerchief from her reticule and dried her damp cheeks. "Thank you. Now, we need to go inside. I want to greet the people I knew, and then we will dress for dinner."

Conversation over the informal dinner table ranged from Marie's chatter about meeting some of the girls to Her Grace's reminisces of the come-out Season she shared with Lady Olivia, until Shelburne cleared his throat.

"Your Grace, may we know how you began your home for unfortunate girls?"

"Yes, we will discuss that and your own efforts over tea trays." She led the way to the small parlor adjoining the dining room. There she settled into a wing-back chair and lifted her feet onto an ottoman. "Olivia has most likely told you of the influenza that caused the death of my infant daughter. I decided to open the doors of Dorchester Park in her memory."

There followed two hours of questions and answers. When Sir Julian asked his first question, the duchess raised her eyebrows at him.

He smiled. "Your Grace, my wife and I had already discussed the possibility of opening a home for girls when Shelburne mentioned his and Rebecca's plans. In subsequent conversations, Becca and I considered the possibility of opening a home for boys."

"Commendable," the duchess assured him. "There are at least as many little boys in need as there are girls. The information I share about girls applies to boys also."

The evening ended on a note of satisfaction for Shelburne and Rebecca and for Julian and Becca.

The following day they toured the premises and talked with staff and teachers. They were content they had sufficient information to begin the process of opening their planned schools.

The remaining days of the visit passed quietly, but Sir Julian kept a close watch on his daughter. Marie's exuberance knew no bounds when she learned of the ruins of the Bishop's Palace that dated from the twelfth century.

"Are there truly ruins we can explore? Not just rubble like we saw when we visited the Desmonds in Hertfordshire?"

"Oh, yes," the duchess assured her. "Both the Saxons and the Danes destroyed the area, but each time the town grew again. In the mid-1600s, parliamentarian troops destroyed the palace to capture a bishop and a band of Royalists, and the diocese did not restore it. The remains include part of the twelfth century tower, traceried windows of the Great Hall, and sections of a brick wall as well as part of the moat."

"What is traceried?"

"A Gothic window that has open tracery at the top."

Marie turned to her father. "Papa, may we please go there?"

Sir Julian raised his eyebrows at the others, all of whom nodded agreement except Rebecca, who turned to the duchess.

"Your Grace, you may recall that Louise and I visited the ruins when we lived here. May I stay here?"

"Yes, of course, you may. I will enjoy hearing of your experiences since you moved to Town. However, I don't believe you went to the two Meon villages, which are well worth a visit. I should think all of you would enjoy seeing the Church of All Saints in East Meon, especially the font. The carving is from a single block of Tournai marble and dates from the twelfth century."

"Those are two excellent suggestions, Your Grace," Sir Julian said. "We will enjoy both before we leave later in the week."

Marie's enthusiasm spread to the others, and it was with reluctance they entered the carriages for the return trip to Town a sennight after their arrival.

"Susan is coming!" Marie clutched a sheet of notepaper a few days after the visit to Dorchester Park. "Her doctor has given her permission to travel, and her Mama said she can come to us for the rest of the Season, providing she rests a great deal."

The breakfast table at Haverford House showed the usual clutter of plates, coffee cups, and letters.

"Is the rest of the family coming?" Sir Julian peered at his daughter over the top of his newspaper.

"No, only Susan and her maid can come. She writes Mr. Connors cannot leave his parishioners because of some discord, and the younger children are throwing out rashes right and left."

"I expect Mrs. Connors wants to be sure Susan doesn't contract whatever the illness is, after being so ill earlier," Lady Becca commented.

"What fun we will have," Marie exclaimed.

Lady Becca smiled at her bubbling daughter. "Yes, dear, but do remember Susan needs rest and cannot take part in many of your activities."

"Surely, she can have one activity each day, which is better than none, Mama. Besides, we will enjoy spending time together, because I've missed her beyond anything. I must choose a room for her on the instant."

Marie collided with Lord Beaufort as she rushed from the breakfast parlor. She clutched his arms for balance and flashed him a dazzling smile. "Good morning, my lord. My dearest friend is coming to visit from Kent—is that not wonderful? You will like her, I'm sure, because everyone does."

Upstairs, Marie sat on the raised hearth of the fireplace, surveying the room. She had visited each guest room and had chosen this one with the sunny yellow drapes and bed hangings. She would fill it with yellow and white flowers on the morning of Susan's arrival. The room was at the back of the house, away from the street noise, and looked out on flowerbeds and scattered trees. She nodded in satisfaction. This was the perfect, peaceful atmosphere for anyone recovering from an illness.

Lost in making plans for entertaining Susan, Marie ignored murmuring voices. When they persisted, she opened the door and glanced down the corridor, but seeing no one, she closed it and went back to the hearth.

Again, voices disturbed her, and this time she went to the windows. There was no one in the garden. She frowned in exasperation as she realized she must be imagining things. Had the Season tired her that much? She wandered around the room, trying to visualize Susan sitting in the chairs or reclining on the *chaise longue*, and then went back to her perch on the hearth. There were those voices again. This time she realized they were coming from behind her, so she stuck her head inside the fireplace.

"I cannot understand it." Her father's voice came clearly although softly to her ears. "How are they getting the information? We do not dare send more funds until we know that one thing. Have you learned anything in your social rounds, John?"

"Nothing. You would not believe the amount of simpering chatter I endure from all those chits. For that matter, the men are almost as bad. Not a brain in their collective heads."

Sir Julian chuckled. "You will survive."

"I shall be grateful when this mess is cleared up and I can get away from this frivolous lifestyle. I need the wilds of Yorkshire."

Marie frowned. So that was why he attended balls. What did he expect at social functions? Discussion of world affairs? He wouldn't listen to a serious word from a frivolous chit if one of us did utter one. She pulled her wandering thoughts back to the conversation and flinched. Eavesdropping again!

"The Minister is impatient after this latest robbery and murder." Lord Beaufort's voice faded away but became stronger as he continued. "I'm afraid he will suspect one of us if we do not soon get definite proof against Stokely or someone."

"I thought of that too. But how can we gather proof without knowing how the scoundrel gets the information?"

Marie's eyes widened as she listened. Someone suspected her father of murder! She jumped to her feet and ran down the stairs.

When the study door burst open, Sir Julian leaped to his feet. "Marie, what is the meaning of this intrusion?"

She flung herself into his arms. "You would never murder anyone, and the Minister should know it."

"Marie, explain yourself," Sir Julian's voice thundered at her, as he held her arm's length.

She nodded, all the time holding to his arms. "You remember I intended to get a room ready for Susan? I decided on the room above this one because it's quiet." Marie paused for breath.

"Yes, yes, go on." Sir Julian was seldom abrupt with his daughter, but he was short on patience this morning.

Marie stared at her father's tense face. "I was sitting on the hearth—you know that's my favorite place to sit—and I heard your voices. Will the Minister accuse you of murder? You would never murder anyone!"

Sir Julian gathered his trembling daughter into his arms and exchanged grim looks with Lord Beaufort. "The chimney acts as a conduit. The traitor could be right here in my own household. I will go upstairs and listen while you two talk. Marie, sit in my chair."

He soon returned, his set face showing his concern. "Your voices were clear though soft." He turned to his daughter. "You will not mention this matter to anyone. Do you understand me?"

She nodded and hurried to him, keeping her gaze fixed on his. "Papa, you won't be accused of murder, will you?"

He managed a smile and hugged her to him. "No, Poppet, I don't expect so. You gave us the clue to the whole mess, and we appreciate it. You already know how dangerous the situation is, so you must put it out of your mind now. Promise me?"

Subdued, she promised.

In a low voice, Beaufort said, "There is one other thing your daughter can do for us. She can go back to that room and be sure no one goes in while we confer."

Sir Julian agreed. "Poppet, will you do that? Go back and listen to see if you can hear anything we say.

You should also tell us if anyone tries to come into the room or tries to lure you out of it. We need only a few more minutes."

She nodded at her father and glanced toward Lord Beaufort. "Of course, it would never do to bore you with my simpering chatter, would it?"

She walked out, thereby missing the chagrin on his lordship's face.

Sir Julian and Lord Beaufort stared at each other in grim silence and then, of one accord, moved to the far end of the study, where they conversed in low tones.

Lord Beaufort spoke first. "We need to meet where there are no fireplaces, and we still don't want to be seen with Colonel Hayes. Perhaps a closed carriage ride would be best, although it, too, might garner attention."

Sir Julian nodded. "We must send a message to the colonel to join us in an hour, but where?" He thought for a moment. "This might be better. Most people don't know that Shelburne is working with us, since we kept quiet about his part in the Rushton affair last summer, so why not meet at his house in Grosvenor Square late tonight, rather than in an hour."

"Sounds reasonable, but they might entertain guests this evening. Do we have an alternative?"

"They're our guests at the theater, so that isn't a problem," Haverford told him. "We will meet our separate responsibilities early in the evening and then return home in the event someone watches us. We can meet at Shelburne's at midnight."

Lord Beaufort agreed. "That sounds workable."

"All right, a message to the colonel is my priority. What are your plans for the evening?"

"I dine at the club and join a card party in Brownlee's rooms afterwards."

"Will that not last until well after midnight?"

"Ordinarily, yes, but he leaves for the races at first light, so the evening must of necessity end early."

"So, we go our separate ways now and meet this evening."

Meanwhile, Marie sat in the upstairs room, straining to hear at the fireplace. When her father walked in, she ran into his arms, her nerves giving way. "I had no idea your work is dangerous, Papa. Are you a spy too? Like Lord Beaufort?"

"Easy now, Poppet. My work is not dangerous because I only do paperwork. The people who died do different work. But why do you think we're spies?"

"I thought intelligence work was spying." Before he could answer, she added, "Is he engaged in dangerous work? Lord Beaufort, I mean."

"His work is no more dangerous than mine. Still interested in him, are you, Poppet? You could do far worse, but I'm afraid you might be a little young for his tastes." He smoothed her ruffled curls and grinned at her mulish expression. "Yes, my dear, I know you consider yourself a mature adult, and in many ways I agree. However, there are several years difference in your age and his."

"Not too many!"

Sir Julian laughed. "All right, Poppet. Now tell me, could you hear anything after you came back up here?"

"No." She gave a decided shake of her fair curls. "I even stuck my head right into the fireplace and could not hear a sound. And nobody came in either."

"Did you see anybody hanging around this room, or did anyone come in while you were here earlier?"

Again, she shook her head. "No. I've been on this floor since breakfast. This is the only room I was in for more than a minute or two, and I did not see anyone. The maids work up here while we're in the breakfast parlor."

He gave a satisfied nod and reminded her not to mention the matter to anyone. When he received her solemn agreement, he smiled and left the room. His daughter might be frivolous at times and disobedient that one time, yet he was satisfied she'd learned her lesson in this matter and that he could now trust her word.

Chapter 13

At Last—Susan!

Marie lingered in the guest bedchamber, staring at the fireplace, and thinking over the events of the morning. The tension left her body, causing her knees to become wobbly, and forced her to sink onto a small armless chair. Visions of her adored father hanging from a tree on Tyburn Hill caused a sob to escape, and she allowed a few tears to slide down her cheeks.

At last growing impatient with herself, she brushed the tears away and went to her own rooms. There, she splashed cool water on her face and paced the length of her sitting room and back. After a couple of turns, she saw her mother standing at the door.

"I came to see if you need company," Lady Becca said, settling onto a small sofa. "I believe you've been crying. Do you care to tell me about it?"

Marie stopped pacing and joined her. "Did Papa talk to you before he left?"

"He told me about the help you gave him in finding a solution to a problem, if that's what you mean."

Marie gulped back a sob. "I keep visualizing him hanging from that big tree on Tyburn Hill for murdering someone." Her words ended in a wail, as she threw herself into her mother's arms.

"Easy, my dear, easy now. Your father did not murder anyone, and the Minister could not possibly accuse him of doing so. You can put that thought right out of your head." She soothed her daughter, much as she had done when Marie was a tiny girl and ran to her for comfort when her kitten disappeared.

Marie's crying subsided into sniffles and then hiccups. She sat upright. Accepting the proffered handkerchief, she blew her nose. "I know that, of course, but that horrible picture still comes to mind."

"We must turn your mind to something pleasant. I gather you decided on a room for Susan."

"To be sure I did. I chose the yellow room, because it's so cheerful and just what an invalid needs. Provided Papa holds his conferences away from the fireplace," she added with a watery chuckle.

Symms's announcement that luncheon awaited their pleasure ended their discussion. Marie revived it over pudding albeit from a slightly different perspective.

"I wish we had waited a few more days to have our ball, so Susan could attend. May we have another?"

"Two balls in one Season?" Lady Becca's eyes widened in mock horror. "Your father would have something to say about his home's being invaded by the masses again so soon."

"Now, Mama, you know you trained him properly. He will do whatever you ask."

That ridiculous statement brought a hoot of derision. "My dear, there is no such thing as a properly trained husband, and you would do well to remember."

"Yes, Mama," she answered with assumed meekness. "If not a ball, how can we entertain Susan? We should do something here, not just take her to other places, although we will do that too."

"What do you think of a dinner party for your special friends, followed by a musical evening? I recall Susan has a beautiful singing voice."

"Oh, yes, that is a marvelous idea! We must invite Rebecca and Louise as well as my special friends. I don't know if Rebecca is musical, but Louise is."

"Speaking of Louise, she paid me a visit while you were busy with Deborah yesterday afternoon."

Marie raised her eyebrows. "When Deborah and I saw her earlier, she didn't mention she planned to come here."

"I believe she wanted to talk about her mother. I mention her visit only to tell you that there is question that she will be able to bear children, and I caution you not to mention her recent difficulty."

"Poor thing. I'll include that situation in my prayers tonight."

"Yes, do that. She had other news that might interest you. She and Stafford have decided to open their home to a child of Stafford's friend who perished in Spain. Apparently, the child's mother simply pined away for him, leaving the child alone."

"That's generous of them, to be sure," Marie said. "She stays so busy with the major's army friends that we seldom see her, and this would be a good opportunity to know each other better. I told Susan about Louise and Rebecca, and she's anxious to make their acquaintance."

"If they are to come, we must also invite Lord Shelburne and Major Stafford. Who else?"

Marie avoided looking at her mother. "Lord Beaufort?"

"We can invite him, but I wish you will not be surprised if he declines."

"And we need to invite some of the older generation to keep you and Papa happy," Marie teased.

Lady Becca refused the gambit. "We can expect some two dozen or so sitting down to dinner, depending on how many can come at such short notice. Since we're providing our own entertainment, we need not be concerned about obtaining a professional."

Marie considered for a moment. "I shall beg off whatever engagements I might have for Susan's first evening here, and we can have a delightful coze while she rests. This dinner party would be ideal for her second night. What shall we do after that? There are still several weeks of the Season."

"Do I remember correctly she enjoyed the Opera last Season?" Receiving a nod, she continued, "We will arrange a party for that. I wonder who is appearing at Covent Garden now."

"It does not matter as long as it isn't that creature Mrs. Patterson had at her musicale."

They continued their plans until time to dress for the evening.

The streets were quiet, and only someone watching could have seen the men moving through the shadows on their separate ways to Shelburne's home. No one watched, so no one saw the activity at the rear door. Soon after midnight, all had arrived—Colonel Hayes, Sir Julian, Lord Beaufort, and Shelburne himself.

"Gentleman, what do you have to tell me?" Colonel Hayes settled his lanky frame into a large leather chair and glanced around the room. He sat quite still, his Mephistophelian eyebrows raised to their highest point, while Sir Julian described the morning's events.

"There is no reason to suspect anyone in your household, so someone at Whitehall must use the room above my office for his own purposes. Treason, to be exact."

His grim voice chilled his listeners. One by one, they rejected the thought, but soon had to accept the idea one of their own men murdered his co-workers. However, who else could move so freely throughout the department? Employees would find it easy to sneak in and out of any unoccupied room.

"What do we do about it?" the colonel inquired. "Haverford, let's have your thoughts first."

"Someone must see who enters that room while we talk in your office and give false information and then follow that person to identify the eventual recipient of the information."

Colonel Hayes agreed. "A room across the hall would give access, but how could this person follow the culprit out without being seen?"

Lord Beaufort spoke. "Would it not require two people, sir? One to identify the man and another to follow him? Or even three, one upstairs and one watching each entrance."

"It would be easy to signal from the window above the rear entrance, but the watcher would have to scurry to get to the one over the front entrance. That would require two people watching, or are we getting too many people involved? Also, who can we trust?"

"Good point, Haverford." The colonel sat in thought, interrupted by Lord Shelburne.

"Since you three regularly meet together, you must do so on this occasion too," Shelburne said. "May I be the person in the upstairs room? I know we can trust my tiger to follow the person without his knowledge. If I leave my post as soon as the miscreant enters the other room, you can talk long enough for me to alert Sanders at one entrance and position myself at the other."

The colonel raised his extraordinary eyebrows at the others, and as they concurred, he said, "Our usual meeting time is in midmorning, so, Shelburne, I want you in place an hour earlier. We presume this villain is on the premises daily and goes into that room after we begin our meeting."

"Why not smuggle Shelburne into the building before anyone arrives? If nobody sees him going in, no one will watch for him to leave."

"Good thinking, Beaufort," Colonel Hayes congratulated him. "All right, gentlemen, I need a few days to confer with the Minister. Afterward, I will send you word about a further meeting."

With this settled, the men slipped away, one at a time, leaving Shelburne House as unobtrusively as they had arrived.

Marie paced the floor of her bedchamber. The house was quiet, and through the opened window, she could hear the night watchman making his rounds. Occasionally the slurred words of inebriated gentlemen reached her ears. Her father had returned from his late night meeting some time earlier. She didn't know why he had gone out after escorting his ladies home, but it sounded dangerous to her. That had kept her alert until she heard his footsteps on the stairs. She still could not quiet her mind enough to sleep. Her thoughts centered on Lord Beaufort. Had he, too, attended the meeting?

Earlier in the evening, her father had escorted his ladies to Drury Lane to see the famous actress Sarah Siddons who came out of retirement to perform *Lady Macbeth* for charity. Although it was Marie's only opportunity to see the famous actress in her best-known role, she could not sit still during the early part of the performance, turning her head this way and that, trying to locate someone. Was he with her? Was Beaufort entertaining Lady Arabella this evening?

During the intermission, she turned each time the door to their box opened, only to turn away when she did not see the face she sought. Her mother took her to task over her ill manners, so she forced herself to greet each newcomer with a smile. Later, she could not recollect who visited their box. She only knew the one person she wanted to see did not.

Noting her anticipation each time the door opened, Sir Julian advised her that Beaufort had other plans for the evening.

She hoped no one else read her actions so clearly. She suddenly became quite animated and whispered with a mischievous grin, "Papa, you are in luck this evening."

He quirked an eyebrow in her direction but followed her gaze to the next box. Controlling his twitching lips with an effort, he murmured, "Ah, yes, the crimson satin gown with the indecent décolletage."

"Now admit it, Papa. That gown is perfect for me!" She burst into soft laughter at his wry grin and allowed her glance to survey the rest of that party. She cringed inside but kept her composure when she met the cold gray gaze of a gentleman just entering the box. She could only hope she and her father had spoken in a sufficiently low tone that Stokely couldn't hear them. She nudged her father. "Papa, do you see who is in the next box?"

He nodded. "I had already noted his presence, Poppet, but you're safe. I won't let him near you."

She squeezed his hand and turned her attention to her other side and chatted with her own visitors until the actors returned to the stage.

The end of the performance brought thunderous applause, which Marie joined despite her earlier inattention. She avoided looking at the occupants of the adjoining box, as Sir Julian ushered her out of theirs and to his carriage.

The guttering candle brought Marie back to the present. Her spirits lifted. Her father was safely home, and Lord Beaufort must be safe also. And she would see Susan tomorrow!

Midmorning found Marie pacing from the drawing room door to the window overlooking the street and back again.

"Marie, you will wear a hole in the carpet. Can you not sit still and wait for Susan?"

Her mother's sharp words brought Marie to a standstill, and she seated herself on a small sofa. "I'm sorry, Mama. I've missed her beyond words."

Lady Becca's expression softened as she studied her daughter's eager face. She recalled how she had missed her own special friends when they disappeared from her life all those years ago. Her heart still ached at the memory. She'd never seen them again. Before she could speak, Marie jumped to her feet and ran to the window.

"She's here, Susan is here!" Marie rushed down the stairs with her mama following at a more sedate pace and reached the front door before Symms could get there. Marie threw open the door and ran headlong to

Susan, as a footman assisted the latter from the carriage.

"Susan, I vow this is the happiest day of my life. These weeks without you seemed like years."

"Marie, calm yourself. Susan, dear, welcome back to our home." Lady Becca ushered their guest into the house. "We are so pleased you can join us for the remainder of the Season. You shall have a cup of tea first. You must have a good rest after your journey."

Twenty minutes later, Lady Becca rose and placed her arm around Susan's thin shoulders. "No, Marie, you may not escort her to her chamber. I will do that because she does not need any more of your chatter quite yet."

Susan flashed her friend a big smile. "We can have a good coze in an hour or so, Marie. As soon as I finish resting, I want to see all the gowns you described in your letters. My mouth watered with each description."

Marie possessed her soul with as much patience as she could muster, until Susan entered her sitting room a couple of hours later. Throwing her arms around her dearest friend, she declared, "I do not know how I've managed to survive all these weeks without you!"

At the dinner table Lady Becca managed to make herself heard. "Susan, do tell us how the children are. Has the doctor identified their ailment?"

"Yes, Ma'am. They have the measles, and although each case is mild, the illness has gone from one to another. James, the first to fall ill, appeared to be past them, but he threw out another rash when Howard became ill. This morning, Charles woke with a rash."

Sir Julian spoke. "Your parents were wise to send you to us until they're sure the contagion is over. I understand measles can be devastating with lasting effects."

"My parents are fearful the boys might have vision problems." Susan chuckled. "Can you imagine those three imps staying calmly in a darkened room? Mama has a maid sitting in a chair blocking their door."

Marie shared her amusement. "I dare say the vicar has locked away all the books, and that alone is enough to push Howard into a decline."

Their chatter continued through dinner and over the tea tray later. Their babble came to a temporary halt only when Lady Becca decreed they must go to bed.

Glancing around the breakfast table the following morning, Sir Julian complimented his daughter. "I see you stopped talking long enough to eat, Marie. For a while I feared you might expire of starvation."

Her silvery laughter filled the room. "I realize I must keep up my strength for our shopping expedition this morning."

He rolled his eyes heavenward. "Am I to understand you have some clothing allowance remaining? I would never have credited it."

"Oh, no," his audacious daughter replied. "I expect you to recognize, in your infinite wisdom, that I cannot stand by and purchase nothing while Susan outfits herself in the latest mode. Of course, *her* father gave her a draft on his bank."

"I believe she has outmaneuvered you on this." Lady Becca grinned at him, while the girls chuckled.

"Infinite wisdom, the baggage says. If I had any such, it would persuade me not to listen to such unscrupulous reasoning. And, no, I will not give you a draft on my bank. I do claim sufficient wisdom to avoid that prelude to bankruptcy!" He turned to Susan. "My dear, I depend on you to persuade my daughter not to purchase a crimson satin gown that does not reach her ankles."

Susan's eyes brimmed with amusement. "You may depend on me, Sir Julian. I have already heard a detailed description of that gown. I believe that color and style would suit me rather more than Marie, so I may well purchase the gown myself."

As the ladies went into whoops, Sir Julian grinned and shook his head. "I can see I'm outnumbered, so I will take my leave. You may expect me for dinner, my dear."

"I should hope so," his daughter told him with a saucy grin. "You're hosting a party this evening."

"Then it behooves me to return quite early, so I can curb your excesses," he rejoined, and with a wink for his wife, he left the room.

"Marie, you and Susan should begin your shopping now because Susan must rest most of the afternoon." Lady Becca replenished her coffee cup and reached for her correspondence.

"How many are coming to the dinner party, Ma'am?" Susan turned eager eyes toward her hostess. "I am excited about meeting Marie's new friends, so I hope they will be here."

"We invited thirty for dinner, and afterwards I hope you will sing for us. Louise agreed to perform on the piano, and I understand Deborah Langford—do you remember her?—worked up a recitation for us."

"Some of the others want to perform too," Marie assured her. "We can expect a full evening of entertainment. I hadn't realized my friends had so much talent. Now, we really must go shopping. Do you come with us, Mama?"

"No, dear, I have things to do here." Turning to Susan, she advised her not to allow Marie to tire her too much.

With a laugh and a wave, the young ladies and their maids entered the waiting carriage and prepared to give the Bond Street modistes a pleasurable morning. A footman joined the coachman on the box and gave him the office to start.

A few hours later, they joined Lady Becca for a light luncheon. Susan's coloring had risen, but she did not appear tired. "I even found a gown already sewn that fits me perfectly except for the length," she exclaimed. "Madame Bouchét remedied that on the spot, so I have a new gown for dinner this evening. Is that not wonderful? I dreaded wearing a year-old gown to a dinner given in my honour."

"She found two other gowns that require little alteration," Marie said. "Just wait until you see her in them, especially the one that is a shade of deep rose! She is truly magnificent in that one."

"She flatters me, Ma'am! Marie, don't overdo your compliments, else your mother will be disappointed when she sees me in that gown."

"I have never been disappointed in you, no matter what gown you wore," Lady Becca commented. "Not even when I saw you in tatters after one of your escapades with my daughter!" Amid their laughter, she placed her folded table napkin beside her plate and sent Susan to her bedchamber to rest. "Marie, stay away from her for at least two hours. For that matter, you should spend some time on your own bed, considering how little rest you get during the Season."

The girls parted company at the top of the stairs, and satisfied that they would obey her, Lady Becca sought her own bedchamber for a rest.

With sparkling eyes and no trace of fatigue, they joined Sir Julian in the drawing room prior to the arrival of their guests. Marie, in a blue gown reminiscent of the sky, and Susan, wearing pale pink, which brought roses to her pale cheeks, stood in beautiful contrast as they greeted their guests.

"My lord, this is my dearest friend, Miss Susan Connors, who is visiting us from Kent. Susan, this is John, Viscount Beaufort." Marie spoke proudly but didn't identify even to herself whether her pride was for Susan's meeting him or his meeting her. She could hardly wait to learn Susan's opinion.

"Good evening, Miss Connors." His lordship executed a perfect bow, as he acknowledged the introduction. "Miss Haverford mentioned you are here for the remainder of the Season. I trust you will enjoy it."

"You are most gracious, my lord."

When he strolled away, Susan leaned toward Marie's ear. "I can see why you are enamored, of course, especially of his eyes, yet do you not prefer Mr. Desmond's cheerful countenance?"

The whispered question elicited a negative shake of the fair curls as more guests arrived. They chatted until Lady Becca nodded to Symms to announce dinner.

Becca had exercised due caution by placing her daughter well away from Lord Beaufort. Marie had Lord

Shelburne on one side and Mr. Anstey on the other, and since each gentleman had his betrothed on his other side, Marie had plenty of time to reflect on the assembled company. She noted with surprise that Susan talked animatedly with Mr. Desmond, who ignored Miss Patterson on his other side. That didn't present a problem because that young lady conversed with Mr. Buxted on her other side. Really, thought Marie, where are their manners? Neither of her dinner partners uttered more than a cursory word to her. She rose with relief when her mother gathered the ladies with a glance and escorted them to the drawing room.

While waiting for the gentlemen to join them, Marie and Susan sat with Rebecca and Louise. "Marie has told me so much about you ladies that I have longed to meet you," Susan said.

Louise Stafford chuckled. "Did she say anything nice about me?"

"Of course, I did!" Marie turned appalled eyes toward her auburn-haired guest, who met her gaze with a twinkle.

"Louise, behave yourself." Rebecca admonished her with a slight tap on the arm with her fan. "Pay her no attention, Miss Connors. She's in one of her playful moods. I've long known it's best to ignore them."

"I'm sorry to hear that," Susan replied with a wide smile. "I was about to ask what Marie could tell me about her that was not nice. Those are usually the most interesting *on dits*, you must realize."

Louise's ready laughter rang out. "I agree. Oh, I definitely agree."

Marie turned to Rebecca. "I'm inclined to believe they're two of a kind. Whatever shall we do with them? We must not allow them to corrupt the entire party."

Their private conversation came to a stop when Sir Julian ushered the gentlemen into the drawing room. Mr. Desmond joined Susan on the small sofa, and Rebecca and Louise smiled to the special gentlemen in their lives. That left Marie standing alone, until Beaufort joined her.

"Miss Haverford, you gathered a sterling group of people for the dinner honouring your friend."

"Thank you, my lord. Susan is such a dear that I wanted her to meet some of my newer friends. Of course, she met Mr. Desmond last Season." With Lord Beaufort at her side, she did not spare a glance for her former beau.

Lady Becca clapped her hands. "Ladies and gentlemen, we persuaded some of the talented members of the party to supply our entertainment this evening. Our guest of honour agreed to begin by singing while Marie accompanies her on the piano. Girls."

Marie took her seat on the piano bench and ran her fingers across the keys. After performing together since early childhood, she and Susan needed no music. The instant the first notes rolled off Susan's tongue, silence reigned among the listeners. When her voice faded, Marie beamed in proud recognition of her friend's ability, and enthusiastic applause filled the room. After a brief hesitation, Susan sang another aria and then begged to be excused from further participation.

Marie glanced at her mother with a question. How could anyone follow Susan's performance with any degree of confidence? Fortunately, no one else planned to sing. Receiving a nod, she continued to play a couple of airs in a reasonably competent manner, which should be an encouragement to the others. Then, she moved to a chair near Lord Beaufort, who congratulated her on her play.

"Oh, my lord, my play is adequate at best. Only wait until you hear Louise Stafford a little later. I believe Deborah Langford is next with a dramatic recitation from one of Shakespeare's plays."

She smiled inwardly, when Lord Beaufort raised his brows in surprise, and could almost read his thoughts. The hoydenish Miss Langford will recite something from the Bard? Marie admitted to knowing little and caring even less about Shakespearean drama, despite her earlier debate with his lordship. In truth, she much preferred Sheridan's comedies, but she listened in some awe as Miss Langford declaimed a portion of Kate's speech from *The Taming of the Shrew*.

"I admit to being impressed. What will your guests surprise us with next?"

"Miss Patterson is next with something quite out of the ordinary." She nodded toward the harp.

"Ladies and gentlemen," Miss Patterson began in her soft voice. "Most of us are aware that Handel composed many works for full orchestras as well as concert pianos. However, he also composed some fugues for the small organ, and I find these are also adaptable to the harp. Please allow me to perform two of those fugues for you."

When the last notes floated away on the air, there was an instant of silence before fervent applause replaced it. With a proud air, Mr. Buxted rose and escorted her back to a chair near his.

Lady Becca stood near the piano, waiting for their attention. "When I was a child at Shelburne Park, one of my two closest friends was Marie Sanford, whose name I gave my own daughter. I often heard her play the piano in our music room, although she never had the privilege of lessons. She simply heard a tune and soon could perform it. Her daughter, Louise Stafford as she now is, inherited her natural talent. However, unlike her mother, Louise received lessons from music masters while she lived in the orphanage sponsored by the Duchess of Dorchester in Hampshire. We are fortunate that she agreed to demonstrate her talent for us now. Louise."

Louise, a serene expression on her face, seated herself at the piano. A soft melody filled the room, repeating itself and growing in volume as Louise lost herself in a Bach fugue. The tone softened but grew louder as she moved into a Beethoven concerto without a noticeable break. It increased to a crescendo, slowly growing quieter as she returned to the Bach fugue. The last note faded to nothing, followed by a moment of stunned silence and then spirited applause. Louise's breathing became normal again, and she smiled as she acknowledged the ovation.

"By jove, I have never heard the like!" Lord Beaufort turned to Marie. "I admit my heart seemed to fall into my shoes when Lady Becca explained this evening's entertainment. I never expected anything remotely compared to this."

"I'm pleased you enjoyed our entertainment, my lord," Marie assured him with a smile. She had recognized his earlier chagrin and had enjoyed watching his facial expression turn from disbelief to total admiration.

"I never realized young ladies could attain such a high level of expertise," he confessed. "Any one of these outshines any professional I ever heard."

"La, sir, young ladies can accomplish most anything they choose. Always provided they are permitted to do so, of course," she added. She did not add that she was surprised at Miss Patterson's expertise on the harp or that she marveled anew when she heard Louise at the piano again. That lady's performance far surpassed Marie's memories from their few days together at Shelburne Park the preceding summer.

"I must give my congratulations to each of them," Beaufort exclaimed and moved toward the crowd surrounding Louise.

Marie watched with amusement, as he strolled away. She had never seen him so animated, but his response proved he could notice and appreciate something other than business.

Later, when the door closed behind the last guest, Sir Julian gathered his ladies and Susan toward the staircase. "All of you truly outdid yourselves this evening. I'm sure no one expected so much excellent talent under one roof."

Marie chuckled. "I can assure you Lord Beaufort waxed eloquent over each performance." She did not add, except mine, but the thought crossed her mind. She set it firmly aside with the reminder her talent did not compare in the least with that of the other performers. God had given her other talents, although, at this moment, she could not think what they might be.

Chapter 14

Pleasure and Plans

Over breakfast coffee cups, the ladies discussed their success of the previous evening, while Sir Julian perused the newspaper.

"Your friends' talented performances impressed me, Marie." Susan forked up the last bit of buttered eggs and pushed the empty plate aside. "I met Deborah Langford last Season, although I did not know her well. I had to look twice to recognize her because both her appearance and her demeanor have improved beyond measure. Still, it never occurred to me she possessed such an extraordinary voice for recitation."

"That tone is not her normal use for her voice, that is certain. Once I gave the matter some thought, I realized what a good thing her betrothal is. She might have deserted us for the stage otherwise!"

"Miss Patterson appeared to have a more subdued personality, or was that because she was in company? I believe the softness of the harp was part of her being, not like a piano, which can be quite loud."

"That's a good description. I promised her that you and she can get together for a coze while you're with us. You see, she, too, has brothers who play pranks, and I believe you have much in common."

"Yes, I would enjoy that. I do miss my brothers." She chuckled. "We can share notes on how we have thwarted their tricks through the years."

"We will invite her to tea one morning when you can compare experiences without interruption." Marie pushed away the thought she would have nothing to contribute to their conversation.

Symms came through the door and handed to Sir Julian a folded and sealed sheet of paper.

Sir Julian read it, refolded it, and tucked it in his pocket. "No reply is needed, Symms."

"Well, ladies, what are our plans for this evening?" He glanced toward his wife for an answer.

"Did you determine who is appearing at Covent Gardens?"

"No," he answered with a glint in his eyes. "However, I did discover that Madame Catalani is performing at The King's Theatre." He turned an innocent gaze upon Susan and continued in an offhand voice. "I don't suppose you would care to hear her perform one of Mozart's operas."

"Oh, yes, please, sir," Susan breathed, her hands reaching toward him.

"Papa, you abominable tease! I do not know one opera singer from another, but even I recognize the name of the one who has ruled the opera world since her debut! Which opera is she singing?"

"Oh, that does not matter," Susan assured them. "To hear her sing anything is beyond my most cherished dreams."

Sir Julian reached over and patted Susan's arm. "Marie is right, my dear. I am an abominable tease. We will occupy our box at an early hour and remain there to the very end, I promise you. I believe even my non-musical daughter won't consider it caterwauling."

"Well, dear, I believe you got your own back after the way the girls teased you yesterday at breakfast about that crimson gown." Lady Becca twinkled around the table.

"I thought so," he acknowledged while the girls directed outraged glares in his direction. A smug grin crossed his face.

Breaking into her quicksilver laugh, Marie turned to Susan. "Is Papa not the most complete hand you ever saw?"

"To be sure," she agreed. "But we will get our own back one of these days, so be warned, Sir Julian!"

On this laughing note, she and Marie left the table to begin another shopping expedition.

A few moments of silence reigned in the breakfast parlor before Lady Becca leveled a steady gaze at her husband. "The note was of some importance else it would not have been delivered so early, yet you did not leave at once. Can you tell me what it is?"

He reached out a hand to clasp hers. "Of course, I can my dear. You know I never keep secrets from you! Colonel Hayes has arranged a meeting at midnight, so we must be sure to be back at home in plenty of time for me to get to Shelburne House."

"The Opera ends at an early hour, and we can use Susan's need for rest to avoid any late supper that someone might suggest. Shall I get a small party together for the evening?"

"That's a good idea. I noticed Stokely watched us at the theater the other evening, so be sure to include males, especially Beaufort, if he is available."

"Are you looking in that direction for our daughter?"

"No one could please me more for Marie, but she's rather young for a person of his serious nature."

"Perhaps she's what he needs."

"You could be right." He didn't hide his doubt.

She flashed her dimples. "I seem to recall you were a sober-minded gentleman when we first met."

"Baggage! If so, you changed me."

"For the better, I hope?"

"Of a certainty!" He smiled and cupped her cheek in his palm and then captured her lips in a long kiss. "To get back to Beaufort, my thoughts were centered on camouflage. I would prefer that Stokely believe Beaufort is here so often because of his interest in our daughter. By the by, young Desmond seemed enthralled with Susan last evening."

"Yes, he did, and I don't believe Mr. Connors would have any objections to that match." A frown crossed her face. "I know Marie is not interested in the Desmond boy, yet it bothers me to see her stand by herself while he ogles another young lady."

"Well, Beaufort went to her rescue last evening, just as he did at our ball when she stood alone among the crowd of betrothed couples."

"I noticed that too, and that is what gave me some hope for a match between them."

Sir Julian drained his coffee cup and set it on the table. "I must spend some time in my study for a couple of hours, after which I'm off to Parliament. A debate affecting the use of machinery as opposed to people is on the schedule again. I want to hear the possibilities, since the outcome has such an impact on some of our farms. I don't expect to be home to lunch, but you may expect me for dinner."

Lady Becca sat a few moments longer, sipping coffee and thinking of the theater party. Her husband's reference to Lord Stokely bothered her. With a sigh, she went to her desk in the morning room, where she penned notes to Lord Beaufort and Mr. Desmond. Their box would seat eight, yet she could think of no one else who might be available on such short notice.

A solution came in the form of a note from young Desmond. He felt he must decline because his parents were in town. She sent him another message, inviting the senior Desmonds to join their party. "For you must know, if I had known they were visiting Town, I would have arranged some entertainment for them."

Thus, there were eight enthusiastic people in the Haverford box that evening waiting for the dark blue curtain to rise.

Lady Desmond clasped Becca's hand. "I am so pleased you invited us this evening. This is my first opportunity to hear Madame Catalani, after dreaming of it for several years."

"Ha! I will wager this Catalani female cannot sing any better than Miss Connors. Just wait until you hear her, Ma'am, and see for yourself." Robert Desmond turned toward his parents who sat in the back row of chairs with their hosts.

"I look forward to hearing you, Miss Connors," Lady Desmond assured her.

Marie exchanged smiling glances with Lord Beaufort. "I doubt Susan would outshine the Catalani female, as Mr. Desmond calls her, yet Lady Desmond is in for a pleasant surprise when she does hear Susan. Do you agree, my lord?"

He agreed, although admitting he had no notion of how well or how poorly Madame Catalani sang.

Tonight, there were no catcalls shouted from the pits nor oranges thrown at the stage. The singer held her audience enthralled, until the last note died away and she swept off stage for the intermission.

In the Haverford box, Susan and Lady Desmond sat as though in a trance. With indulgent smiles, the others talked around them.

Marie glanced around the horseshoe shaped theater. "I hoped the Prince Regent would be in attendance or at least one of the other royal dukes, because Susan has never seen any of them."

"If they were here, you would have known when they arrived," Lord Beaufort assured her with a smile. "They demand and receive due acclaim."

"I daresay I would do the same if I were in line to become the reigning monarch. Oh, well, considering the state Susan is in, she wouldn't see them if they stepped on her toes."

Beaufort chuckled, and they turned to greet visitors entering the box until the theater manager called the house to order. The diva returned to the stage to thunderous applause, which she waited to end before she began the next aria.

When the final note faded and Madame Catalani took her last bow, the curtain closed on a crescendo of admiring chatter. As the Haverford party gathered its possessions in preparation to leave, Sir Ambrose Desmond shook his host by the hand. "This has been a rare treat for us, my dear sir. Will you and the rest of the party join us for a late supper?"

"A late supper would be our pleasure, Sir Ambrose; however, I must decline because of the hour. You see, Miss Connors is still recovering from a severe bout of influenza, and we must get her home before she becomes too tired."

Lady Becca added her regrets and asked how long they would be in town.

"Our plans are for the remainder of this week, my lady. We don't maintain a house in town, but we hope you will honour us with your presence at a dinner at Grillon's Hotel tomorrow evening."

Lady Becca glanced at her husband for confirmation and answered in the affirmative. "Perhaps you and Lady Desmond will come to tea tomorrow, and we can settle the arrangements then. Your son is also welcome," she said with a quick smile in his direction.

Lord Beaufort stood with Marie's hand tucked in his arm throughout this interlude and Sir Julian's standing on her other side. They also stood this way while they awaited the arrival of their carriage. After Beaufort handed the girls into the carriage, he spoke *sotto voce* to Sir Julian. "You saw Stokely too?"

"I don't believe he took his eyes off her," Sir Julian replied in savage undertones, as he motioned for Beaufort to enter the carriage.

When they reached Haverford House and alighted from the carriage, Sir Julian kept his hand on Marie's arm. Turning to Beaufort, he inquired, "Will you come in for a drink?"

"I don't believe so, thank you." Beaufort smiled at the sleepy Marie. "But perhaps I will see you at tea tomorrow." He brought her hand to his lips and held it a long moment. With a nod at the others, he tipped his hat and waited for them to enter the house. Only then did he walk away, swinging his Malacca cane.

From the corner of his eye, Sir Julian saw a lurking shadow, as he hurried the ladies into the house.

The house was dark within an hour. Sir Julian stood behind a curtain and watched the figure leave, before softly opening the door and easing into the darkness.

A short while later, he tapped on the rear entrance at Shelburne House and slipped through the opened door. "I apologize for being late, Colonel Hayes. Someone is keeping a close watch on my house, and I waited until he left before I ventured out." He turned to Beaufort. "Did anyone follow you when you left us?"

"I stayed in the shadows and paused every few minutes to listen for footsteps but never heard any. I kept as close a watch across my shoulder as I could and don't believe anyone was nearby. I didn't see anyone lurking around my house, either, and I made sure the lights were out for fully half an hour before I left."

"You did all you could to obscure your actions." Sir Julian turned back to the colonel. "What do you have to tell us, sir?"

"I apprised the Minister of the situation, and he approved our subterfuge. We will meet at ten tomorrow morning in my office and see if we can snare the culprit with some false information."

"What time should I be there, sir?" Shelburne broke the silence following the colonel's grim words.

"The first people arrive at nine, so I will meet you at the side door at eight. That should give you time to check the layout of the building. You already know the location of my office, of course, so there's no need for me to go inside with you. I will officially arrive at my usual time."

With brief murmured good nights, the conspirators slipped away into the night.

The following morning, Shelburne dressed in old clothing, which his valet pronounced too disreputable to wear even by the dustman, and slouched alongside his tiger for the walk to Whitehall. He pointed out the place for Henry to wait and continued across the road, where he met the colonel at the appointed door.

Slipping inside with a silent nod, he ascended the stairs and traversed the hallway to locate the other stairway. There, he counted the doors until he found the one directly over the colonel's office and inspected the room from the doorway. He could see dim footsteps in the dust that lay on the floor and noticed the pair that pointed out into the room from the hearth. It was obvious the miscreant sat on the hearth with his head inside the tall fireplace to listen. Nodding grimly, Shelburne closed the door and stepped into the room across the hall where he prepared to wait.

He glanced at his pocket watch several times and forced himself to sit still. One last glance at his watch showed it was ten o'clock, so there should be action soon. He opened the door a crack and stood with his gaze fixed on the shadowy hallway. He heard stealthy footsteps on the uncarpeted floor and barely breathed as a stoop-shouldered man approached in long strides.

In his early forties, he wore the usual clerkship garments of black trousers and coat with a dingy white shirt and carried a shapeless hat of faded green. Shelburne eased the door shut and stooped down to peer through the keyhole. He saw the man glance around and then sidle into the other room, closing the door without a sound.

Shelburne waited a moment before he slipped down the back stairs and out the door where his tiger waited. He gave Henry the description of the clerk and repeated the instructions, before he hurried to the front of the building, where he crossed the road and lounged in a doorway.

In the room above Colonel Hayes's office, the clerk stuck his head inside the fireplace and almost held his breath as he listened. Would they give him the information he needed this time? He had slumped in this uncomfortable position several times of late without learning anything to his advantage and feared his contacts were growing impatient. Besides, he needed the money. Yes, this was what he needed to know. They would transport the funds to Plymouth three nights hence and in the usual manner. He slipped from the room and hurried down the back stairs.

Shelburne did not have long to wait. From the corner of his eye, he saw the culprit hurry down the side road, the tiger not far behind. With a raised finger, Shelburne indicated he would follow on the opposite side of the road. He grinned at a brief thought of his betrothed. What would Rebecca think if she knew he had again involved himself in a possibly dangerous pursuit?

It was fortunate for her peace of mind that Rebecca did not know. She was at Hatchard's, where she encountered Marie and Susan browsing through the shelves.

"Have you found anything interesting, Susan? I will not ask that of Marie because I can see she is enthralled with a volume of poetry."

Marie glanced up at her. "The poems were written by 'A Lady' who was a victim of unrequited passion. I can sympathize," she added.

Susan joined Rebecca's low laughter. "I believe I will take this novel written by Lady X, whoever she may be. It appears to be filled with scandal, and I have already remarked how much I enjoy that."

Marie could not remain moody in the face of such an audacious statement. "I believe we have time for ices at Gunter's, before we must go home for Susan's afternoon rest."

A grimace crossed that young lady's face. "I don't feel the need to rest. That's all I've done for months."

"Are you trying to get me in trouble with my mama, you ungrateful creature?"

Laughter preceded them out the door where a footman and two maids waited. While the footman motioned for a carriage to come forward, Rebecca raised her eyebrows toward her own maid but refrained from speech until all the females were settled on the cushioned benches.

"Which of you is so carefully guarded?" she inquired of Marie.

"Fathers can be so difficult," Marie complained in a light tone. "Mine believes I might be in danger, so I have a double escort every time I set foot outside Haverford House." She changed the subject. "Here we are at Gunter's."

She continued to chat about the Season, and the others shrugged away their questions, while they enjoyed their strawberry ices.

Marie glanced at the bottom of her empty dish. "I could easily eat another, but I shall refrain."

She bore their hoots of derision with a twinkle. "You're mocking my appetite again."

"I don't know who could eat more ices at one sitting—you or Louise. She ate three just yesterday." Rebecca exclaimed with a laugh and turned to Susan. "I believe we should set up a contest between them. What say you?"

Susan controlled her twitching lips with an effort. "We might even enter our bets in the book at White's. If we can manage to sneak our way in, that is."

When their laughter died, Marie wiped her streaming eyes on a small square of lace-edged linen. "Rebecca, may we take you to Amesbury House in our carriage?"

"Yes, that would be nice if you can spare the time before your mama calls in the runners."

Marie chortled. "Oh, yes, we have time for such a short detour without Mama's going into alt."

A masculine figure sidled toward the ladies as they came out of Gunter's Confectionary. The footman and the groom exchanged glances and hurried to Marie's side. The man disappeared into the crowd.

Sir Julian soon learned of the incident, because he arrived at his door at the same time as the returning carriage. Catching the footman's eye, he hesitated as the girls hurried up the stairs.

"You have something to tell me, James?"

The footman kept his voice low. "Yes, sir. A man tried to approach Miss Haverford as she left Gunter's, but he hurried off when he saw us stepping toward her. He was the same man we saw a little earlier outside Hatchard's. Sam agrees with me on that, although we don't recall seeing him any other place."

"In full daylight and in a crowd too. They grow bolder, do they not? Thank you, James. I know I can depend on both you and Sam to guard my daughter." He went in search of his wife.

"Here you are, dear." He found her in the morning room and greeted her with a kiss. Sitting beside her on a small sofa, he caressed her hand as he repeated James's story. "We must accept that Marie is in danger."

Lady Becca stared at him with fear-filled eyes. "Are we doing the right thing by allowing her to complete the Season in her usual way? Perhaps we should keep her at home."

"I believe we will clear up the whole situation very soon," he soothed her. "In the meantime, we will keep a constant watch over her."

She nodded her agreement. "The Desmonds are coming to tea to discuss our dinner party with them. Are you still free for this evening?"

"Yes, only we must not stay out too late because I do have a meeting later."

"We can use Susan's need of rest as our excuse. Her state of health is a benefit to all of us, in one way or another. Marie and I are getting more rest, and you have a good reason to end our evenings early."

The Haverford party entered Grillon's Hotel at seven o'clock, arriving as Lord Beaufort approached on foot. The proprietor escorted them to a private dining room, where Sir Ambrose and Lady Desmond waited with their son at their side.

Robert Desmond nodded to the others but hurried to Susan's side. "Miss Connors, I am indeed pleased to see you this evening. Here is a comfortable chair for you." He barely gave her enough time to greet his parents, before he seated her in a small, upholstered chair and sat as close to her as he could manage.

"Young Desmond seems smitten with your friend," Beaufort commented to Marie.

"Yes, I believe he is, and Susan does welcome his attention. I expect they will make a match before the Season ends."

"How do you feel about that?"

She glanced at him in surprise. "I think the possibility is marvelous, sir. They're so comfortable together, as you can see. When Susan rested the first afternoon she was with us, I recalled her questions about him in letters and realized she must have hidden feelings for him. As a result, I have paid attention to them together and have come to realize he attracted her last Season, and she held back in deference to me. The past few days I've had my work cut out for me to convince her I have no interest in Mr. Desmond beyond the simple friendship of long acquaintanceship. I believe she has finally accepted my assurance and is ready to accept his attentions."

Conversation was general over dinner and ranged from the Catalani performance they had seen the previous evening to the possibility of a house party after the Season finished.

"You entertained us royally a few weeks ago in Hertfordshire, and we will be pleased to have you with us in Kent for a few weeks," Lady Becca told them.

Sir Julian added to his invitation to Sir Ambrose. "I want your advice on setting up a croquet lawn. My daughter has enthused over the game to the point I have decided I must learn to play it myself."

Beaufort glanced at Marie. He surprised himself by issuing his own invitation. "I realize Yorkshire is a considerable distance from Kent, yet as soon as that house party is over, I want all of you to visit Beaufort Park for the remainder of the summer."

Marie wordlessly appealed to her father.

Sir Julian's face softened. When had he ever been able to deny his adored daughter anything? "I've never traveled so far north and would enjoy seeing the differences."

"I can promise you one major difference. Yorkshire summers are cooler than in the south of England."

Sir Ambrose and his lady exchanged quick glances and accepted the invitation. "You probably have space for a croquet lawn too, my lord. However, if you don't, I must warn you I am also a fair hand at pitching horseshoes. I here and now challenge all comers!"

Amid much laughter, the gentlemen accepted his challenge, and the dinner party went their separate ways a few minutes after ten o'clock.

Sir Julian was on the alert for loiterers around his house but didn't spot movement in the shadows. Safely inside the house, he ordered a tea tray in the drawing room, where they chatted for half an hour in the event someone watched the house. Soon thereafter, candlelight disappeared room by room, and the house lay in darkness.

Sir Julian changed to dark clothing and stood inside the closed drapes while he studied the outside of the house. In a matter of moments, he saw a shadow detach itself from a tree and move down the street. He let himself out a side door and slipped into the darkness, making his way to Grosvenor Square.

"That is the situation, gentlemen." The men gathered in Lord Shelburne's study listened as Colonel Hayes explained the occurrences of earlier that day.

Shelburne added his information. He and his tiger had trailed the clerk to a coffee house in a side road, where the tiger followed the stoop-shouldered man into the dark room. Henry had stood in the shadows until his eyes adjusted to the dimness. A glance around showed the clerk in conversation with two men. The tiger noted their descriptions and slipped out the door. Shelburne had identified Lord Stokely and Mr. Rayson as they left the premises separately moments later.

"The men's identities don't surprise us, because we received reports of suspicious conversation between them. Now we have the link between them and Whitehall, which is what we need." Colonel Hayes paused, as the men thought over what they had heard.

Lord Beaufort broke the silence. "We gave them the false information, and now we must consider our next step. Do we follow our usual procedure of sending a courier openly? The previous attendants never got close enough to protect them."

"Since we know whom we are watching, it should be easier to protect the next courier." Sir Julian's quiet voice carried confidence. "We can delegate someone to follow Stokely and Rayson, as well as Anderson, since we have identified him as part of their coterie."

"I wonder why he was not with them this morning."

"Good point, Shelborne." The colonel glanced at the man who had not spoken throughout the discussion.

"Bishop, before the murders, you volunteered to be a courier. Are you of the same mind?" Seeing Bishop's nodding agreement, Colonel Hayes continued, "We need to designate the men to protect you."

Beaufort spoke. "I would like to volunteer, sir."

Shelburne added his voice. "Colonel, my tiger and I want to follow through with what we started this morning. Henry is small enough to get into tight places, and I can bring two grooms from Shelburne Park who are stout enough to take on any comers. We will be armed, of course."

The colonel rested his thoughtful gaze on his newest recruit to Whitehall. He would hate to lose Shelburne, who could prove to be so valuable over time, but if they did not settle this problem, there might not be any reason to keep him.

"All right, Shelburne, it rests in your hands. As you said, you will be armed, but I would prefer they be taken alive if possible. I believe some extra men might not come amiss. You and your men will travel with Bishop and follow the three mentioned. Also, we need a couple of others to follow along a short distance away."

"I can supply them," Sir Julian commented. "No one in town will recognize my men from the country."

"You and Shelburne can acquaint your men with the plan. Is that agreeable with you, Shelburne?"

With a nod, Shelburne agreed to meet with Sir Julian the following morning.

"We must discuss plans for the rest of us." Colonel Hayes glanced around. "What social function is on tap for the evening in question? I should think that would be where we would find both Stokely and Rayson."

Sir Julian spoke first. "I believe that is the night of the Pemberly ball, and I cannot imagine my wife denying her close friend, so I will be there. Do you plan to attend that function, Beaufort?"

"I had not but do have an invitation, so I will be there. What about you, Colonel? Should you be in evidence too, in the event someone watches you?"

"I have it on good authority that, if I miss that particular soirée, there will be dire consequences." Chuckling at their surprised expressions, he continued, "Charlotte Pemberly is my godchild, and no matter what other social functions I choose to ignore, I know better than to miss her annual ball."

Chapter 15

Headache and Heartache

Marie studied her image in the full-length mirror. With difficulty, she pulled her thoughts away from what Lord Beaufort might think. She smiled her pleasure that her father had succumbed to her blandishments and allowed her to purchase a new gown. After all, no fashionable young lady could appear at the Pemberly ball in a gown she had already worn!

The deep rose silk sheath peeking through the overdress of light pink spider gauze flowing from the high waist emphasized her slenderness, while the puffed sleeves showed her arms to perfection. The double strand of pearls adorning her throat was the only jewelry she needed. She nodded at her reflection, as she pulled on the elbow-length white gloves and left the room.

Marie tapped on her guest's door and called, "May I come in, Susan?" When the maid opened the door and stood back, Marie gasped in wonder at the sight of her friend.

"Do you like it?"

Susan's shy question brought Marie across the room to give her a big hug. "You are always beautiful, yet this evening you take my breath away. I'm so glad we chose the same shade of rose, even though our gowns are entirely different."

Susan's rose-colored gown opened in the front to reveal a cream underskirt with tiny embroidered roses and twining ivy leaves. Her pale complexion, which appeared wan earlier in the day, now was creamy with a hint of roses in her cheeks. Her only ornament was a rose carved from ivory, hanging from a chain around her neck.

"I am much too short to wear that style," Marie murmured. "I would look like a dumpling!"

"Think of it this way, Marie. If I wore the styles you choose or your mama chooses for you, I would give the appearance of a Long Meg!"

On this note of laughter, the young ladies strolled down the hall, arm in arm, to peek in on Lady Becca, who suffered from a rare, but painful, headache.

"Mama, I am truly sorry you must miss the Pemberly ball. Is your poor head not any better?"

Lady Becca did not dare turn her head, so she turned only her eyes toward her daughter. "I, too, am sorry, but Lady Carstairs will chaperone you. You girls enjoy yourselves, but be sure you pay her all due respect, because she is doing us a favor by acting as chaperone. You may tell me about it tomorrow when I feel much more the thing."

"My lady, I hope your headache goes away quickly." Susan gazed at her with worried eyes. "Is there anything we can do for you before we leave?"

"I appreciate your concern, Susan, but there is nothing you can do." Lady Becca roused herself to stare at the girls. "You will both remember Susan is still recovering from a serious bout of influenza. Do not stand up for every dance, Susan. And do tell either Sir Julian or Lady Carstairs you are ready to leave the instant you become tired."

"I promise I will be very careful, Lady Becca. I had already decided to sit between dances. As you know, I did spend almost the entire afternoon resting in my bedchamber, so I should not tire quickly."

"We promise to behave just as we ought," Marie assured her mother, and with smiles and blown kisses, they sped down the stairs to join Sir Julian.

He watched with amusement as they came headlong toward him. He held up a restraining hand. "Ladies, I dare say I should be thankful you did not slide down the banisters as I have known you to do. Let me look at you. I take note that your gowns are not quite crimson, although near enough."

"They are not above our ankles either, Papa," Marie pointed out with an unrepentant grin.

"Baggage! Now let us not tarry longer. After all, we must not keep your string of admirers waiting, must we?"

When they alighted from the carriage at Pemberly House, Sir Julian escorted his ladies into the ballroom. He waited while the sprigs of the fashionable world vied for dances and then decreed they must greet Lady Carstairs before setting foot on the dance floor.

Marie and Susan flashed brilliant smiles toward the young gentlemen and followed Sir Julian.

"Good evening, Lady Carstairs." Sir Julian drew her from a whispered discussion of the latest *on dits* and presented the girls.

"Beautiful gels, both of you," she pronounced after studying them through her lorgnette.

"Thank you, my lady," they murmured in unison and in relief, after managing to remain still under her scrutiny.

"My lady, I leave them in your care." He lifted an eyebrow toward Marie, which she recognized as an instruction to be on her best behavior.

She acknowledged the admonition in her usual way by squeezing his hand and watched him stroll away.

Marie's dance partner arrived as the music started for the opening minuet. She dropped a quick curtsy to Lady Carstairs and joined him on the dance floor.

Marie knew Lord Beaufort was there, although he didn't approach her. She kept a smile on her face and tried to hide her chagrin, being sure people were feeling sorry for her. He was back to his old habit of being friendly at one meeting and ignoring her at the next. She turned with a smile when he spoke from behind her.

"Good evening, Miss Haverford. Are you enjoying the ball?"

"Yes, my lord, and you?"

"Dancing is not exactly my forté," he confessed with a slight smile while his restless gaze scanned the room.

Marie hid her pique. She supposed he was searching for lady Arabella, but could he not do that without embarrassing the lady at his side? She decided to tax him with it. With a slight smile, she drew his attention toward her. "Are you looking for a particular person, my lord? I do not believe I have seen Lady Arabella this evening, in the event she is your quarry."

A slight flush covered his face. "No, I was not searching for Lady Arabella."

Marie darted a glance at him. She would never know if she didn't ask. "I do not recall hearing much about her. Do you know her well?"

"Reasonably well, I suppose. We grew up in the same village, and she married my close friend."

Marie's heart lightened. "I was not aware she has a husband, my lord."

"Nor does she now. He died in the Peninsula last year. She only came to town to do some shopping and has returned to Yorkshire."

Marie's heart plummeted. A widow and, therefore, eligible was her first thought.

"Ah, Miss Haverford, I believe your cavalier has come to claim your hand for this dance." Beaufort sketched a bow and strolled away when the blushing young gentleman offered his arm to Marie.

Dance followed dance. Marie sat one out with Susan, who wafted her fan as they surveyed the crowded floor. The colored gowns interspersed with the white muslin required of the debutantes created an interesting myriad of color against the background of the gentlemen's black evening apparel.

"Are you enjoying your first ball of the Season, Susan? You do not appear to be tiring yet."

"Oh, yes, even more so than last Season. I'm not at all tired and confess to surprise after the length of that last dance. I decided, though, to sit out the rest of the longer dances rather than test my luck."

"I didn't see you dance with Mr. Desmond, although he was the first to approach you. Do not tell me you refused him," Marie teased.

Susan flushed. "He put his name down for the next dance and for the supper dance." She slanted a glance toward her friend. "Is Lord Beaufort's name on your card?"

"No." Marie shook her head. Before she could elaborate, the music started, and Mr. Eagleton and Mr. Desmond bowed before them.

Marie smiled at Susan and accepted Mr. Eagleton's arm. He danced creditably, if woodenly, and managed not to step on her toes. He touched her hand when they met in the line, never clasping it for too long, and gave her his undivided attention. Truth to tell, she had only one complaint about dancing with him and that was not his fault. She would rather dance with a certain other gentleman. When the dance ended, her partner strolled with her to the vicinity of her chaperone and stood for a moment.

"Dancing in this heat makes me thirsty." Marie said with a smile. "Will you obtain some lemonade for me, please?" Wafting her fan, she scanned the ballroom. Her glance lighted on someone she did not recognize. He had a face of marvelous ugliness dominated by Mephistophelian eyebrows. He was staring at Beaufort, but then, as though he sensed someone watching him, he looked into Marie's eyes. She turned away, embarrassed at being caught staring yet curious. Why was he watching Lord Beaufort in such a malevolent way?

Marie accepted the lemonade from Mr. Eagleton and stood quietly as he chattered about his latest equine acquisition. However, she gave him only half her attention as her thoughts strayed to Lord Beaufort. She must warn him about that other gentleman on the instant. She murmured encouraging words but allowed her gaze to wander until she spotted Beaufort, who had moved around the room.

Catching his eyes, she moved her eyebrows the slightest bit and then breathed a sigh of relief when he strolled in her direction. She wondered about the odd, fleeting expression in his eyes when he arrived at her side.

"Lord Beaufort, are you acquainted with Mr. Eagleton?"

"Yes, we met some days ago at Tattersall's. I understand you purchased Storbridge's chestnut mare, Eagleton. I've had my eye on her but decided I didn't need another mount at present."

Marie fumed as the men discussed the finer points of a horse, which she wished she had never heard mentioned. Did Beaufort not realize she didn't call him over to discuss horses? She cleared her throat but to no avail. She touched Eagleton on the shoulder and requested another glass of lemonade. He hurried toward the refreshment room.

In answer to Beaufort's raised eyebrows, Marie muttered, "My lord, I have already heard too much about that horse!" She saw his lips twitch and dared to smile at him. "I wanted to talk to you, but let us move away from this spot before Mr. Eagleton returns."

They strolled around the room, her hand tucked under his arm. "There was something you wanted to say to me?"

Marie drew her attention away from his warm hand covering hers and raised her fan to guard her lips. "Have you noticed that gentleman near the door? The one with the ugly, uh, I mean plain face and Mephistophelian eyebrows?"

Lord Beaufort glanced in that direction and then down into Marie's face. "What about him?"

"I noticed he watches you quite closely. Do you think he could be one of them?"

"One of whom?" he asked coolly.

"One of the spies, of course. Who else would watch every move you make?"

He shook his head. "Have you not heard a word your father and I have said to you? Stop meddling in something you cannot understand. Instead, find one of your friends and giggle over your latest conquests or whatever it is that causes you so much merriment."

Marie stopped in her tracks. Pulling her hand from his arm, she dropped a brief curtsy, lowering her lashes to hide the hurt in her eyes. "Please excuse me for boring you, my lord. I will leave you so you may find someone worthy of your brilliant conversation." With her teeth clenched and her chin raised, she walked away.

Chapter 16

Plans Go Awry

A few hours earlier, Shelburne and his men had conferred one last time at Shelburne House and then made their way to their individual destinations.

The night was as black as the devil's heart. Shelburne, dressed in nondescript clothing, stood in the shadows outside Bishop's house and watched the courier place the purported funds in saddlebags for transfer to Portsmouth. He had kept watch for the past hour and had seen no one, although he felt sure the scoundrels were close by. With a brief, silent plea for God's protection throughout the night, he mounted the large bay gelding he had chosen for this expedition.

Bishop swung into the saddle of his roan, motioning for Shelburne to join him. Riding at a modest pace, they passed through the town limits without incident. Each previous assault had occurred closer and closer to London, but there was no reason to expect trouble in this densely populated area. They talked until they were on the Portsmouth road and then fell silent, each straining to hear the least sound.

"Stand and deliver!" The muffled voice came from the shadows. As two men moved onto the road, they met with gunshots that startled their horses into throwing the villains and running away. Pandemonium reigned for several moments. Shelburne and Bishop collared the would-be robbers, as the extra men rushed forward to help.

In the shadows on the other side of the road, Stokely cursed under his breath as he saw the foul-up of his plans. He rode his horse away through the trees. Confronted by a man on horseback, he lashed out with his whip and caused the other horse to rear on its hind legs, throwing the rider into a senseless heap at the base of a tree.

Stokely realized he must leave the country because he could not trust Rayson and Anderson to keep their mouths shut. Even if they did, his creditors would be on his trail on the instant if he failed to pay them something on account. He could not do that without the funds he had expected to receive this night.

He fumed over his bad fortune as he hurried back to town, making plans for his departure, vowing he would not be alone when he took ship at Dover. The Haverford chit was at the bottom of his troubles, and he would make her pay for it. He preferred more sophisticated women to warm his bed, but perhaps a chit barely out of the schoolroom would renew his jaded appetite.

Returning to St. James Square in record time, he gave his servants hurried instructions and changed into evening attire. He arrived at the Pemberly ball in time to see Marie walk away from Beaufort. She appeared to be in a snit over something he had said. Stokely watched her slip out the door unnoticed by anyone else. He sauntered around the room, speaking to a few people, and sat next to Sir Jocelyn Yarborough, who woke from a sound sleep and blinked his eyes in surprise.

Lord Stokely had spotted his watchers—Colonel Hayes on the other side of the room and Beaufort near the refreshment room—before they saw him. He kept the men in sight, as he waited for the Haverford chit to return to the ballroom. When she did not, he decided she had found a place to recover her temper in private.

He rose to his feet and continued his stroll around the room. When he reached the door through which Marie had disappeared, he glanced around the room. Neither Hayes nor Beaufort was watching him, so he slipped into the hallway. He checked each room until he found his quarry seated alone in a small withdrawing room, her back to the door.

Marie had scurried away to hide her hurt from the all-seeing eyes of the *ton*. She sat alone, wallowing in her misery. Why did she ever think Lord Beaufort could care for her? She scolded herself for being such a pea goose. The first she knew that she was not alone in the room was when someone clapped a hand over her mouth, pinning her head to the back of the chair. She raised horror-stricken eyes to Lord Stokely's grim face. How could she have forgotten her danger? Beaufort would be angrier with her than he already was. She cringed at the thought of her father's reaction.

"Your interference got me into trouble, and you will get me out of it." Stokely spoke with deadly calm, his large hand holding her still. His cold gray eyes held her gaze. "Pay attention. We are going to leave this room, go down the back stairs, and out into the alley where my carriage waits."

She struggled against his hand, but to no avail.

"We leave for France this instant. You will enjoy Paris with its society and fashions. Just as I will enjoy your company. I intend to walk out of here with you by my side. However, if you make a sound, I will not hesitate to knock you out and carry you. Is that clear?"

Marie managed to nod as his hand slackened its hold. She trembled when he pulled her to her feet and placed his left arm around her shoulders in a grip she had no hope of breaking. In truth, she would have fallen if he had not held her against his side. She must think. She must find a way to escape. Her heart was pounding, but her brain was numb.

They reached the outer door without incident, and he again cautioned her to silence. "There are people abroad on the streets. If you call out, I will kill anyone who tries to rescue you. Do you understand me?"

She nodded. She knew he would do as he threatened without compunction. She couldn't live with herself if she were the cause of an innocent bystander. Her own death would be better, and she would manage even that, if necessary, rather than submit to this evil man.

Marie realized people on the street saw a solicitous gentleman helping her into the carriage. She huddled in the corner of the wide seat, as far from the hated lord as she could get, and prayed. They rode down the street and turned a corner before they picked up speed and traveled at a much faster pace toward the Dover road.

Marie hid her fear and gathered her thoughts as she clutched the strap when the carriage lurched over bumps in the road. Moonlight lit the inside of the carriage, and she saw the shape of a pistol in the pocket of the door. Was it loaded? Could she reach it?

As if he had read her mind, Stokely said, "Don't even think of it. I'm not fool enough to leave a loaded pistol near you."

He waited for a reply, but none came, and he continued his gibes. "You can forget trying to escape because you won't succeed. Instead, you can better use your time in accustoming yourself to the idea of going to France with me, because that is my intention. I will kill anyone who tries to interfere with me." He spoke almost in a conversational tone, as though they discussed the weather.

Marie refused to speak, and his taunts increased in his effort to force her to answer him. In truth, she hardly heard his words, as her mind swung back to Pemberly House. How much time would pass before Susan missed her?

Susan began searching for Marie at the beginning of the supper dance. A short while earlier, Susan had approached Lady Carstairs and told her she would sit in the comfort of the ladies' withdrawing room for a short period. With that lady's nod of permission, Susan made her way around the ballroom. She saw Marie talking to Lord Beaufort, but was unable to catch her eye, and decided that Lady Carstairs would report her whereabouts if Marie inquired.

When Susan returned to the ballroom for the supper dance, she scanned the crowd but could not see Marie. She danced with Mr. Desmond and again scanned the crowded ballroom as they approached the supper room. "Mr. Desmond, can you see Miss Haverford? We planned to sit together at supper."

He surveyed the immediate area. "No, I do not see her, so she's probably waiting for us inside." However, a quick scan of the supper room did not reveal Marie's presence.

Susan cast a worried glance around before yielding to Mr. Desmond's pressure to find a table for themselves. Susan tried to maintain a light conversation, while she enjoyed lobster patties and green peas in mint sauce, but failed. When they finished their meal and returned to the ballroom, she approached Lady Carstairs. "My lady, have you seen Marie Haverford in the last little while? We planned to sit together at supper, but I have been unable to find her."

"No, my dear, I haven't seen her, but I only this moment returned from the card room. Sit with me, and we will watch for her together. I'm sure she will join us soon."

Susan listened to Lady Carstairs's discourse on everyone within their view. With a sigh of relief, she welcomed Mr. Eagleton for the next dance. She could get beyond the sound of Lady Carstairs's droning voice.

When the dance ended, Susan suggested to Mr. Eagleton they stroll around the room. She listened with small attention while he discussed the merits of a horse which he had purchased a few days before. She scanned the room as she murmured encouraging words and glanced into the refreshment room. Where could Marie be? Susan knew she did not care for gambling, yet the card room also received a quick glance but to no avail. At length, she returned to Lady Carstairs.

"My lady, did Marie return while I was dancing?"

"What did you say, child?" Lady Carstairs turned a vague glance in her direction. "Oh, Marie Haverford. No, my dear, I have not seen her." She started to turn back to her gossiping crony on her other side, but Susan persisted like a bee buzzing around a flower.

"Lady Carstairs, I am concerned about her. I considered seeking out Sir Julian, but I could not find him. I wonder if they're together."

"Oh, no, I'm sure they're not together, Miss Connors. Sir Julian approached me before I went to the card room and told me he was leaving. He asked me to tell his daughter, but how can I do that when I have not seen her? Troublesome chit. She should return to me after every dance. Surely, she knows that!"

"But, Ma'am, she would not know you were in the card room. Did Sir Julian say when he would return?"

Lady Carstairs became fretful at the delay in her gossip. "I only know he left and asked me to see you chits home."

Susan strolled around the ballroom again. When she still did not find her friend, she returned to Lady Carstairs with a determined air and broke into her conversation without compunction.

"I cannot find Marie. Please escort me to Haverford House. I must determine if she has gone home."

"Miss Connors, this hour is much too early to return home. Besides, I feel sure you worry without cause. She has probably found a quiet place to flirt with one of her many beaux. Perhaps you should do the same."

"No, Ma'am. I am certain she would not do that. Will you call your carriage, or shall I?"

Their eyes sustained a battle of wills for a long moment before Lady Carstairs shrugged and admitted defeat. However, she prolonged their progress out of the room by holding conversation with several people, while Susan chafed at the delay.

Susan suffered in silence throughout the long carriage ride. Lady Carstairs did not. She lamented the necessity of leaving the Season's premier ball so early. She complained about the inconsideration of the younger generation. She berated herself for having such a soft heart that she consented to chaperone a pair of chits who gave her nothing but trouble.

Susan sighted Haverford House with a sigh of relief. She expressed, as politely as she could, her appreciation for Lady Carstairs' benevolence and wished her a pleasant evening.

Another carriage pulled to a stop behind the Carstairs' carriage; thus Susan and Sir Julian arrived at the same time.

"Sir Julian, I have never been so pleased to see anyone! I can't find Marie." She broke into sobs that stopped when she saw Lord Beaufort arrive. She turned on him and demanded, "What have you done with her? Answer me, you scoundrel! What did you do with Marie?"

Sir Julian intervened before Beaufort could answer. "What makes you think he did anything with her, Susan?"

"The last time I saw her, she was talking to him, and when I returned to the ballroom, she was gone."

"Beaufort would not harm my daughter, Susan," he soothed her. "Come inside now."

Chapter 17

On the Hunt

While Susan rested in the withdrawing room, Colonel Hayes and Lord Beaufort searched for Lord Stokely.

"I went through all the rooms, and I cannot find him." Colonel Hayes's quiet, yet urgent, voice conveyed his concern that the culprit had escaped their vigilance. "How could he get out of the ballroom without one or the other of us seeing him?"

Lord Beaufort shook his head. "I don't believe I took my eyes off him for more than an instant, yet he's gone. I cannot find him, and my casual questions elicited no help from anyone else. No one saw him leave. It's almost as if he faded into the woodwork."

"He must have left the house on his own two feet. Do we depend on his shadow to be following him, or do we search for him ourselves?"

"He might have lost the man following him," Beaufort replied. "I suggest we make some discreet inquiries at his usual haunts. He's still accepted at most of the clubs but prefers Watiers."

They met Sir Julian on the landing outside the ballroom door and explained the situation.

"Have you seen my daughter?" His urgency communicated itself to the others.

"Not since we started watching Stokely," Beaufort admitted.

"I don't believe I'm acquainted with your daughter, so I cannot answer," Colonel Hayes said. "Describe her to me."

"You might have seen me talking with her moments before you approached me about Stokely," Beaufort told him. "The petite fair-haired lady dressed in a rose-colored gown."

"Yes, I did notice her with you, but I don't recall seeing her afterwards." So, it was Haverford's daughter who had left his lordship staring after her with a bemused expression on his face.

"I must find Lady Carstairs." Sir Julian entered the ballroom and saw Lady Carstairs in front of him. "My lady, have you seen my daughter in the past few minutes?"

Regrettably, Lady Carstairs had little sense of the passage of time. "Oh yes, Sir Julian. I saw her but a moment ago at the end of the last dance."

"I don't see her close by, but I don't have time to search for her. I must leave, so will you escort her and Miss Connors back to Haverford House?"

She assured him she would do so, and he sketched a quick bow before hurrying from the room. Moments later, the three men entered his carriage. They first went to Stokely's house, where the elderly butler opened the door enough to peep through after considerable pounding.

"Good evening," Sir Julian greeted him. "I wonder if we might see Lord Stokely."

"He is not here, sir," the butler quavered and attempted to close the door.

"Is he truly not here, or is he simply not home to company? You see, we had an engagement with him for cards, and he did not arrive. It occurred to us he might have forgotten the appointment."

"He is not here," the butler repeated and this time succeeded in closing the door.

"Did he seem upset to you?"

"Yes, Colonel, he did," replied Sir Julian. "There's no question he was nervous, yet I don't at the moment see what we can do about it." He directed his coachman to take them to Watier's, where a quick scan of the rooms did not reveal their quarry. From there they went to White's with the same result.

"We could try Boodles, I suppose." Sir Julian frowned in concentration. "He is not a member, but he might be there as someone's guest."

"If he isn't there, I'm afraid he escaped us, and we can only hope our man is still on his trail," the Colonel muttered.

A few minutes later, they agreed he was not at Boodles and settled into a quiet corner to discuss the matter. They had just begun their deliberations when a shrill voice at the door interrupted them.

"I could scarcely believe my eyes—the Haverford chit eloping with Stokely! *Sans doute* he is old enough to be her grandfather!"

In the stunned silence that greeted his words, every eye turned toward the door. Gervais Hadley, a vision in a pea-green coat worn over a crimson waistcoat and yellow unmentionables, raised his quizzing glass and surveyed the room. His enlarged eye lighted on Sir Julian, and he minced across the room to offer his congratulations. Before he could speak, Sir Julian met him half way across the room.

"Explain yourself, Hadley." The grim expression on Sir Julian's face and his low, but deadly words forced Hadley to open and close his mouth twice before he could utter a word.

"Faith, sir, do you not know of your daughter's preference for Lord Stokely?" He tittered as he glanced around but fell silent when he encountered only condemning stares.

Sir Julian lifted the shorter man off the floor and thrust his face to within an inch of the cowering fop's gaping mouth. "You have thirty seconds to explain yourself before I flatten you. Talk!"

Stuttering and with his blunt hands fluttering in agitation, Hadley told of seeing Marie entering Stokely's carriage in the alley behind Pemberley House. "She stumbled, but he had his arm around her shoulder until she entered his carriage. There were several people about."

"What time was that? Which way did they go?" Haverford rapped out the questions.

"It must be a couple of hours ago at least." Hadley gulped and continued. "They went southeast."

Sir Julian and Beaufort stared at each other. Dover. Stokely intended to take her to France. Sir Julian glanced around the room, then thrust Hadley toward Simon Abernathy saying, "Shut him up."

Sir Julian hurried from the club with Beaufort and Hayes at his heels.

"If they left two hours ago, Lady Carstairs could not have seen my daughter when she said she did," he said through clenched teeth. "We should never have trusted the girls to her care, but she has never failed us in the past. I will explain to my wife, and then I will go after them."

"We travel with you," Beaufort assured him.

Colonel Hayes agreed. "We will change and meet you at Haverford House. That should be the quickest way."

With that agreement, the three men parted company.

Now, Sir Julian put his arm around Susan's shoulder and led her into the house consoling her in a soft voice.

Lord Beaufort threw the reins of his bay mare to a groom and followed them inside. His quick change of clothing and the speed of his mount allowed him to arrive at almost the same time as Sir Julian, who traveled in the heavy carriage that was necessarily slower. "Shall I wait for you in the study, Julian?"

"Yes, do that. I shan't be more than a few minutes."

"This is my fault, Sir Julian. I should never have left her side!" Susan covered her face and wailed.

"You would have disappeared too, my dear, and we would not want that to happen. Think about this. If you had stayed with her, more time would have passed before we knew both of you were missing. We don't know the circumstances of how she left the house, so let us not apportion blame. Now, you don't need all this upheaval after being ill, so go to your bedchamber and try to rest."

"You will bring her back, Sir Julian. I know you will," Susan stated through trembling lips and with tears still streaming down her face.

He nodded and hastened to his wife's bedchamber. He found her awake, but with closed eyes, and could see that the headache still bothered her.

"My dear, I hate to disturb you, yet I must."

Her eyes flew open at the austere tone of his voice, and she struggled to rise. "Has something happened to Marie?"

He explained as quickly as he could, giving her the little information he possessed.

"This is my fault," Lady Becca said. "I should never have allowed a mere headache to keep me at home."

"There is nothing 'mere' about your headaches. Susan is also blaming herself, and I shall tell you what I told her. We do not yet know all the details, so let us not place blame anywhere."

"I should have been there," she maintained in heated tones.

Sir Julian held his wife for a moment and wiped away her tears. "Now, my dear, I hate to leave you, but I must change and go after them."

"You do not go alone?"

"No, no," he soothed her fears. "Both Colonel Hayes and John Beaufort ride with me. We will bring her back tonight, I promise." With a final hug, he stepped to the door and beckoned her maid. "Please give her ladyship some laudanum and take some to Miss Susan also."

"No!" Lady Becca said. "You know how I detest dosing myself."

"I know, dear." He hurried to her side and held her an additional moment. "However, you will only make your headache worse by lying awake and worrying. Trust me on this, please."

She nodded, and he was able to leave her bedchamber. In a matter of moments, he dressed for the road and descended the steps where his black gelding stood, saddled and ready. Colonel Hayes waited astride a large, raw-boned horse, which looked like nothing on earth but which Haverford knew had carried the colonel through many battles before the Minister assigned him to a desk job over his strong objections.

With Beaufort on his bay mare, the three traveled abreast and at speed down the Dover road. They kept words to a minimum, realizing they were almost three hours behind Stokely. They stopped anytime they saw an open inn and inquired for the carriage but with no luck.

Sir Julian began to despair. Had that misbegotten cur Hadley misled them? His life would be forfeit if he had. He brightened considerably when they reached the village of Oakfield. There they heard, amid much snickering, of the young lady who had been screaming like a fishwife because she wanted tea instead of ale. "Ladies do not drink ale," she said. "I'm a lady, and I demand tea!"

A grin tugged at the corners of Sir Julian's mouth. Trust Marie to make sure everybody remembered her! How far ahead were they? Only an hour, the hostler assured him. His hopes soared as they continued southeast, restraining their urgency by alternately galloping and walking their mounts.

"Listen!" Beaufort raised his hand, and they pulled the horses to a stop. "A ruckus of some sort just ahead." They rode around a curve where they stared in amazement at rearing horses and shouting men.

Beaufort had said little since arriving at Haverford's house because Miss Connors's accusation had stunned him to silence. He had already berated himself for upsetting Marie Haverford at the Pemberley ball. Was he responsible for her abduction? For whatever Stokely did to her? Had his thoughts of her prevented his seeing Stokely leave the ballroom? While he and the colonel waited for Sir Julian to join them, he had prayed the same prayer time and again. Now, as they rode toward Dover, those words repeated themselves in his brain. *Dear God, Take care of Miss Haverford. Don't allow that scoundrel to harm her.*

Now as they rode toward the ruckus, he made himself a promise. If God would keep her safe, he would never again be upset with her, no matter what she said or did.

Chapter 18

The Hoyden Climbs a Tree

Marie stayed as far from Stokely as the carriage permitted and stared out the window. Not that she could see anything, but at least she did not have to see those cold eyes assessing her. How could she have been so stupid? Papa had warned her. No, he had *ordered* her not to be alone, and she had agreed. She did not intend to disobey him but had allowed her wounded feelings to overshadow her judgment, and look what happened.

Lord Beaufort was at fault. If he hadn't upset her . . . his somber face flashed before her eyes, his eyes cold and stoney. No, she had only herself to blame, and she knew it.

"This rackety coach makes me sick at my stomach. If you don't want me casting up my accounts, you must stop the horses on the instant!" A vision of Lord Beaufort riding *ventre à terre* to her rescue occupied her thoughts for only a moment because why should he? His low opinion of her was clear to the meanest intelligence. If she had ever doubted this assessment, she no longer could after his remarks in the ballroom— *giggle over your latest conquests.* She didn't giggle over her conquests or anything else. Well, maybe . . . . However, surely Papa would come after her. Yet how could he know where to find her, which direction to take? She had made sure everyone would remember her at the only stop which Stokely had allowed. Where did she learn to scream like that? Certainly not from her ladylike mother. Still, Papa might not search in this direction. No, regardless of how obnoxious she could be at every possible opportunity, her father would not be able to find her.

With that conclusion, she realized she must put hope of rescue out of her head and concentrate on how to rescue herself. The moment she reached this decision, the carriage stopped with a jerk.

"Stand and deliver!" The muffled voice brought a shiver of fear to Marie, and she crouched further into the corner. When a masked man wrenched open the door, he met a shot from Lord Stokely's pistol and fell backwards. The coachman shouted for the groom to fire the blunderbuss at another scoundrel. The horses reared and jerked the carriage just as Stokely attempted to step out the door. That knocked him onto the side of the road where his head struck a stone, and he lay still.

This was the opportunity Marie needed. She peeped out the window, and seeing that no one paid her any attention, she slipped out the door and sidled around to the other side of the carriage. There, she pulled up her skirts and jumped across a shallow ditch landing on solid ground.

The woods beyond would offer shelter, if she could only get deeply enough into them before Stokely revived. Should she go straight ahead or turn back in the direction they had come? Neither, she decided. Stokely would expect her to try to return to London, so she turned toward the woods. The canopy of trees was too dense for moonlight to penetrate, so she walked slowly, while holding up her skirts with one hand and guiding herself around trees with the other. She hadn't gone far enough yet. She could still hear shouting voices.

Some distance into the forest, Marie leaned against the broad trunk of a tree to catch her breath. Her feet sank into decayed leaves causing a pungent, earthy scent to envelope her, and she smothered a sneeze. When the blood stopped pounding in her ears, she heard a strange voice shouting for quiet. Could this be a rescue, or was it more trouble?

She could go no farther because, somewhere along the way, she had lost her dancing slippers, and her feet were already bruised and sore. She was also miserably tired. She did the only thing she could do.

Marie tucked her tattered ball gown into the top of her white lace drawers and pulled herself onto the lowest limb. Climbing up several more limbs, she found a place where three limbs joined the tree close together, thereby creating a small corner. She sat on the broad lower limb and wedged herself between the other two, leaning her head sideways against the trunk, and waited. She didn't ask herself what she expected to happen. She only knew that was all she could do at this moment.

The birds she had disturbed settled back in their nests when she grew still. The only sound was the drone of insects settling for the night. Much to her surprise, the sound soothed her, and she drifted into a light sleep.

Back at the roadside, the colonel assumed charge. "Beaufort, Stokely appears to have regained his senses enough to talk, so tie him to that tree over there. We don't want to lose him at this point." The colonel barked his orders in a voice he hadn't used since his days on the battlefield. "Now, Stokely, where is Miss Haverford?"

"My dear man, I protest I don't understand you!" His shaky voice carried great surprise, and he rubbed a spot on the side of his head. "Highwaymen held up the carriage, I remember that much, and they apparently knocked me unconscious, yet you constrain me as though I were the criminal instead of a law-abiding citizen. Perhaps you will explain?"

"Let me at him!" Sir Julian had searched the immediate vicinity, and his grim face showed his consternation upon not finding his daughter. Now he raised his fists.

"Calm yourself, Haverford. We will find her." The colonel's voice turned to steel as he again addressed Stokely.

"Stokely, don't try to gammon us. The bump on your head didn't even break the skin, and your voice was clear when you first spoke, so answer me. Where is Miss Haverford?"

"How should I know that? Her father stands beside you, ask him. If he has allowed her to wander, that's his problem, not mine."

"I'm fast losing my patience with you, Stokely," the colonel informed him in a voice of steel. "People saw you getting into your carriage with Miss Haverford in the alley behind Pemberly House. I will ask only once more. Where is she?"

"Cannot a gentleman dally with a bit of muslin without all this fuss? I was merely following her wish to see Paris and would have returned her in due course." He sneered into Sir Julian's face. However, it was Lord Beaufort's fist that cracked Stokely's jaw. The unconscious man's head fell sideways, and they left him that way. He wasn't going anywhere until they found Marie Haverford.

The colonel glanced around. The coachman and groom had disappeared, as well they might. They must know of their master's perfidy. "Now we search for the young lady. Haverford, you call her."

Sir Julian cleared his throat and raised his voice as loud as he could manage. "Marie! You can come out now. You're safe!" They listened but did not hear a reply. "Surely, he did not set her out someplace?"

"No," the colonel replied, his voice positive in denial. "That would not suit his purpose. He had to have her with him to ensure his safety when he boarded the packet for France, in the event anyone tried to rescue her. She's here somewhere. We just need to get close enough for her to hear us calling her."

"Still, Stokely's coachman or the highwaymen might have abducted her, intending to hold her to ransom."

Disturbed by the agony in his friend's voice, Lord Beaufort laid his hand on Haverford's arm. "Your daughter has a good head on her shoulders, so do not get discouraged. She will have contrived her own escape."

"That's true, Haverford. It seems to me she would not attempt to escape from this side of the carriage because the men might see her, so we should look on the other side of the road." They detached three of the four lanterns from the carriage and began their search. The colonel led the way, as he had so often led his troops into battle. This was a battle of a different sort, but still a battle. When they came to the ditch, they separated—Sir Julian to the left, the colonel straight ahead, and Beaufort to the right—each calling her name.

"Miss Haverford! This is John Beaufort. You're safe now!" He continued to call as he went deeper into the woods at a right angle. He kicked something soft and got down on his knees feeling around until he found it. "I found one of her slippers!" His joyous voice rang out again moments later. "Here is the other one!" The others hurried to him. "They are hers, are they not? I believe that is the color of gown she wore tonight."

Sir Julian nodded, as he caressed the small slippers in his large hands. "Marie! It's Papa. You can come out of hiding now. You're safe." After a moment of silence, his anguished voice rose again. "Poppet, answer me! Please answer me."

Marie straightened her tired body. She wondered how long she had slept. Long enough to dream of Lord Beaufort's calling her name at any rate. Wishful thinking, to be sure. He wouldn't try to find her. She frowned. There it was again; only this time it was her father's voice calling her. She heard the anguished voice call again.

Papa! By God's miracle, he had come. Marie slid down the tree and hurried in the direction of his voice.

"Papa! Papa!" She darted into a small clearing and straight into her father's open arms. "How did you find me? I was afraid I would never see you again." Marie burst into tears and buried her face in his shoulder.

With tears streaming down his own face, he cradled his daughter in his arms. "Oh, Poppet, I've been so worried."

The colonel cleared his throat. "Perhaps the young lady would care to adjust her clothing before we start back." He had averted his eyes when he saw her running toward them.

Marie popped her hand over her mouth. "I forgot! Please excuse my lack of decorum." She pulled her ball gown into place. "You see, I had to tuck up the hem in order to climb the tree."

"You were in a tree?" Lord Beaufort's incredulous voice brought a blush to Marie's face, and her father laughed.

"Oh, yes, John, my little hoyden can climb trees with the best of them. We reprimanded her over it in the past, but we won't do so again." He sounded jubilant, as he continued, "I doubt Stokely would have thought to look for her among the leaves!"

Colonel Hayes grinned. "I agree. Now we had best be on our way. You need to get your daughter home, and I need to get Stokely back to town. Rayson and Anderson should have talked by now, and it will be interesting to compare their stories with Stokely's."

"You caught him? He planned to take me to France." She shivered and clutched her father around the waist.

When they arrived back at the coach, Sir Julian lifted his daughter inside. He turned to Stokely. "She escaped you, but that will not prevent me from dealing with you in my own way once the government has finished bringing you to justice." He climbed onto the driver's seat. "I will drive my daughter. You can return Stokely to Town on my horse."

"Truss up the scoundrel, Beaufort, and sling him across the saddle. I don't believe in coddling traitors."

Stokely roused and spoke with a snarl. "I am not a traitor."

"Try to convince Whitehall of that!"

They proceeded at a walking pace, each lost in thought except Stokely, who muttered curses every inch of the way.

Seated in the coach with only her thoughts for company, Marie cringed. What must Lord Beaufort think of her? Young ladies do not climb trees. Young ladies do not run around with no shoes on their feet. Young ladies do not expose their undergarments to gentlemen.

She felt her face grow hot. Lord Beaufort was so disgusted he had not even spoken to her after that one astounded question. She could never face him again, although she couldn't bear the thought of her future without him either.

On the long ride back to town, Marie relived every tender moment between them, every warm smile, every slight touch of their hands. They must continue, but how could she manage something so hopeless?

They returned to Haverford House at dawn. Marie climbed out of the carriage and hurried up the steps before the others could see her face. They rearranged themselves, with Beaufort driving the carriage that now contained the trussed up Stokely. He left his mount in the hands of Haverford's groom, who led it and Sir Julian's gelding to the stables.

"I will hear from you tomorrow, Colonel?" inquired Sir Julian.

"Most assuredly you will, just as soon as I have something to tell you." He cleared his raspy voice. "You have a very brave daughter, Sir Julian, and you may tell her I said as much." He touched his crop to his hat and rode after the carriage.

When Symms opened the door in answer to Marie's knock, she saw tears standing on his eyelashes. She so far forgot herself as to give him a quick hug, which he returned with equal fervor. "Oh, Symms, I'm happy to be home again!"

"Is that Marie? Has Marie come home?" Lady Becca hurried down the stairs, tears streaming down her face, and gathered her daughter into her arms. "Are you hurt, my darling? If that demonic man harmed a hair on your head, he will answer to me."

Sir Julian laughed at her ferocious scowl. "You're supposed to be asleep," he chided, as he gathered both his ladies into his arms and took them upstairs. "Symms," he called over his shoulder, "I believe we would enjoy some tea."

Marie saw Susan standing at the top of the stairs, tears streaming down her cheeks, although the only sound she made was like the mew of a kitten. Marie held her close, and they cried together for a moment before all of them went into the drawing room.

Sir Julian knew none of them would sleep until they all knew the entire story, so he settled everybody into comfortable chairs. "Marie, you begin by telling us how Stokely managed to get his hands on you."

She flushed a deep crimson but faced him with determination. "Through my own fault, Papa. I was upset with Lord Beaufort and went off by myself to regain my composure." She continued the story of her abduction as they listened with rapt attention. "I apologize for disobeying you once again, Papa. I simply did not think of consequences, only my need to hide."

He reached over and clasped her hand in his. "I believe you have been amply punished, my dear, so we will say no more on that score."

"How did you know where to find me?"

He stared into the distance for a moment. "I never thought I would murder any man. My faith sustains me that God will wreak havoc on wrongdoers. However, I felt like killing a man this night, and I do not mean Stokely." He recounted Hadley's behavior at the club and went on from there with the rest of his story.

The sun peeked over the trees when at last they sought their separate beds.

Chapter 19

A New Day

Symms concealed his surprise when Sir Julian appeared for breakfast after only a few hours of sleep. "Good morning, sir. The *Times* is on the table, and I shall bring coffee immediately."

"Thank you, Symms. Lady Becca asked me to tell you she would prefer to have tea with her breakfast."

This time Symms did not attempt to hide his surprise. "Do I understand the ladies are coming down to breakfast, sir?"

Sir Julian grinned. "I peeked in on my daughter a few moments ago. She is her usual sparkling self despite the excitement of last evening. Oh, to be so young again. Truth be told, I don't believe I was every as young as she is!"

"Papa, if you were any younger you could not be my father, and just think what you would have missed." Marie cast a smile toward the butler as she entered the room. "Symms, I'm famished."

He smiled. There was nothing wrong with her this morning.

Lady Becca and Susan arrived in the breakfast parlor soon after Marie received a heaping plate of buttered eggs and ham with a stack of toast close to her hand.

Lady Becca shook her head in mock horror. "Marie, I cannot understand how you can face so much food this early in the day. Symms, I will have toast and marmalade, please."

"I, too, Symms," Susan said.

"Oh, no, Susan," Marie challenged. "You must eat to regain your equilibrium after the worry I put you through last night!"

Symms added his encouragement. "Miss Susan, if I may be so bold, an egg and a bit of ham is just what you need to set you up for the day ahead."

"I can see I'm outnumbered, Symms. I submit to a larger breakfast."

The matter of food settled, breakfast proceeded apace until a loud banging at the front door caught their attention even though they were at the back of the house.

Symms hurried to answer the knock; a frown marring his face. People ought to know better than to disturb other people before they have eaten their breakfast, he muttered as he passed a footman who smothered a grin. The knocker slammed against the brass plate again, and Symms smoothed his frowning face to calmness before opening the door.

"Good morning, Symms. Will you be so good as to tell Sir Julian I'm here?" Beaufort did not betray by so much as a flick of an eyelash that he realized he should have waited until later in the day. To excuse his behavior, he prevaricated. "I need to see him on the instant."

"Yes, my lord. The family is still at breakfast. Do you care to join them?"

"No, thank you. I have already broken my fast."

"Will you take a seat in the study?" Symms deposited the visitor's hat and gloves on a small inlaid table and trod in his usual majestic manner into the breakfast parlor.

"Lord Beaufort is waiting in your study, my lord. He declined to join you here."

"I will join him. Poppet, you will stay indoors today, will you not? You need to recuperate from your harrowing experience."

Lady Becca intervened. "I wonder if, instead, we should all put in our usual appearances during the day and pretend nothing happened. Would we avoid gossip that way?"

An arrested expression crossed Sir Julian's face. "Perhaps you're right. Consider this alternative. You ladies receive visitors this afternoon, and we will all put in an appearance at various soirees this evening. There must be several entertainments available."

"I'm sure there are. Do we pretend Marie was not abducted?"

"I would prefer to do just that," Sir Julian agreed. "However, Lady Carstairs knows she disappeared from the Pemberly ball. She will not keep her lips closed on a bit of juicy gossip."

"I can attest she enjoys a good gossip," declared Susan. "She told me more about everyone we saw than I could ever want to know." She paused a moment. "I'm at fault here, since it was I who told her that Marie was missing."

"You are not to think you are at fault for anything, Susan." Marie clasped her hand. "You could never do anything wrong, in my estimation. I question whether we could keep my abduction a secret anyhow. Do remember Mr. Hadley and his penchant for spreading gossip."

Lady Becca agreed. "Yes. He is even worse than Lady Carstairs, and that is a conservative view of the matter."

When their chuckles stopped, Sir Julian voiced his opinion. "I agree we cannot keep the abduction secret, yet it is not necessary to say how long Marie was in Stokely's company. Nor need we give any details of her rescue, other than to say I went after her and brought her home." He turned to Marie. "Will you be comfortable with that, Poppet?"

"Yes, Papa." She placed her table napkin beside her plate. "I believe I will go back to my bedchamber and rest now."

"Is there anything I should do for her?" Sir Julian gazed after his daughter.

Lady Becca smiled at him. "No, dear, things will right themselves in a few days. However, you might advise Lord Beaufort about how we intend to react to last night's occurrences. Also, the colonel when you see him."

Sir Julian turned to "Symms, who stood by the door. You will know how to deal with anyone who has the audacity to question you."

"Yes, sir. The butler assured him in a voice of steel. "No one will get information from me, I assure you."

In the study, Beaufort's heart lurched at the worried expression on his friend's face as the latter opened the study door. Had that scoundrel harmed Miss Haverford after all? He pulled himself together.

"Good morning, Julian. I realize I'm early. I wonder if you have heard what transpired after you came home last night, rather this morning."

"I have not yet heard anything from the colonel. Has Stokely talked?"

Beaufort shook his head. "No, and I am not sure he ever will. Rayson and Anderson have, though, and tell the same story, so I do not see how Stokely will go free, titled though he is."

"They didn't have an opportunity to concoct a story, did they? I mean, Stokely cannot make that accusation, thereby clearing himself of duplicity?"

"No, they were kept separate from the moment of capture and have not spoken together at all. Shall I tell you the most astounding thing of all?"

"It all seems astounding to me," replied Sir Julian. "I doubt you can surprise me, but tell me what it is."

"They stole the money for themselves! Napoleon had nothing to do with it. They're nothing but common thieves." Beaufort's disgusted voice fell silent. "I am wrong, of course, because they are murderers, too, and will stand their trial for that even if not for treason."

"They cannot be hanged for traitors, but will they not hang for the murders?"

"Rayson and Anderson almost certainly will," Beaufort said. "Yet Lord Stokely will be tried by his peers, who are renowned for their unpredictability."

"What about the Whitehall clerk?"

"The colonel fired him, and he will stand his trial also." Beaufort shook his head in wonder at the stupidity of men. "I wonder if he now thinks the meager sums which he received were worth it."

"Who confronted him?"

"Colonel Hayes and I went to his lodgings after we heard what Rayson and Anderson had to say. Each of course blamed everyone except himself." Beaufort shook his head. "I can scarcely credit this, but I was almost sorry for Anderson. He seemed so innocent until he made the statement government money belonged as much to him as to anyone, and he needs it as much as anyone else."

"We can lay that at Stokely's door. I imagine he convinced Anderson of that. Scoundrels find it easy to influence people who are not awake upon every suit. Naïveté continues to be the downfall of too many young men who have not developed Town bronze. Anderson will learn his lesson the hard way."

"Yet, Society frowns upon what they perceive as wildness among the young! How else can they learn to recognize the pitfalls they will encounter?"

"Especially those whose fathers never leave their country estates and, from what my daughter has told me, that is true of Anderson." Sir Julian concurred. "However, let's get back to Stokely. I understood the colonel intended to interrogate him immediately."

"That was his intention. However, he decided to let his lordship meditate on his sins for a while." There was no mirth in Beaufort's smile. "That will take a considerable amount of time, in my opinion."

"How did Anderson become involved? He seems like such an unlikely conspirator."

Beaufort agreed. "I have a slight acquaintance with his family in Yorkshire. They own a small estate that has deteriorated over the past couple of generations due to simple lack of interest. I understand

Anderson has aspirations to make their property productive again, so he needs the money."

"Still, how did he become involved in this affair?"

"The Whitehall clerk is from the same village as Anderson and encountered him in a coffee house here in Town. As well as I understand the situation, Stokely had his eye on the clerk and befriended Anderson when he saw them together. I dare say a promise of great riches was all that was necessary to involve Anderson."

"Enough for most young men, I suppose."

Beaufort nodded. "Individually, each is a disgrace on their village. I hesitate to think what will happen when word of their combined actions trickles to their homes, which must when their trials begin even if not before. It will certainly be a new day for the residents, having so much excitement."

"One which will last in their memories," Beaufort agreed. "A subject for whispers and gossip to the discomfort of both families."

"What can you tell me about the clerk?"

"Not much, I fear. His name is Barstow, a man past his prime and married to a meek little woman, who barely raised her head while we were there." Beaufort sighed and shifted in his chair. "We will have to do something about her and their eight children."

"Did the clerk admit his wrongdoing? It seems to me that would help in Stokely's conviction."

"He denied all knowledge, stating over and over that he did not know anything about it." The new lines in Beaufort's face seemed to deepen. "The colonel sent me home after we escorted Barstow to Whitehall and said he would fill us in later today."

A tap on the door interrupted their conversation. "Excuse me, sir. Have you forgotten your luncheon appointment?"

Sir Julian tapped his head with the heel of his hand. "Thank you for reminding me, Symms. I had, indeed, forgotten." He turned to Beaufort. "I would rather discuss this matter further, there are still things I don't understand, yet I must leave. Perhaps we can get together this afternoon by which time the colonel will surely have interrogated Stokely. Being without food and other comforts might have worn him down."

"There is little further I can tell you, anyway. I shall consult with the colonel and arrange to meet with you here at any convenient hour."

"My appointment should not require more than an hour. Thereafter, I will be free the remainder of the day. I doubt the colonel has slept and will need to get some rest, so ask him to name the time."

With a quick handshake, they left the study.

Chapter 20

A Cause for Hilarity

As the gentlemen left the study, the ladies came down the stairs. Marie slowed her steps when she saw Beaufort.

"Do you gentlemen require the carriage?" Lady Becca acknowledged Beaufort's bow with a smile. "If not, we will use it for a shopping expedition."

"We navigate on foot today, so you ladies are welcome to the use of the carriage." Sir Julian accepted his hat from Symms. "We will return later in the day."

With a nod, the gentlemen left the house.

Lady Becca motioned for the girls to join her. She noted that Marie's natural color had returned, but the shadows were still in her eyes. "Come, girls, the Bond Street modistes are eager for our custom."

When they reached the salon of Madame Bouchét, Lady Becca prepared to alight.

"Girls, we will meet the situation head-on, I believe. Prepare yourselves." As she stepped to the ground, she heard her name.

"Oh, Lady Becca, say it isn't so!" A gushing matron eyed her with gleaming eyes.

"Say what isn't so, Mrs. Cogswell?"

"I heard your daughter was abducted and taken to France last night."

"Oh, no, you have that wrong, Mrs. Cogswell," broke in Lady Gertrude Hathaway. "Not France at all—Germany."

"You are both wrong," stated an arrogant matron whose name Lady Becca could not recall at that moment. "A white slaver took her to Africa to be in somebody's harem."

Lady Becca made an instantaneous decision, confident God would understand. She raised her hand for quiet. "Ladies, wherever did you hear such stories? They are naught but Banbury tales. Marie, come here, please."

"Yes, Mama." Marie stepped to the ground, hilarity clear on her countenance.

"See, ladies? This is my daughter, whom all of you know quite well. How could she be here if someone had abducted her? The simple fact is, I was not well last evening, and she left the Pemberly ball early to look in on me. Is that not correct, Marie?"

Marie's dimples flitted in and out of sight. "Of course, it is, Mama. I didn't mention to anyone that I was leaving because I intended to return to the ball after I saw to Mama's needs."

"I fear the entire thing is my fault," Susan confessed with a shy smile, as she joined the others on the roadway. "I was resting in the ladies' withdrawing room, so Marie didn't tell me she was leaving. Then, when I missed her, I insisted upon returning to Haverford House, and there she was. Since I have not been well myself, we decided not to return to the ball."

"You look familiar, yet I cannot quite place you." Lady Hathaway lifted her lorgnette and studied her.

Lady Becca came to her rescue. "Please forgive me. Our guest is Susan Connors from our home village in Kent. She had a serious bout of influenza and could not come to town for the beginning of the Season."

"I must admit your daughter does not appear to have been abducted." Mrs. Cogswell's face registered her disappointment.

"But, my lady, Mr. Hadley said he saw your daughter being pulled into a carriage!" The third lady, whose name Becca suddenly recalled, Mrs. Dawkins, made the assertion as though it could not be in dispute.

"I do not mean to carry tales about anyone, but I must tell you he asked for our daughter's hand in marriage, and her father refused even to consider him. I understand that Mr. Hadley thereafter made some vague threat of ruining her in the eyes of the *ton*. So perhaps you should not listen to anything he says."

The ladies easily accepted this story because it was no secret Hadley must marry a fortune. After all, what father in his right mind would allow his daughter to marry such as he?

"Ladies, if you hear more Banbury tales about my daughter, I do hope you will scotch them."

With a nod, the crowd dispersed, and Lady Becca ushered the girls into the salon.

"Mama, you are a complete hand!" Marie's laughter bubbled. "Did Mr. Hadley truly offer for me?"

"Yes, on the very day he rescued you from the rearing horse. He seemed to think his heroics had earned him you for a wife."

"Well, I was and am appreciative of his action, but not to the extent I would care to share my life with him," Marie declared. "I cannot imagine seeing a man-milliner across the breakfast table for the rest of my days."

"Those were your father's thoughts exactly. We must remember to tell him what we told these ladies," Lady Becca commented with a chuckle.

They celebrated their ingenuous story by purchasing a new gown for each of them and returned home in high spirits. They had scarcely settled into the drawing room when Symms announced the first afternoon visitors.

Rebecca Blackwell was the first to arrive and rushed straight to Marie's side. "I heard a frightful story, Marie, but must say you do not appear to have collapsed from a fever of the brain." She stared in amazement when Marie broke into gales of laughter.

"A fever of the brain? When we were shopping earlier today, I heard that someone had abducted me and taken me to France. Or in the alternative, the abductor took me to Germany, or even to Africa. White slavery played a part in the story."

Louise Stafford had come in while Marie was speaking and now grinned. "That's even better than what I heard. I have it on the best of authority from my maid, who heard it from the footman who works for Lord Buckley, who had it from a Mr. Simpkins, who saw the whole thing," she drew a deep breath "that you sailed away with a pirate." After that bit of recitation, she chortled at the stunned expressions crossing her listeners' faces.

"Do you always get your information in that fashion?" Marie asked with awe.

Several more people had crowded into the room and listened in fascinated horror at Louise's tale.

Lady Becca decided she must intervene. "All the tales we heard today are amusing, yet that is all they are. You can see that Marie is her usual self, which even she could not be if she had endured any sort of upsetting experience. The truth of the matter is so simple that I don't know how such ridiculous rumours could start."

The visitors listened avidly as Lady Becca repeated her earlier explanation. Some turned away in frustration because they did not have a scandalous *on dit* to pass along at their next stop.

When the crowd thinned somewhat, Deborah Langford erupted into the room and grabbed Marie in a embrace. Tears streamed down her cheeks as she stammered, "I heard that you were d-d-dead. Symms told me b-b-better, but I had to see you for myself."

Marie wiped her tears away. "The whole thing is the figment of people's imagination, Deborah. Nothing drastic has happened to me, but do tell me how I am supposed to have died."

Deborah gulped. "Some men fought a duel over you, and you ran between them and were sh-sh-shot. D-d-dead."

"What?" Sir Julian thundered from the doorway. "What are you saying about my daughter?"

Lady Becca hurried to him and laid a restraining hand on his arm. "Everything is all right, dear, nothing has happened to our daughter, I promise you. Come, let us go into your study, and I will explain what has happened today." She pulled him out the door, casting a speaking glance at Marie over her shoulder.

Lady Becca quickly related to him and Lord Beaufort the gossip that was making the rounds of the *ton* all ready. "I decided to deny that anything out of the ordinary occurred."

The tension left Sir Julian's shoulders, and he grinned. "I dare say you're correct, my dear.

The crowd in the drawing room talked for a few moments longer, before leaving in chattering groups of two or three.

Lady Becca rejoined the girls when only Marie's closest friends remained. "I believe the gossip will clear in a few days."

Marie agreed. "I certainly hope so. If the stories get any wilder, I shan't have a shred of reputation left." With a light tone she was far from feeling, she turned the conversation. "What are our plans for this evening?"

Chapter 21

The Outcome

While the ladies discussed evening activities in the drawing room, Symms escorted the unshaven and exhausted Colonel Hayes to the study.

"Good afternoon, gentlemen." The colonel's voice was weak from overuse.

Sir Julian offered him a chair. "You've had a long night and day, sir."

The colonel nodded. "I decided to come over and give you the most recent developments before going home. Once I get to my bed, I expect to sleep around the clock. I'm too old for these shenanigans."

Sir Julian smiled his understanding. "Beaufort told me the preliminaries, up to Barstow's denial."

Beaufort nodded. "I expected his denial. He would hardly blurt out a confession, would he? I suppose he needed the extra money for his children."

The colonel shook his head. "No, his salary was sufficient for their needs. He told us he needed money to satisfy the demands of his mistress."

"His mistress," Sir Julian snorted. "Did his wife know of his activities? At Whitehall, I mean."

"Apparently not. At least she appeared stunned. As for knowing about his mistress, I imagine she considered her a blessing, if she knew about her."

Beaufort inquired, "Did Barstow ever admit his involvement?"

"At length, but only after we confronted him with our knowledge of his acquaintance with Anderson and his meetings with the other conspirators."

"That should help with Stokely's conviction," Beaufort exclaimed with satisfaction.

The colonel agreed. "Barstow admitted knowing Anderson but denied knowing the others. Apparently, they gave him false names."

"Has he confronted them?" Sir Julian asked. "Has he definitely identified them?"

"Oh, yes, we escorted him to Newgate in midmorning. He identified them as his other two contacts, so there is no problem there. He even told us of their meeting places."

There was a brief silence as the men contemplated the probable events over the succeeding days.

"One other thing came to light. Barstow's mistress was previously in Stokely's keeping. She introduced Barstow to him. At Stokely's request, I need hardly say, so both men were paying her."

The colonel heaved himself to his feet and ran his hand through his hair. "I never cease to be amazed at what some men will do for a woman." He took his leave of them with plans for a meeting the following day.

Chapter 22

Yes!

Beaufort broke the silence which reigned after the colonel left.

"Sir Julian?"

Haverford's head snapped up at the unfamiliar address from his old friend. He stared in amazement as Beaufort's face changed color, first red and then white.

"Sir Julian?" He cleared his voice.

"Yes, Lord Beaufort?"

"I, uh, want to talk to you about your daughter."

Sir Julian's eyebrows rose, and a smile passed across his face. "What about her?"

"I want to marry her." The blunt statement brought Haverford's smile back to the surface. Now he knew why Beaufort's attention had wandered throughout the day.

"That certainly is agreeable with me, but Marie has a mind of her own, which she will no doubt exercise."

"Do I have your permission to address her?"

For an answer, Sir Julian tugged the bell rope summoning Symms and requested his daughter's presence in the study.

After returning to her bedchamber when the afternoon visitors left, Marie tried to relax on the *chaise lounge* but to no avail. She was soon on her feet, pacing back and forth, her thoughts in turmoil. If people ever learn the truth, she would be ostracized. But, would that be so bad? Beaufort despised her, of that she was certain, and life without him was too much to bear.

Hannah watched until the third time she found it necessary to dodge her restless mistress. "Miss Marie, pacing the floor will not alter anything. Sit down, and tell me about it."

Marie focused her eyes when Hannah led her into the sitting room and pushed her onto a chair. Sighing, she asked, "What do you want to know?"

"Everything."

"Remember our official story is that Mr. Hadley tried to ruin me with gossip because Papa refused his suit," she cautioned.

Hannah nodded and listened in enthralled silence as Marie recounted her experience. "This is better than *Castle Rackrent*," she declared. "I would wager you could write as good a book as that Edgeworth female, if you would but try."

"Heaven forbid!" Marie's eyes widened in horror. "I'm already in disgrace, and that would put me beyond the pale. What does it matter though? Lord Beaufort will never speak to me again anyway."

Hannah began to comfort the distressed girl. "Haven't you always told me God would work things out in His own way and time?"

Before Marie could answer, a knock on the door heralded a message from Sir Julian. He wished to see his daughter in the study.

Marie pinched her cheeks to add color and went to her father.

Beaufort rose to his feet when Marie entered the study.

"You wanted to see me, Papa?"

"Yes, my dear. Rather, Lord Beaufort does. I will leave you alone for fifteen minutes."

Fifteen minutes! The time limitation stunned Beaufort. He needed more time than that just to gather his thoughts and marshal his arguments. Despair had overwhelmed him when he held her slippers in his hand after her abduction. He had feared he would never see his love again.

Yes, his love! When had she become that to him? He did not know, but he did know one thing. She was his, and he had decided the instant she ran into the clearance that he would waste no time in letting her know she belonged to him. And to think she rescued herself, and by climbing a tree, no less. What other female of his acquaintance had that much gumption?

Perhaps she did not care for him, what would he do? He had never been a coward about anything else and didn't intend to start now. He cleared his throat, and in his usual direct manner said, "Miss Haverford, will you marry me?"

He lowered his head and stared at the floor, his mind wrestling with the need to convince her.

Marie's heart seemed to leap into her throat before settling down to its usual place. If he wanted to marry her, he was not disgusted with her behavior, she reasoned. Taking a deep breath, she concentrated. She must be calm. Dignified. Restrained. No giggles.

"Yes."

Beaufort was so intent on his thoughts he did not hear her answer. "I know I have not treated you with much respect. Respect for your mental faculties, which are far above any female I know. Nevertheless, I have come to the realization I care deeply for you and want you to be my wife."

"Yes."

"I want to apologize for any of my careless words that may have upset you. I have long since realized I was resisting the attraction you stirred in me, and I could understand if you refused my suit." Taking a deep breath, he continued, still without looking at her. "I will not make those same mistakes again, although I undoubtedly will make others. I do want you to marry me. You fill an emptiness that has been with me for many years."

"Yes."

Lord Beaufort sat staring at the carpet, "When we were searching for you, I knew I might never see you again, and that did not bear thinking on. Never hear your bubbling laughter again? I don't believe I could live without that."

"John," Marie interrupted. "I said yes three times, but I will say it again. Yes, I will marry you. Nothing would give me greater pleasure than to marry you. I would like to marry you above all things."

He stared at her, a myriad of emotions crossing his face as he comprehended her words.

"I will even propose to you if that will convince you." Marie slipped onto her knees in front of him and clasped his face between her hands. "The thought of living without you is more than I can bear. Will you marry me, my lord?"

The slow smile Marie had learned to wait for crossed his face as he rose to his feet, gathering her into his arms.

Marie smiled into the glowing mahogany eyes fixed on her face and slid her arms around his neck. "God has answered the deepest needs of my heart. With you by my side, my heart is whole."

Author's Note

Your opinion matters, so if you enjoyed *The Divided Heart*, please spread the word by posting a short review on Amazon, Good Reads, and other sources to which you have access. Reviews are enormously helpful to the reading community, and your support really does motivate me to keep writing. Thank you!

♥ Peggy ♥